FALLING INTO YOU AGAIN

S. N. CHRISTENSEN

CONTENTS

AUTHOR'S NOTES

This book can be read as a standalone in the fALLINg series and ends with a HEA. This book takes place six years after the first two in the series, fALLINg into Summer and fALLINg into Senior Year. The first two take place in high school from Everly's POV and explains how James and Everly got to where they are in this book.

Some content in this book may be triggering to some readers.

Trigger Warnings include mention of suicide, mention of rape, kidnapping, DUI, violence, and the use of drugs and alcohol.

Chapter One

EVERLY

New York. The place in the United States I vowed never to return to. The place where I'm currently sitting in a coffee shop, questioning my life choices once again. The place that offered me a job when no one else would. Not only am I in the state that I desperately wanted to get away from, but I'm working at the high school I desperately never wanted to think about again. I've only been back in this state once since leaving for college. One time too many. Life surely has a sense of humor.

I sip my coffee as I watch Declan sit on a bench outside the coffee shop taking a phone call. I wonder who he is talking to, but I never ask anymore. The man has given up his life for me. I owe him everything. I have two security guards who have been with me since high school, but Declan is the one I'm closest to and who has never let me down.

I take my last sip of coffee and pack up my supplies on the table. It's time to head to work. It's been a full month since I've been back in New York and even with my very specific routines, it's not getting any easier. I throw my coffee away in the trash can and turn around, bumping into someone. Coffee splashes back onto the man's expensive suit, but he doesn't make a sound. I would have yelped if it had been my hot coffee splashing on me.

"I'm so sorry!" I say while reaching for the napkins right next to me.

I grab the napkins and start blotting his shirt, right over his rock-hard abs. I blush at what I'm doing. I can't believe I'm basically feeling up some stranger's abs. I throw the napkins away and go to apologize again, but the words get stuck in my throat when I finally look up at his face. James.

I've only been back in New York for one month and I've already run into him. In a coffee shop close to where I work and at least thirty minutes from his office. Why and how is he standing in front of me right now?

I continue to stare at his face as a slow smile grows on his lips. "Everly."

My name coming out of his mouth still makes my body react. I can't breathe, and I feel goosebumps rising on my skin. Is it possible that he's gotten even hotter than the last time I was with him six years ago? Those piercing green eyes and that dirty blonde hair... It's gotten longer, but he keeps it professionally styled back. The urge to run my hands through it again still hasn't left me after all this time.

I look away and close my eyes for a split second. I take a deep breath to force myself to breathe and look back at him with a friendly smile. "Hey James, it's good to see you. How are you doing?"

He keeps his smile on his face as he says, "I'm doing good. You're back in town."

I'd be surprised if no one told him I was back here. "Yep. I'm surprised Jake didn't tell you."

He frowns. "Jake and I haven't spoken much in the past few years."

That's surprising, as I didn't know that. "Oh."

Oh? Really? Is that all I could think of saying? I need to get out of here before I say something stupid. "Well, I don't want to be late for work. Sorry again about your shirt, but it was good to see you."

I don't wait for his response and start to walk by him. He grabs my arm and that little spark I always used to feel with him officially turned into a full-blown fire. I can feel his touch throughout my whole body. Once again, I hold my breath as I look toward him.

"You're back in town for good?" he asks, hopeful.

I nod, even though my brain is telling me to lie. I can't.

The smile reappears on his face as he says, "Let's catch up sometime. You still have my number?"

I nod again and realize how stupid I must look. "Yeah, sure. Sounds good. See you, James."

I quickly pull from his grasp and basically run out the door. I don't stop to look over at Declan as I walk down the street to work. Declan runs to catch up with me and puts his phone in his pocket.

"Hey, everything okay?" he asks when he catches up to my side.

"Yep," I reply.

He cocks an eyebrow and puts his hands in his pockets as he keeps the pace beside me. "What happened?"

I slow down and sigh. "I ran into James."

He nods, and he doesn't look surprised. Did he see James walk in? Of course he did. He sees everything, but why didn't he warn me? He knows I want to avoid him at all costs. We don't say a word the rest of the way to the high school.

I'm polite and say good morning to everyone in the front office as I make my way to my office and close the door. I'm fifteen minutes early, and I need to get back into the right headspace if I'm going to be able to do my job.

In these situations, I instinctively reach for my notebook and do what I always do. I write a letter to my dead friend. I could easily text Ashley about what happened, but the best part about writing to dead friends is that they can't respond. Ashley could respond. And I have a feeling I know what she'd say. I'm not in the mood to deal with that right now.

Dear Lauren,

It's been a month since I've been back in New York. A month since I've been back in this high school, which I promised never to return to. It's been almost seven years since you've died. I miss you, friend. Being back here makes me miss you even more, especially when I walk past your old locker. When I grab lunch from the cafeteria and when I walk by our old classrooms. I just... miss you.

You will never guess who I ran into today. James. Yeah, I know. I also know what you would have been saying to me these past six years that I haven't spoken to him. When I saw him, it felt like no time had passed at all, other than how handsome he has become. How can he be even more handsome? I still felt the same way I did when I was around him back in high school. I doubt he feels the same. Even so, I need to avoid him... right? Catching up would be a big mistake, especially since I know he can still make me feel that way. I can't deal with another broken heart. He's still probably with that girl, anyway. He didn't have a ring on, so I know he's not married. Why am I even considering seeing him? Of course I shouldn't! Thanks Lauren, you always know what to do. I love you. I miss you.

I place my notebook back in my desk, feeling better about my decision. Pretending I never ran into James is for the best. A knock sounds on my door as I tell whoever it is to come in. My first student of the day enters my office and sits in front of me. She always looks so sad, as though she's just going through the motions of being here until she graduates. Is that what I used to look like in high school? I force a smile on my face and know this is why I'm here. While taking this job was not ideal, students like this show me exactly why I'm here. I'm going to do my best to help them. Not just to help them get through high school, but to be happy again. To find the joy in life and not go down the path that I did.

Today went by faster than I thought it would. When I walk out of the school, Declan is on the front steps waiting for me as he always is.

"How was your day?" he asks, just like he does every day.

"It was good. How about you? You getting bored yet waiting around staring at a bunch of teenagers all day?"

He laughs. "It can be quite entertaining, actually. I especially like seeing those skipping school to make out in their cars or to do drugs."

I laugh and shake my head. I don't know how he can handle this job. There's a lot of waiting around for me and being bored. Then, when he's not bored, I keep him on his toes. I'm thankful for him, and I literally owe him my life.

"You know, if you see students doing drugs, you should really report them," I say seriously.

He smirks. "Just like I reported you?"

I roll my eyes. He's right, he never reported me. He probably should have, though.

While walking to the car, I overhear some seniors talking about homecoming.

"We need to find the perfect dresses! Since we're not going with dates, maybe we can get dates while there if we look hot enough," says one girl to her two friends.

"I don't care to find a date. I need to concentrate on my grades this year," one of her friends replies.

The other friend rolls her eyes. "You're never any fun. We're seniors. We're going to do this right!"

They all giggle and get into one car, driving off. I can't help but smile at remembering this time when I was a senior here. Most of my memories are bad, but not all of them.

Chapter Two

EVERLY

Sweat drips down my forehead as I block the punch Declan throws at me. I try to take the opening he left on his side, but he blocks that, as he does pretty much every punch I throw at him. He grabs my shoulders and throws me to the floor, knocking the wind out of me. He straddles me and pins me down with his hand gently on my throat.

I cough a couple of times as the burning air re-enters my lungs. I hit the mat beside me with my hand to tap out. Declan gets off me and holds out his hand for me to take. I shake my head and sit up, taking a moment to regain my composure.

He's been pushing me a lot harder since being back in New York. We felt a lot safer in Georgia since we were across the country. It's not as dangerous as Boston is, where my dad lives, but it's a close second considering his boss lives here. I got more curious over the years about what my dad does, but he's been able to keep it well hidden from me saying the less I know, the better. Of course I've snooped around. He's definitely doing some illegal things with some shady people.

"So, what are the plans tonight?" Declan asks like he does every Friday morning.

"Pajamas, ice cream, and movie night," I state just as I have the past few weekends since being back.

I haven't figured out what my goal is with being back in New York yet, so it's easier to stay in when I'm not working. I really would've been much happier staying away from this state for the rest of my life, but since every job I applied for didn't hire me, here I am. All my old friends are here and I'm not sure if I want to reinsert myself into their lives yet or not.

My goal when heading off to college was to cut them all out completely. It didn't work with any of them, except James. Looking back, I could've done that a lot differently. I could've done a lot of things differently. I've come to terms with there being no use regretting my decisions, but I'd be lying if I said I wish I couldn't go back in time to change things. Then again, I wouldn't be who I am now and where I am now.

"You're going out," Declan states.

I choke on the water I'm drinking. Declan has no problem telling me how things are, but he rarely tells me what to do, especially with my time.

"Excuse me?" I ask, wiping the water off my chin.

"Go to Asher's club. Sit at the bar. Eat a meal and have a drink," he states.

I look him over, and I know I have a confused look on my face. "Are you coming with me?"

He stares at me. "Of course."

"Are you asking me on a date, Declan?" I ask with a teasing smile.

His lips quirk up. "You'll be alone at that bar while I watch from my usual corner. Have some fun Everly."

I continue to tease, "Well, that's no fun. I was hoping you were finally giving in and couldn't resist me."

Declan pulls his shirt back on while motioning to himself with his hand. "Sorry Everly. You'll never have this."

I make a fake pouty face as I stand and gather my things. Declan is the definition of the best and most trustworthy security guard. He's also the definition of the hottest security guard. With his dark brown hair kept short, he always sports that attractive three-day-old stubble look on his face. He has those deep, panty-melting brown eyes. We're not even going to talk about his perfectly sculpted body. He trains every morning with me, but I swear at night when Barry is on shift, Declan comes down for hours of weightlifting.

I'd be lying if I said I didn't check him out every time I see him shirtless, which is pretty much every day. A girl can look. He's seven years older than me, so that means he's thirty. I need to figure out a way to get him a girlfriend because a man that looks like that should definitely be shared with the female population.

I'd be even more of a liar if I said I didn't have a crush on him at one time. In my poor decision-making days in college, I even made a move on him. I try not to remember planting that kiss on him one day when we were training, and he was straddling me on the floor like he was today. The worst part is that I was completely sober, which was a rarity during those days. He immediately pushed me off and turned me down gently. I, figuratively of course, banged my head on the wall for weeks after that.

Running into James today pops into my head with all this reminiscing. I feel those stupid butterflies in my stomach thinking about him. I'm not dumb enough to think that I've ever gotten over him, even though I've tried my hardest. Including wanting to screw my security guard among many, many more regrettable poor life decisions I made. Regardless, pushing him out of my head is the best thing I can do right now.

As I walk toward the door, I yell over my shoulder, "One drink."

Declan doesn't respond, and I don't need to look back at him to know he's smiling. I've had quite a few people I consider my best friend in my lifetime, but Declan is and always will be number one. He may be paid to protect me, but I know that even if my father couldn't pay him anymore, he'd still be here.

My phone buzzes in my pocket. Speaking of best friends, when I pull it out to see who's calling, I find Ashley's name flashing on the screen.

I answer on the third ring. "Hey."

I hear her laugh. "Hey to you too. You sound so excited to talk to me."

I laugh this time. "Sorry, just finished my training with Declan."

"Oh!! Was he shirtless today?" She asks, a little too excited.

Speaking of crushes on Declan, Ashley has had one on him since high school. Honestly, I'd be wondering what was wrong with someone if they didn't have a crush on him.

"He sure was, but he made it clear again I'll never have a shot at that perfect body of his."

I hear Declan choke on his water as I made sure to say that loud enough for him to hear. I love messing with him, but he deserves to know how great he is, too.

"I don't know how he resists you, Everly. You're hot too," she says.

"Thanks Ashley. I can say the same to you. So, what's up?" I ask because I know she doesn't randomly call in the mornings for nothing.

"I'm thinking of flying in for a few days around Halloween. You free?" she asks.

"Yes! Of course I'm free! Have you had any luck with finding a job?"

Ashley's like me, where she would be fine living the rest of her life without stepping a foot back in New York. She saw how I struggled to find a job though, which still baffles me since I had forty-nine other states I could've been working in. Regardless,

I'm here now and she wants to be where I am. Plus, she can be closer to her family again.

"I have an in-person interview lined up for when I'm there. It'll be the third, so I think I have a good shot," she says.

"That's awesome Ashley! You're staying with me, right?" I ask.

"Of course! I'll probably stay one night at home, though. My brother and his wife will be in town, too."

That's right, Dillon recently got married. He and James were best friends for a while. I wonder if they still are. There is an unspoken rule that we don't talk about James. Dillon came down and got a job in Georgia so he could be closer to Ashley. He's the big brother who always comes to her rescue, the one she turns to when she's desperate and needs help. There is nothing he wouldn't do for her. He met his wife while working there, but about a year ago, they both moved to Indiana. The last I heard, they hate it there, and he's trying to relocate back to New York. Everything freaking leads back to New York.

"So, how's everything going?" she asks.

I sigh. I suppose she'll eventually know, so I might as well tell her now. "I ran into James this week at a coffee shop. Literally ran into him."

She's silent for a moment before asking, "How'd that go?"

"It was okay. Honestly, it felt like no time had passed, and unfortunately, he looks even hotter now than he did when we were together."

I can feel her smile on the other end of the phone. "How'd you feel?"

"Like I wanted to jump him and pretend like we've been together this whole time."

Did I just say that out loud? Because I'm pretty sure I haven't even said that in my head. Dang Ashley and her getting my true feelings out of me.

"So, what are you going to do about it?" she asks.

"Nothing. Absolutely nothing. I'm going to forget we ran into each other and pray it never happens again. You know what happened Ashley..." I say, not needing to explain my reasoning to her.

We finish the call, and I'm excited she will be coming in a couple of weeks. I know it's only been a month since I've seen her, but it's a month too long. We've been living together ever since we left for college, in the house my father bought for us. I miss my best friend, who is basically a sister now.

I take a quick shower and get ready for work. I send a text to Asher, letting him know that I'll be stopping by the club tonight because of Declan's insistence. He responds that he'll be there later in the night, so he'll come to say hello. I finish with my hair and makeup, putting on more than normal because I don't feel like fixing it up again before going out tonight, and I head out the door.

CHAPTER THREE

JAMES

I stare out of the floor to ceiling windows in my office at the city below me. Mindlessly, I watch the cars sitting in traffic and the people walking on the sidewalks. I haven't been able to concentrate on work since running into Everly at the coffee shop the other morning. I knew it would be hard seeing her again, but I didn't know it would be this hard.

She took my breath away the moment she bumped into me. Her long brown hair with a hint of red and loose curls draped over her shoulders. Those hazel eyes draw me in every time I look at them. Her skin is pale like she hasn't seen the sun in years, but it glows, making her the most gorgeous woman I've ever laid my eyes on.

The moment she spoke to me, it felt like we were back on the day she left for college. Like no time has passed, and the universe was giving me a second chance to do things differently. I thought I was doing the right thing back then by letting her go, but I've regretted it every day since. I regret the choices I made after even more. It took everything I had not to touch her and claim her as mine again. I'm not making the same mistakes I did back then when I was young and stupid.

My phone vibrates with a text from Declan.

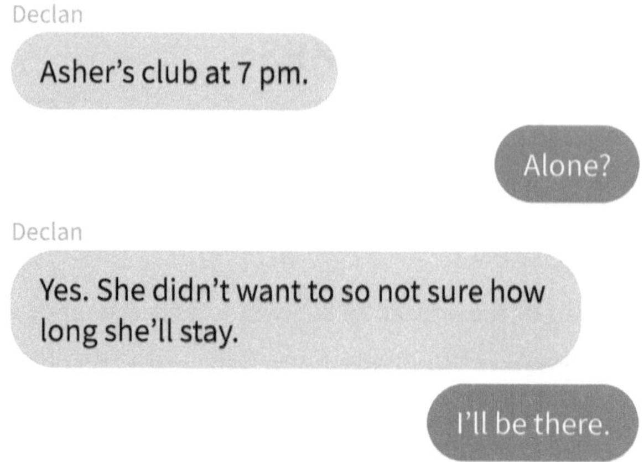

I don't believe in fate. I believe in making your own destiny, and sometimes that means doing what you need to do to get what you want. In this case, I want Everly back. The moment she broke up with her fiancé, I started putting things in motion to get her back. That meant I first needed to get her to New York.

The only way to do that was to get her a job here. She probably wonders why she never heard from half the schools she applied to in basically every state other than New York. Those that did reply, replied with a professional thank you for your interest, but we've gone with another candidate. She would never know that her applications never even made it to their destination. I knew with her being a month away from graduating with her master's, she'd be getting desperate for a job, so I pulled some strings with our old high school. While they were happy to have an old student come back to work, especially with her 4.0 GPA she would be graduating with in her master's program, the hefty donation I offered ensured they'd reach out immediately with the job offer. Thankfully, she had signed up on a job website that they claimed to have found her on.

I gave her a month to get settled before inserting myself back into her life. It was easy enough considering I have an inside source that knows where she is at all times, Declan, her security guard. While I can track her, it's easier knowing exactly when and where she's going to be, giving me time to prepare. He's loyal to Everly, and it took him a while to break her confidence by talking with me, but even he knows we're meant to be together. She's it for me. Now I just need to convince her I'm it for her.

My phone buzzes with another text. This time from my best friend, Bash.

Bash

I heard Everly is back in town.

He knew she was coming back to town, and while I haven't told him, he knows I had something to do with it. This is his way of asking me if I've made my move yet.

I bumped into her earlier this week.

Bash

Bumped into huh? How'd she look?

Beautiful as always.

Bash

Not what I meant.

I know what you meant. She looked good.

Bash

Any plans to see her again?

I may bump into her tonight.

Bash

Laughing emoji Good luck. Let me know when we can all start getting together again.

Soon.

His last text makes me feel nauseous. Thinking about all of us getting together means thinking about Jake, who she fucking had to bring up immediately in our first conversation we've had in six years. Yeah, Jake used to be one of my best friends too, since we were kids. He's Bash's younger brother, the same age as Everly and my little brother, Ben. We all grew up together and are basically like brothers. Except, brothers, don't fuck the girl you love. We've been on rocky ground for a few years now. It's been hard to completely avoid him, but I'm doing my best. Every time I see him, I want to punch him in the face, which I've already done.

A knock sounds on my door. "What?" I snap.

The door cracks open, and my assistant peeks her head in. "I'm sorry to bother you, Mr. Crawford, but your ten o'clock is here."

I shake my head as if that'll get rid of the sour mood that thinking about Jake put me in. "Thanks Tina, I'll be right there."

She nods and closes the door. I take a deep breath and take my suit jacket from the back of my chair and put it on. I need to stay focused for a few more hours, and then I can let thoughts of Everly distract me. I need to come up with a plan for tonight.

It's close to seven, and I spent way too long getting ready for tonight. I feel like a teenager again, trying to figure out what I should wear to impress the girl I have a crush on. Should I go casual? Business casual? Full on suit and tie? Clearly, the last one isn't the best course of action considering we're going to a club.

In the end, I went with the safe option of what she told me she loved to see me in back when we were dating.

"I really love you in those button-down shirts with jeans," Everly said as she ran her eyes up and down my body.

I made a mental note that night and made sure to wear outfits like that more often. That was one of the best nights I had in college. She surprised me for my birthday with our best friends as we partied together, got drunk and high, and made stupid decisions. I remember she was self-conscious about the way she dressed because she didn't expect to be going to a frat party with me that day, but she always looked perfect in anything she wore. The guys at that party couldn't keep their eyes off her. Then when my buddy Brad came up hitting on her, I almost lost it. I had to get her out of there before I punched someone.

I pull out my phone and dial Ryder, who answers on the first ring, as always.

"Yeah?" he answers casually.

"We're going out tonight," I state.

"Where to?"

"Asher's club," I reply.

I hear him cough as if he was taking a drink and choking on it. "I'm sorry, did you just say a club?"

I'm getting impatient. "Yes, Ryder, a club. I'm leaving in five."

"Alright, I'll pull the car around," he says before hanging up the phone.

Ryder has been with me since high school, and he's the best at what he does. Which is any role that I ask him to be: driver, bodyguard, personal shopper, stalker, IT support, etc. And while I'll never admit it to him, he's one of my best friends. He's only four years older than me, and my father gave him a shot because his father is a good friend. Once I moved from home, I took him with me and put him on my payroll. He had no objection to coming with me.

He's also great at keeping himself unnoticed. I'm fairly positive that Everly doesn't know that he exists, but he knows everything about her. As I mess with my hair in the mirror right before heading out the door of my apartment, I feel like an idiot. I ride the elevator downstairs and hop in the passenger seat of his dark gray Porsche, which I had to buy him when I lost a bet against him.

He drives off, and I notice the smirk sitting on his smug face.

"What?" I ask.

He shakes his head and doesn't answer.

"If you have something to say, say it," I snap.

"When's the last time you've been to a club?" he asks with a knowing smile.

Yeah, I don't do clubs. I don't do much of anything other than sleep, eat, and work. Occasionally, I'll get together with Bash or Ben, but that's usually at one of our places. I don't go out, and I really have no desire to do so.

"What's your point?"

He shrugs his shoulders. "No point. Just an observation. Does it have anything to do with a certain someone being there at seven tonight?"

I rest my elbow on the car door and lean my head on my hand, staring straight ahead. I don't give him the satisfaction of responding to that because he already knows the answer. After I mentioned going to the club, he must have looked at my texts. He keeps tabs of my text messages, emails, and everything. The guy knows me better than I know myself.

He pulls up and drops me off at the entrance. It's only 7:20 pm, so there's no line yet into the club. Her coming here this early in the night shows she doesn't want to be here anymore than I want to be, which works to my advantage. Maybe I can convince her to come back to my place.

When I walk into the club, I spot Declan in the corner with his arms folded, standing against the wall. He looks my way as I enter and tilts his head toward the bar. My gaze follows where he indicated to find Everly sitting with her back facing me and Asher sitting in the chair beside her. As if Asher can sense me, he glances my way, smiles, and excuses himself from her. I take the opportunity to casually slide into the seat he just left. My breath hitches the moment her hazel eyes meet mine.

CHAPTER FOUR

EVERLY

My stomach is in knots as I look up at the man who just sat down in Asher's seat that he just left moments ago. James.

I'm not one to believe in fate, but the way we keep running into each other is almost like the universe is messing with me. I can't help but take a moment to admire how handsome he looks in his light gray fitted button-down shirt and dark jeans. I remember telling him when we dated how much I liked him in that. Did he remember? No, he didn't know he'd run into me here today, so that wasn't for me.

I turn around to look at Declan, who shrugs his shoulders with a smirk on his face. Once again, he failed to alert me to James' presence, and clearly, he had no intention of doing so or trying to interrupt to get me out of a conversation with him. He knows how much I've been wanting to avoid James. A good friend would come up with a scenario about why we need to leave, but he's not being a good friend right now. I'm going to have to have a talk with him later about this.

Before turning back toward James, I catch Asher in the corner of my eye, also watching from a distance. That jerk must have seen James enter too, and that's why he excused himself in the middle of our conversation. He didn't even warn me he saw James walk in. I'm going to have to reevaluate the company that I keep.

Finally, my attention is back on James, and he already has a beer in hand. Was I really glaring at my supposed friends long enough for him to capture the bartender's attention and order a beer?

James stares at me as he takes a sip and doesn't say a word. Am I supposed to be the one that makes the first move in the conversation? He's the one who sat down beside me without being invited. I take a sip of my margarita, and we continue our stare-off, neither of us wanting to break first.

The longer I stare at him, the more uncomfortable I get because my damn heart is betraying my head. It's beating as if I just ran three miles and haven't taken a break. I let out a silent groan as my thoughts wander about how handsome he is and how he's currently making me feel. Just the way he's staring at me, and his professional hair that looks like he's run his hand through a few times after a long day at work, makes me want to jump into his lap and do things I should not be thinking about when it comes to him.

I go to take another sip and realize that my margarita is completely gone. When did I drink the whole thing? I must've been gulping it down while thinking things I have no business thinking. I take this opportunity to break away from looking at him and order another. If this is how the night is going to go, I really need another margarita even though I only planned to have one.

After the bartender brings me another, I can't take it anymore. I feel like I'm about to crawl out of my skin with this silence between us, even though the club is plenty loud.

"What are you doing here?" I ask while taking another sip and giving him an accusatory stare.

He grins. "I'm here to relax after a long day at work. What about you?"

I narrow my eyes before asking, "Do you come here often?"

He takes another sip of his beer before saying, "Nope."

What the hell kind of answer is that? If he doesn't come here often, then what is he doing here on the same night that I'm here? I take another glance at Declan, who just raises his eyebrows at me like he's asking me what. My heart skips a beat for a moment as I remember Declan is the one who forced me to come here. Did he set this up? Does he still talk to James? I never forbade him from speaking to James, but I didn't think that I needed to. I especially didn't think that I needed to tell him not to tell James my whereabouts. Declan wouldn't do that, right?

I look back at James as he continues the conversation. "Do you want to sit at a table where we can talk easier?"

Sitting at one of the VIP tables Asher used to pull me to is a lot better than sitting at a bar when you're trying to have a conversation with someone. It's also a lot more private, which means that is the worst idea to do with James when I'm already a margarita in. I glance down at my current margarita and retract that statement. That's the worst idea to do with James when I'm already two margaritas in. Considering it's completely empty, I push it to the end of the bar for the bartender to come by and take.

"No thanks, I'm comfortable here," I say.

When the bartender comes back, he asks if I want another, and I sigh as I nod. I came for one drink, not three, and to get drunk. Clearly, I'm getting drunk tonight. I put my elbow on the bar and my forehead in my hand, shaking my head. What am I doing? Drinking a third is the last thing I should do around James.

James places his hand on my knee, which verifies that statement as true. I can feel a spark and tingle climb my leg all the way through my entire body. My body still reacts to his touch, and drinking so much will only intensify it.

"Everly, if you prefer for me to leave, I will," he says softly.

I look up at James and see that his facial expression is also soft. Geez, he really means that he will leave if I ask him to. Butterflies start fluttering through my stomach again and make my heart clench.

I want, no need, to say yes please leave. My head is screaming at me to tell him to leave or better yet force myself to leave, but my heart and body are both over here betraying my common sense by telling me it's a fantastic idea to sit here, drink another margarita, and talk with my ex who I'll never be over.

I down half my third margarita in what feels like one gulp as I say, "No, it's okay. It'll be nice to catch up."

Yeah, obviously we're playing the game of just keep piling on the lies and throwing out words I want to say the complete opposite of. What is wrong with me?

He removes his hand from my knee and smiles. I miss the connection already, and his smile goes straight to my needy vagina, who hasn't gotten action in a year. I internally roll my eyes at myself. I'm doomed.

"So, what made you want to come back to New York?" he asks casually.

I laugh. "Want is a strong word. I needed a job, and New York was the only place that offered me one."

"Where do you work?"

I have a feeling he knows exactly where I work and what I do, but I play along.

"I'm a school counselor at our old high school."

He doesn't look surprised. "I can see that. I bet you're great at your job and will help a lot of kids. They need someone who cares and someone who can relate."

Of course, he knows me well enough to know why I chose this profession. He knows everything about me, and that's just one more reason that I need to stay away from him. After I moved to Georgia, I left my past exactly where it belonged, in the past. It was nice making new friends who knew nothing about me. I could be whoever I wanted to be, and no one needed to know about anything that happened in high school. I pretended like I had a perfectly normal high school experience. Sometimes I felt guilty pretending Lauren never existed, but it was for the best.

"So, you're working at your father's company?" I ask, but already know the answer.

I tried hard not to look at what James was doing, but sometimes I reserved certain nights for a special kind of torture. The day Lauren died was typically when I spiraled and decided that I needed to torture myself by seeing how happy James was without me and what he was doing. I always found a lot of evidence proving that I made the right decision by letting him go. He's incredibly successful in his business, and he always looked so happy with whatever girl was on his arm in the tabloids.

"Yes, I'll be taking over completely in a couple of years once he thinks Ben and I are ready."

"That's great. Are you enjoying it?" I ask.

James is silent for a few moments before answering. "I enjoy the tech side of things, yeah. Being the boss has its upsides, too. The job itself is fine."

The way he said that makes me think that he's not entirely happy. I'm not sure if it's because of his job or something else in his life. My heart sinks, thinking that he's not completely happy because that's all I ever wanted for him.

I finish my third margarita and ask for a glass of water. Feeling fuzzy and loosening up, I find myself staring at James again and know I'm wearing my emotions on my sleeve. I decide to look away before I make any stupid decisions because while he is all man, he still has that boyish smile that does something to me. That something is nothing I need to be thinking about three drinks in.

As I look around the club for a distraction from James, I find a man sitting at the other end of the bar that I'm pretty sure has been looking over here most of the time we've been here. Underneath a baseball cap, he looks handsome with long, shaggy black hair. He has a bit of scruff that's neatly kept like he hasn't shaved in a couple weeks but grooms it. He's tan and I'm pretty sure if he stood up, that would also add in the tall to the tall, dark, and handsome cliché.

I must have been looking at him for too long because he notices. He smiles and winks at me. I feel myself blush, so I quickly look away to find James also looking at him with a death glare. Is he jealous? The guy hasn't even talked to me. He just winked. I can't help the smile that creeps up on my face.

Chapter Five

JAMES

I'm trying my best not to get worked up at the fact that Ryder is sitting across the bar from us, being way too obvious. It's clear that Everly has caught onto his gaze, and she's observing him more closely than I'd like her to. I'm also pissed off that he just winked at her. I didn't think I was a terribly jealous man, but after seeing that wink, I want to take that Porche back.

Everly is already three drinks in, and I can tell she's feeling it. I will not take advantage of her tonight, but I want to get her back to my place so we can continue talking. She's battling with herself, which means she still has feelings for me, and that's great news for me. With how tipsy she currently is, it shouldn't be too hard to convince her to come home with me.

Before I can ask her, my phone buzzes in my pocket. I sigh as I pull it out, fully intending to ignore it until I see the name that pops up on the screen.

"I have to take this," I say as I walk toward the back offices to hear.

Normally, I wouldn't leave her alone at the bar, but both Declan and Ryder are watching after her. They won't let anything happen to her or anyone hit on her.

"What's up, Ben?" I answer.

"Hey James, how's it going?" he asks me in his "I'm going to pretend everything is alright, but I'm in deep shit right now" voice.

"What do you need?" I ask, trying to cut to the chase.

He sighs. "I'm in a bit of a predicament. I'm kind of in a bush in Central Park and need a ride home. By need a ride home, I mean I also need some clothes. Like, everything..." he drifts off and I don't catch what he's mumbling.

I close my eyes to keep myself from getting worked up. "So, what you're saying is you are currently naked in a bush in Central Park?"

He laughs. "Yeah, that about sums it up."

"Do I want to know why?"

"Nope," he responds, popping the p at the end.

"I'll be there in twenty minutes," I say while hanging up the phone.

Leave it to Ben to ruin my chances tonight with Everly. Or maybe he just helped my chances. I guess we'll find out.

When I round the corner and spot Ryder in the seat I was in before talking to my ridiculous brother, the rage that has been slowly surfacing boils over. What the fuck is Ryder doing talking to Everly when he's not supposed to be seen? When I get closer and hear them laughing together, it takes everything in me not to pull Ryder off that chair beside her and get a hit in.

I insert myself between them, leaning on my elbow, facing her. I pretend Ryder doesn't exist and try to rein in my rage before talking to Everly.

"Sorry about that. That was Ben. He needs my help," I say, while trying to block Ryder from Everly's view.

She looks up at me, concerned, before asking, "Is everything alright?"

I shake my head and force a smile. "He said he's currently naked in a bush in the middle of Central Park. I need to go get him."

She laughs. "What? How did that happen?"

I shrug my shoulders. "Not sure. I didn't ask."

She tries to look around me toward where Ryder sits, but I lean closer to her, so she has to only concentrate on me.

She clears her throat. "Um, okay. Well, it was good seeing you. Good luck with Ben."

She looks disappointed and relieved at the same time. Yeah, she's battling with herself. I lean in even closer, and she holds her breath. I can see her face flush as she glances down at my lips that are just inches from hers. If I were to kiss her right now, she probably wouldn't object, but I won't. I'm going to make her want me, and she's going to make the first move. I can be a patient man.

"Come with me," I say softly.

She begins to breathe again as she says, "Okay."

I smile at my victory, stand up straight, and hold my hand out for her to take. To my surprise, she takes it and stands up next to me. I throw some cash on the counter for the bartender and lead her away, still holding her hand.

She tugs on my hand, making me stop as she looks at Ryder. "It was nice meeting you, Ryder."

Anger rises again as he smiles back at her, tipping his hat. Seriously? And he told her his name? What the hell is he thinking?

I was thinking about having Declan drive us to get Ben, so Ryder wasn't stranded here, but screw him. I'm taking the car, and he can find his own way home. Declan follows as I lead her out the door. He meets up with us outside the club, and I tell him where we are headed so he can follow.

I open the passenger door for her and she stumbles a little. I grab her arm to help guide her in. With how much I've seen her drink in the past, I didn't expect three drinks to make her this tipsy. The bartender was putting a little more alcohol in it than necessary, but I'm still surprised.

As I walk to the driver's side, I send a quick text to Ryder that he's on his own. Usually, I wouldn't go without him because you never know, but with Declan following us, we'll be fine. After what he did tonight, he deserves to be left behind. Though I'm betting he's laughing right now and proud of himself.

After a few minutes of silence, I finally break it by asking, "So who was that at the bar?"

Everly looks over at me, studying me. I made sure to ask the question in an even tone and keep my face straight, but I know she's thinking I'm jealous. The tilt of her lips shows she's pleased with that development.

"I'm not sure. His name was Ryder, but we didn't get to talk much," she says, not giving any details.

If they didn't get to talk much, then why the hell were they laughing together when I came back to the bar? I want to ask what they were laughing about, but that would be too much. I'll have to get it out of Ryder later.

Surprisingly, it doesn't take too long to get to Central Park, even with all of New York City's ridiculous traffic. After parking, I pull up the app on my phone to track Ben's phone. It's about a five-minute walk. Thankfully, he's not too deep into Central Park, which makes me wonder if he started walking to get closer, but that would be dumb to do naked.

I get out and open the door for Everly. To my surprise, she waited. She used to purposefully get out quickly so I couldn't open the door for her. I had to tell her I enjoy doing that for her so she would let me sometimes. Clearly, she remembers.

Before walking toward Ben's location, I pop the trunk and pull out my gym bag. It has clothes in there that Ben can use. They aren't clean, but he doesn't have much of a say in the matter. I sling the bag over my shoulder, and we begin the walk to his location. As Everly gets closer to my side, I catch myself before I try to hold her hand. It's hard to believe it's been six years since I've last seen her because everything with her feels so natural.

"So, what do you think happened to Ben?" she asks while keeping her eyes forward like she's concentrating hard on walking.

"I have no idea. He's not any better than when we were kids. He's always getting himself into awkward situations," I say.

Everly laughs. "I thought he'd outgrow that. Did I ever tell you about the time he had a squirrel in his room?"

I look over at her and say, "No."

She shakes her head. "It was right before Homecoming. Ashley and I were getting ready, and I went downstairs for something. I ran into Ben, and he asked for my help to get a squirrel out of his room before your mom found out and freaked. It took a minute to find it, but the thing jumped at my face, and I caught it in the box Ben gave me. He then threw it out the window where it landed in a tree."

Her entire face lights up at the memory, and she's laughing. I can't help but smile and laugh with her. I love seeing her happy like this. I wish all her memories of high school were this light and made her happy. I wish window,I could be enough to make her feel like this all the time.

"Why did he have a squirrel in his room?" I ask while still laughing.

She shrugs her shoulders. "I have no idea. He pulled the don't ask questions, just help friendship rule."

Ah, yes. The five of us made up that rule when we were little. Actually, I'm pretty sure Ben made that rule up. Each of us has used it many times. When we don't want to explain what happened, but need help without judgment, we pull that one out. As much as we really want to know what happened, it's a great rule to have. It's nice to have friends you can trust to help you out in any situation when you need it. I suppose like Ben is now. I'm certain he's going to pull it out here, too.

We finally make it to Ben's location, but we don't see him. I wonder if he lost his phone in one of these bushes and got caught by the police. I wouldn't be surprised if the police picked him up and took him to a holding cell for being naked in Central Park.

Just as I'm about to peek into the bush where it says his phone is, Ben stands up. The bush covers most of him, but you can still see from his chest up.

"Took you long enough, James!" Ben says while grabbing the gym bag from me.

Before he can unzip it, he notices Everly. "Everly! What are you doing here? Never mind, it's good to see you! Let me just... get dressed and we can chat."

Ben sits back down, but it looks like he dove back into the bush. He takes a few moments to get the clothes on, but when he finally does, he comes out and gives Everly a hug.

"It's good to see you too, Ben. So... are you going to tell us what happened?" she asks with a hopeful smile on her face.

"Nope. Don't ask questions, just help," he says exactly as I knew he would.

Neither of us bring it up again on the walk back to the car. Everly and Ben talk the whole way, and I can't get a word in. I'm sure that's exactly what she wanted. Once Ben gets in the car, I grab her arm to stop her before she can go back with Declan.

"Come back to my place for a bit," I say with hope in my voice.

Everly is looking back and forth in my eyes, debating with herself. I purposefully made a statement versus asking a question because Everly used to find it hard to resist doing what I told her to do. Especially when it came to something she equally wanted.

To end her internal debate, no matter which way it lands, I pull her in closer, so her body is against mine. I lean down, inches from her face, just like I did at the bar. I can hear her breathing pick up and can still see the debate warring inside her. Come on Everly, just say yes. Come back with me.

"I... I can't. I need to get home. I have... something to do," she says while backing away from me.

I silently groan and try not to be disappointed. It's only the first time we've been able to spend any time together since she's been back in New York. I can give her time. I need to give her time. I will, but I'm going to do everything I can to persuade her into giving us another chance. Those feelings are still there, just under the surface. Now, I just need to make them resurface.

CHAPTER SIX

EVERLY

It's been a week since I bumped into James at Asher's club and a whole week of me giving Declan the cold shoulder. When Declan brought me home that night, I outright asked him if he was talking with James, and he said yes. When I asked him if he had told James I would be there that night, he didn't say anything, which is also equal to a yes.

I've been training a little more than normal with Declan, just so I can get a few hits here and there on him. I wouldn't say I'm an aggressive person, but there's something about throwing punches and hitting your target when you're angry with them.

It's 6:00 on a Friday night, and we just finished a training session. I sit in a chair, downing some water and wiping the sweat from my forehead. Declan pulls his chair right in front of mine, so close that our knees are touching. That means he's not going to let me leave without speaking to him.

"It's been an entire week, Everly. You need to talk to me," he says, leaning forward with his elbows on his knees.

I stare Declan in the eyes but say nothing. I'm still mad at him, and I feel betrayed. Declan is part of my security, and I consider him one of my best friends. How could he betray me like that?

"Everly... I'm sorry. When James first started texting me, I mostly ignored him. He really cares about you, and I couldn't just not respond to him," he says.

I pinch my eyebrows together and stare at him more intensely. "Um, yeah, you could have. It's easy. You just don't reply."

Declan grins. "There she is!"

I want to facepalm myself for falling into his trap and speaking. He knew that would get me to talk. Whatever, since I already started talking, I guess there's no point in stopping.

"When did he first start texting you?"

Declan doesn't answer, and my heart races. Has he been talking to him this entire time?

My voice grows stern. "Declan, when did you start talking to him?"

Declan's facial expression turns into his I'm sorry expression, which means I won't like the answer.

"I didn't start replying to him for a couple of months after we went to Georgia," he says softly.

A couple of months after going to Georgia? That can't be right.

"You've been talking to him for almost six years?! Declan! What the hell?" I yell.

I rarely yell, especially at Declan, but I'm pissed. What have they been talking about? Has he been telling him everything about me? Are they like besties now? How did I have no idea that he was talking with James all this time?

"Everly…" He shakes his head.

Yeah, he has nothing to say because he knows he betrayed me. We've established that, so now I need to know why he did it.

"Why? Why did you betray me? What have you been talking about for six years? Were you just texting him daily updates or something?" I ask as I feel my anger continue to rise.

He keeps his voice calm. "I didn't talk to him every day. Sometimes we'd go months, but he mainly was just checking in on you. He wanted to make sure that you were okay, and I didn't see any harm in letting him know how you were doing."

That's the problem, though. I wasn't okay. I wasn't okay for the first few years in college. My life was a complete mess. So, if James knew that and he still didn't come check on me himself, then what does that mean? I'm so confused right now about all of this. I feel betrayed by Declan, and now I can't even figure out what is going through James' mind. He cared enough to check in on me through Declan, but not enough in person? There were a couple times I really could've used James by my side, and he wasn't there. Now knowing that he knew exactly what was going on and chose not to be there, makes it even worse.

I stand up, and Declan stands with me, blocking my way to leave.

I sigh. "Declan, I just need some time to process this. Asher's coming over soon, so I need to get ready."

Declan doesn't budge, but after searching my face for whatever he was looking for, he nods and moves out of the way. All I have to say is that I'm glad Asher was already planning on coming over tonight.

Ever since high school, after Lauren's death, Asher has taken the role of my therapist. We met at his club the summer before my senior year of high school. I literally ran into him in the hallway, and he mistook me for someone else for a second. We got to know each other a little that night, or should I say he got to know me, and he's been there for me ever since.

Once Lauren died, I needed a therapist, and the ones my father was paying for just weren't doing it for me. Asher isn't a therapist, but he's a good friend and a great listener, so he agreed to be there for me when I needed him. We did weekly sessions for many years, even when I went to college. We mainly did it on the phone since we were across the country from each other. Now our sessions usually consist of us just hanging out and him listening to me when I need to talk about something.

Even though I've known him for over six years now, I don't know much about his personal life. What I do know is that he basically owns half of New York and knows everyone in it. He owns a lot of clubs, stores, bars, etc. Even the high school I teach at is named after him. Terion High School. Asher Terion. He doesn't have any family as they are all dead, he said, but he has a good friend named Gary. I've met him on several occasions, and he's a lot more serious than Asher is, but he's nice.

The moment I walk into the living room after showering and getting dressed, Asher knocks on my door. I open it and lead him to the kitchen, where we typically sit at the island, talk, drink, and eat whatever dessert I decided to make that day. I just so happened to make his favorite chocolate chip cookies.

"Thanks, Everly," he says while I pile a few cookies on a plate for him.

I sit next to him and ask, "How are you doing?"

He smiles. "I'm doing good. Have a lot going on at work lately, so I'm keeping busy."

I frown. "I hope I didn't pull you away from something important tonight. If you'd rather hang out another night, we can."

He waves me off. "Of course not. I needed a break. So, how are you doing?"

I don't answer because I'm not sure how to answer that. I never have a problem talking to Asher about my problems, but for some reason, I feel stupid talking about this to him. He's so busy, and he just needs to take a night to relax. Is it really fair that I'm always dumping my drama on him? I thought I was over feeling guilty about talking to him about my problems, but ever since being back and seeing how busy he is, the guilt has resurfaced.

"Tell me what's going on, Everly," he demands.

For some reason, I can never say no to him, so I spill every-thing. I tell him about my mixed feelings about James. I tell him about how I found out that Declan has been talking to James the entire time without me knowing. When I tell him how I feel betrayed, I'm honestly confused about everything concerning James. Not only that, but after seeing Ben again, even just for a few minutes, I miss the boys and the way things used to be between us all. I knew coming back to New York would be hard, but this is a lot harder than I thought it would be.

After spilling everything to Asher, his demeanor changes into therapist mode. We move to the living room to get more com-fortable.

"We knew coming back to New York would be hard, espe-cially as you start running more into your past. Let's start with James. We all know that he's still in love with you. How do you feel about him?"

Well, I wouldn't say he's still in love with me. "I don't think he's still in love with me, but we are both definitely attracted to each other. I don't know how I feel. I know that I still love him, but that doesn't change why we broke up and it doesn't change everything that happened while I was away. He never showed up for me when I needed him. He found someone else quickly after and broke his promise to me."

I twist the ring on my right ring finger like I always do. It's the beautiful emerald promise ring that James gave me when I was a senior in high school. I haven't taken it off since, except once.

I tried to give it back to him when we broke up before I left for Georgia, but he refused.

I held the ring out to James, but he grabbed my hands in his and put it back on my finger.

"I made a promise that I intend to keep. I told you that I will love you forever, and I will," he said while still holding my hands in his to ensure I didn't take the ring off again.

My voice cracked. "James... I... You can't..."

He interrupted me. "Everly, I need you to know that I'll wait for you. However long it takes, I'll be waiting. If it takes you ten months or ten years, I'll be here waiting. There's nothing you can say or do that will change my love for you."

I stared at him and had no words. He couldn't really mean that, could he? He was just saying that, so I'd change my mind, right? As much as I wanted to change my mind, I couldn't. It was for the best. For both of us. Why did it feel so wrong, though?

When I had no more words, James gave me one last hug and said in my ear, "Go now. Find yourself and then find your way back to me. Don't say anything. Don't look back. Go."

As he released me from our hug, he turned me around and pushed me toward the car. I felt the tears streaming down my face and I knew that my tears were mixing with his. I did exactly as he said. I walked to the car, got in, and didn't look back as we drove off.

He's the one that put the ring back on my finger and told me his promises still stand. That he'd love me forever. He also promised he'd propose for real one day. He promised that he'd wait for me no matter how long it took. Then, in my sophomore year of college, he went off and got himself a beautiful new girlfriend.

I wouldn't have been mad that he found someone else or was moving on. In order for him to concentrate on his work, I broke up with him, hoping he would do exactly that. I didn't want him having to worry about finding time for me, his last year of college, and working for his father to learn how to take over the company. The part that I did have a problem with is that he made that promise to me right before I left, and I believed him.

While I never intended to come back to New York when I left, that promise changed everything. I spent the first two hours of that drive to Georgia crying my eyes out on Ashley's lap for leaving James. I loved him so much. Then I had the rest of the drive to figure out where to go from there. I decided that if James was going to wait for me, then I would wait for him. I would go to college, get my degree, and come back to him just like he asked me to.

Asher interrupts my thoughts. "What are you thinking, Everly?"

I swallow down the lump in my throat as I say, "I still love him, Asher. When I'm with him, it feels like I never left, but I can't do it. He broke his promise and, by that, he broke my heart. I've had too much heartbreak in my life, I can't risk it again. I'm done talking about James right now."

Asher nods. "Alright, well, why don't we talk about you missing the boys? Text them. Get all of you together again. It'll be different, but it's something you're missing, so you should do it. Even if it doesn't turn out well, then at least you tried."

He might be right. I really do miss all of us together, but I'm also scared. Our relationship isn't what it used to be, and that's my fault. It wouldn't hurt to see if everyone wanted to try to get together, though.

After a couple of hours hanging out and talking, Asher goes home, and I feel a little lighter than before. We didn't talk too much about Declan because somehow, he convinced me to forgive him, and that Declan was just trying to do what he thought was right. I know that, but I'm still not happy about it. Since he's basically with me 24/7, I suppose I should forgive him sooner rather than later.

CHAPTER SEVEN

EVERLY

I sit in front of Lauren's grave and play with one of the flowers that fell out of the vase. I haven't been to her grave since being back in New York. It's well kept, and the flowers look brand new. I know that it's Lorenzo that keeps the flowers fresh, which makes my heart soften even more when it comes to him.

"Hey Lauren... Sorry it's taken me so long to visit. I know I write to you a lot, but there's nothing like coming to your grave. It feels like you're actually here."

The wind blows and I imagine that it's Lauren letting me know she is here with me.

"I can't believe that Lorenzo is still sending you flowers even though it's been seven years since you died... There's no way that you would've guessed he'd be one to do that, huh?"

No... She definitely wouldn't have guessed that. I really wish she could have seen the sides of Lorenzo that he's shown since her death. I hate he didn't show them to her when she was alive. I wonder if he had, if she'd still be here.

I shake my head and respond to her as if she were speaking to me. "You're right, I can't blame him. I don't blame him anymore for your death, or anyone. I sure do miss you. I often wonder what our life would've been like if you were still here. I know you said you never wanted to be a mother, but I can imagine that you would have one or two little ones running around right now. They would call me Aunty Everly, and I would spoil them so bad. They would look just like you and have your kind personality. Ashley would be married to some famous guy, and I bet James and I would be married right now, too. Possibly thinking about starting our own family, if we wouldn't have already."

I smile at the alternate universe I've created in my mind of the three of us living our best lives and raising families together. The smile quickly fades though as I remember the reality. I'm not married to James. Ashley's not married to anyone. Lauren isn't here. She killed herself, and I'm the one that found her the next morning as she did it just behind the closed bathroom door where I was sleeping on the other side.

It's true. She never wanted to be a mother and definitely didn't want to get married to Lorenzo. She told me that the night before, as she was depressed. Her family was forcing her to marry Lorenzo in an arranged marriage. While he wasn't fond of the idea either, he still was going to go through with it, as it was his duty. He needed a wife and an heir, while her family needed help out of debt. She felt so trapped that she took her own life during Christmas break, when she was supposed to be married, in our senior year of high school.

I blamed Lorenzo for a while after her death because he wasn't the nicest to her and didn't really show he cared for her, but the more I found out about him the more I realized she had her own view based on how she was feeling about the situation. Lorenzo isn't a good man by any means, considering he is a mafia boss, but in his world, he does have a good heart.

I've kept tabs on him through the years, wanting to know how he's doing. He got married a few years after Lauren's death, and he has a son and another baby on the way. He looks like he's truly happy. I'm happy for him, but I can't help but wish that was Lauren's life.

My phone buzzes with a text, pulling me from my depressing thoughts. I quickly open the message, thankful for the distraction. When I look at my phone, I notice a new message in the boys' group with Ben, Bash, James, and Jake. We haven't had a message come through this group in six years.

Ben

> Since Everly's back in town let's get together. I checked everyone's schedule and we're all free tomorrow night. My place 6 pm.

I did not expect that message, though considering I just talked to Asher about this, I figure why not? I won't be the first one to respond, though.

More texts come through moments later.

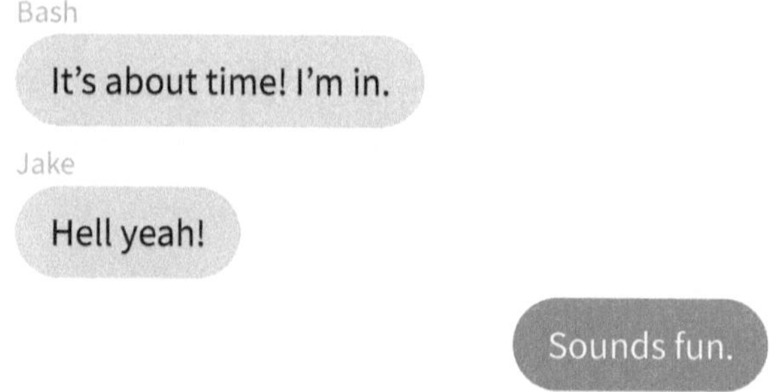

I watch the group chat for a little bit waiting for James' response. I know he and Jake aren't on the best of terms, but I can't imagine that he would pass up this opportunity. As I'm waiting for his response, an incoming call pops up on my phone from my father.

"Hello?" I answer.

"Hey sweetie, how are you doing?" he asks, but I can barely hear him with the background noise.

"I'm good. Where are you?" I ask.

"I'm about to get in a helicopter and wanted to check in on you."

A helicopter? I don't even question it because he's never on the ground, always traveling and flying somewhere.

"I'm good, dad. Why did you want to check on me?"

There's silence for a moment. "Declan mentioned you were at Lauren's grave today for the first time in a while."

Freaking Declan, are you kidding me? "Why is Declan telling you where I am?"

My father laughs. "He's still on my payroll, Everly, and you're my daughter."

I close my eyes and sigh. He's right, he still technically works for my father, so I can't blame him this time, and it's not like it's a secret that I'm at Lauren's grave. I thank my dad for calling and tell him I miss him. He says he'll be back for Thanksgiving and wants to do it at the Crawford's house again like the good old days.

I haven't been back to their house since leaving for Georgia. I talk to Mrs. Crawford at least once a month because I owe her that much for everything she's done for me my whole life. When my mother passed away when I was little, she treated me like her own daughter. My father works directly underneath her husband. We lived in Boston and the Crawford's live in New York. Every summer, I would stay with them for a couple of months while my dad was away on business. The boys became like my brothers, and we always had the best summers when I was in town. James and Benjamin (Ben) are her sons, and I lived in the house with them. Sebastian (Bash) and Jacob (Jake) both lived next door, but Mrs. Crawford always treated them like her sons, too.

After my junior year of high school, I went to the Crawford's house for the summer like normal but stayed my senior year of high school. My father would be out of the state the whole year, so they figured it was best. It was a great summer when James and I admitted our feelings for each other, and I became friends with Ashley and Lauren. The first half of my senior year was great, the second half was hell.

Before my mind can wander down the rabbit hole of depressing memories again, my phone buzzes with another text in the boys' group again.

James

I'll be there.

Seeing his message makes my heart skip a beat and I feel excited. Tomorrow we will all be together again for the first time in six years. I get to see James again, and this time it's planned, so I can prepare. I'm nervous.

CHAPTER EIGHT

JAMES

I walk into Ben's apartment to find him setting up pizza, snacks, and beer on the coffee table in front of the couch. It feels like I'm walking into my college days all over again. Ben lives in the apartment below mine, and both our security teams live in the apartments right next door to each of our apartments. It's a nice setup.

"Hey, can you bring the chips and dip over?" Ben asks with his hands full of beer.

I grab the chips and dip and place them on the coffee table. He went all out, and I have a feeling he's almost as nervous as I am about tonight.

"You nervous about tonight?" Ben asks.

Even though we are two years apart, we've always had a twin-like bond where we can basically read each other's minds. It has its moments when it's cool and then when it's annoying. This is one of those times when it's annoying. I'm not one to show my emotions, never mind talk about them, even to my brother.

"Nah, are you?" I ask, even though I already know the answer.

Ben laughs. "Yeah, it's been forever since we've all gotten together. I miss it, you know? I know it won't be like old times, but I want us to have a good time..."

Ben trails off, and he doesn't need to say what I know he's thinking, but he does anyway. "I know things are still rocky with you and Jake, but... can you try to... I don't know... pretend you two are cool?"

I don't respond and stare at him. I get what he's asking, but no, I'm not going to just pretend we're cool. Honestly, I'm still a little mad that Ben has forgiven Jake so easily. I know they are best friends since they are the same age and all, but I'm his brother. It may be petty, but I feel like he should've had my back a little longer than the few months he gave Jake the cold shoulder.

Ben sighs. "Alright, fine, just don't start a fight in my apartment, please."

I shake my head. "No promises."

Before Ben can respond, there's a knock on the door. I sit on the left side of the couch and pop open a beer. Bash and Jake both arrive at the same time. Bash comes by and gives me a pat on my shoulder as he takes a seat next to me while I'm watching Jake be his loud and obnoxious self with Ben.

"If looks could kill, Jake would be dead," Bash says, pulling my gaze away from Jake.

I smirk. "If only."

Bash shakes his head. "You gotta let it go man, it's not good for you and if you want Everly back... he's one of her best friends too, so he's not going anywhere."

I let out a low growl at his words. Yeah, that's one thing I don't know how I'm going to handle. I've been ignoring that part because right now I'm just concentrating on getting Everly back. Once I have her, we can figure out the rest. Jake is definitely going to be an issue.

Jake sits in the chair next to the couch on my side, and it takes everything in me not to move to the opposite side of Bash on the couch. I know Jake purposefully sat there to piss me off.

"Hey James, good to see you," Jake says like we're best friends and like he didn't fuck the love of my life.

I don't respond because I can feel the anger rising within me. I've avoided Jake as much as possible, and every time I see him, I just want to punch or strangle him. Maybe both. I get up and head to the bathroom to calm myself before Everly gets here. I don't want to be in a pissy mood when I see her tonight.

I stare at myself in the mirror while holding onto the edge of the sink. I hear Jake's laughter out in the living room, and it pulls me back to a memory I wish I could change.

I couldn't stop staring at the stupid tabloid with the picture of Stacey and me. She was completely wrapped around my arm, and they captured one of the few times I smiled. We looked like a happy couple in this picture, which was far from the truth. The article portrayed us like we've been dating and there's an interview with me that they completely took out of context. I threw it on the floor and rubbed my temples like that was going to make this go away, like the massive headache I had.

Someone knocked on my door.

"Come in," I stated without looking up from my desk.

When the door opened and there was no response, I slowly looked up to find Jake making his way toward me. He picked up the article I just threw on the floor and he looked at it, placing it neatly on my desk as he sat in the chair in front of me.

"You want to tell me what's going on with you and Stacey?" he asked, like he was accusing me of something.

"Nothing is going on. You know my father said I needed to bring her as a statement, so I did," I said, leaning back in my chair.

"That's not what this looks like," he said while tapping the article that's on my desk.

"Of course not. What are you doing here, Jake?" I asked, wanting him to get to the point.

He studied me for a moment before answering, "This looks bad, James. You need to tell her the truth."

"No," I quickly stated, interrupting him before he could say anything else.

"She's going to see it," he said with a concerned look on his face.

"So what?"

"So what? So, she's going to be hurt. She's going to assume that all this is true, and you've moved on."

I sighed. "So let her."

Jake looked shocked at my words and then looked angry. Everly is the one who left me almost two years ago, not the other way around. If she wanted to talk to me then she would, but she hasn't texted me once since leaving that day. I'm not going to make the first move. I made it clear what I wanted, so the ball was in her court when she's ready. I meant what I said. I'm going to wait for her, however long it takes.

"You want her to think you're with someone else," he stated instead of asking.

I shrugged. "She can think whatever she wants. If she's concerned, then she can ask me herself."

Jake shook his head. "It's not going to work, James. She's not going to just get jealous and come back to you. This is going to break her heart. She's still not in a good place. She's been through enough. Don't do this to her."

I shook my head again. "She's the one who broke up with me, remember?"

Jake sighed. "You know she still loves you. We've talked about this."

I didn't know that she still loved me. If she did, then why had she gone almost two years without saying a word to me? She left us that day, and I knew she had every intention of cutting all of us out of her life the moment she drove away. She did for a little bit, but eventually she started talking to Ben, Bash, and Jake again. In fact, Jake had been down to visit her multiple times. He claimed she was still in love with me, but I'm doubting it. Not that I would do anything about it because Everly is it for me. I love her, and there's nothing that will ever change that.

"I'm flying in tonight to visit her for the weekend," he stated.

"And?" I asked, wondering why he's telling me this.

"If you still love her, you need to tell her that article isn't true."

There's only been a couple of times I've been angry at Jake, and this sounds like it's about to be one of them.

"I'm good."

Jake stood up and headed toward the door. Before he reached it, he turned around and looked mad.

"I'm disappointed James, I thought you still cared about her. If you don't tell her, then all bets are off."

"What does that mean?" I asked, squinting my eyes at him like it would help me see his intentions better.

"It means that she's going to see you've moved on, and she'll want to do the same. I've stepped aside for you, James, because I know how much she loves you. If you decide you won't tell her and fight for her, then I'm not passing up my opportunity with her," he stated seriously.

It felt like I just swallowed a rock, and it landed hard in my stomach. I always knew Jake still had feelings for Everly, but he's one of my best friends. He wouldn't make a move on her. He was bluffing... right?

I rounded the desk to get closer but kept my distance. "Are you saying you're going to make a move on her?"

He shook his head. "No, I'm not. When she assumes you've moved on, she's going to do the same. If she does, then I'm not turning her down. I love her too, James, and I'm not going to let her be with some random guy if I can have her. So, tell me right now before I leave. Are you going to tell her? Are you going to fight for her?"

I searched his face to find any signs that he's bluffing. I can't tell. I've known Jake my entire life, and he's always so carefree and acts like a stupid goofball. Right now, his face was straight. Regardless, he said he's not going to make the move on her, and I believed that. If she really loves me, some article isn't going to push her into someone else's arms. I'm giving her space to do what she needs to do. I'm not going to put more on her by messaging her. If she really was concerned about Stacey and me, then she'd text me.

"I'm not telling her unless she contacts me," I stated.

Jake reached for the handle and shook his head again. As he opened the door, he said, "I warned you, James."

I didn't say anything else as he closed the door behind him. I swiped my arm across my desk as all the contents to the right side flew off and made a loud thump on the floor. I wanted to punch something, but I couldn't. I took a deep breath and sat back down in the chair behind my desk. I really hope Jake was bluffing because I just called his bluff.

Jake's laughter and Everly's voice pull me out of the past and back into the present. I wash my hands quickly and leave the bathroom, heading back toward the living room to find Jake lifting Everly off the ground in a hug and spinning her around. I close my eyes and take a deep breath. I just went into the bathroom to calm down before she got here, and I failed. I walk toward Everly and give her a hug that lasts longer than it needs to.

"Hey," she says, looking me in the eye with a soft smile as we pull apart.

"Hey," I say back and all the anger in my body dissipates by that single word and the look she gives me.

I keep my hand on her lower back and lead her over to the couch. Bash scoots over to where I was sitting near Jake and I sit in the middle, placing Everly on the right side of me. As far from Jake as possible, while still being able to sit next to me.

CHAPTER NINE

EVERLY

The first hour hanging out with the boys was filled with lots of laughter and reminiscing from the old days. I knew I missed them, but I didn't realize how much until we were actually hanging out again. I worried there would be some awkwardness between us all, but we've picked back up like we haven't gone six years without hanging out all five of us together.

The only way I can tell six years have passed is the way they all look. They haven't changed much, but they are all older looking and more handsome, if that's even possible. Bash and Jake basically look like twins, but Jake has a more boyish look to him. They both have hazel eyes and dark brown hair. Bash keeps his hair short and styled professionally, whereas Jake's is shaggier and goes past his ears. They both are in great shape with abs any girl would drool over, but Bash is a little bulkier than Jake. Ben doesn't look much like his brother, James, at all. Ben has piercing blue eyes and blonde hair. He used to keep his hair short in high school, but it's now like Jake's style, but a little shorter. Both he and James are in great shape too, as I know all of them spend a good amount of time in the gym.

I have noticed some tension between Jake and James. They've barely said a word to each other for the past hour, and I catch James occasionally glaring at Jake like he wants to rip his head off. The only other time I saw James look at him like that was when he found out Jake and I slept together one night during the summer before senior year of high school. It's no secret Jake sleeps around, and I asked him to so I could get over my ex and the horrible things he did to me. Looking back, that was probably mistake number one of a long list of mistakes to follow.

The fact he's looking at him that way shows me he knows what happened between Jake and me a few years ago. I was upset with James and thought we were officially over, so I wanted to move on. Jake and I slept together again, and then continued our friends with benefits situation. He stayed with me the entire summer after my sophomore year of college. That arrangement ended once he went back to New York for college, our junior year. That was mistake number 100. I wasn't in my right mind before my senior year of college after I made an almost life-altering mistake. If I had any idea that Jake had genuine feelings for me, I never would've had that arrangement with him. Somehow, he's stuck around and been one of my best friends.

James pulls me out of my thoughts by placing his arm across the back of the sofa, barely touching my shoulders. That slight movement makes the hair on my arm stand and my breath catch. I'm trying hard not to show my body's reaction to him being so close to me. I peek at him out of the corner of my eye to see him looking straight ahead and smirking. He lowers his arm, so it now rests on my shoulders. Ugh, he knows exactly what he's doing.

"Never have I ever, that's been a while," Bash says, pulling me out of the little bubble I'm in with James.

Someone must have suggested playing a game, and that's always one we liked to play. The last time we played, I'm pretty sure I was drunk.

"Last time we played, we went skinny dipping in the lake and then got drunk. Can we remember some that we said? I wonder if we can say never have I ever still to some of them," Ben says.

"Oh, that's fun. Good idea Ben. We'll take a drink if we have done it," I say while opening a second beer because I just finished my first.

James picks up his beer and says, "I remember one of mine, and it still holds true. Never have I ever kissed a boy."

I drink my beer, and we all look around at each other. No one else takes a sip, which isn't unexpected.

"You still haven't Jake? I'm surprised," Ben teases.

Jake shrugs his shoulders. "What can I say? I like women too much."

I clear my throat and say, "Well, I remember that one came right after mine, which was never have I ever kissed a girl."

They all look at me to wait for my response if that still holds true. I smirk, shrug my shoulders, and take a drink. There is a loud roar between the four of them, and Jake yells out he needs the details.

I laugh. "I was completely drunk with my friends, and I kissed a couple of them. No big deal, sorry there's nothing juicy to tell."

After everyone settles down from that piece of information I shared, Bash says, "One of mine was never have I ever failed a class. That still holds true."

Jake, Ben, and I take a swig of our beers. They all knew Jake and Ben had, but they didn't know I did. What they really didn't know is that I failed more than one class. Like I said before, I made some poor decisions in my past.

We all look at Ben and Jake, but they both say they can't remember what theirs were back then. It doesn't take long for me to remember Ben's because, for some reason, it stuck with me.

"Ben, yours was that you never peed in the shower. Please tell me that doesn't still hold true," I say.

Ben laughs. "Sorry Everly, that's still true. I just can't bring myself to do it."

Everyone else takes another swig of their beers and laughs. We all look at Jake, trying to remember what one of his was. Jake has an odd look on his face, and it makes me think he does remember what it was, but he doesn't want to say it. Apparently, I'm not the only one who notices his facial expression.

"Come on Jake, I can tell you remember. What was it? Clearly it doesn't still hold true if you don't want to say it," Ben says, trying to get it out of him.

Jake shrugs his shoulders. "Nah, I don't remember. I was pretty drunk that night."

"Come on, Jake, what was it?" Bash steps in and pushes.

Jake gives him a pleading look, like he really doesn't want to say it out loud. I cannot for the life of me remember what it was or why Jake wouldn't want to say it. He rarely has a problem with sharing things about himself.

James removes his arm from my shoulder and stiffens beside me before aggressively saying, "Yeah, come on, Jake. Tell us what it was. I know you'll take a swig for this one."

Jake looks at me and gives me an apologetic look. What could it possibly be?

"Alright, if you insist, James. Mine was never have I ever had sex with Everly. Clearly that doesn't still stand," Jake says, taking a long sip of his beer.

James leans back against the couch, placing his hand on my thigh, and takes an equally long sip of his beer. Both Jake and James eye each other while they do. Everyone else in the room is quiet as the tension builds between those two.

Yeah, I was definitely right. James knows what happened between Jake and me a few years ago, and he's not happy with Jake about it. Now that I know that's the truth, I just feel guilty. I hate that I've ruined their friendship over stupid mistakes I've made in the past. If I could take it back, I would. I really try not to dwell on the past, but that doesn't mean I don't sometimes wish I could go back and change things.

After a few moments of silence, Bash clears his throat and tries to change the subject. "Well, that was fun. So, what are you guys doing for Halloween this year? It's my parents' turn for the annual Halloween party, so it'll be at their house this year. Bring a date, I'll be bringing my girlfriend. You all in?"

I sit forward, happy about the topic change. "Yes! I love a good Halloween party. I'll be there, but first I need details about this girlfriend!"

Bash leans back and smiles. I can tell he's thinking about her, and I've never seen that look on his face before. He really likes her.

"We've only been dating for a couple of months, but she's amazing and beautiful," he says with stars in his eyes.

"Okay, more details, please. What's her name and where did you meet?" I ask, leaning over James to get a better view of Bash's reaction.

"Her name's Amelia and we met over the summer while I was on our work vacation at the resort. Everything's still new, but I really like her."

I know I haven't talked to Bash much about his personal life or seen him much in the six years, but I can tell she's different and he really likes her.

"I can't wait to meet her," I say.

Ben changes the subject back. "I'm in for the party."

"Well, it's my parents too, so I have no choice but to be there," Jake says.

"I'll be there," James says while continuing to stare at me.

"Alright, it sounds like we have our next group night planned," Bash says with a smile on his face.

Even with some tension and awkwardness, I love that they all want to continue getting together like the old times. Tonight was a lot of fun, but the Halloween party is going to be even better. It's been a while since I've been to a party, especially one where I can dress up. I'll have to come up with a good costume.

Chapter Ten

JAMES

Chewing the tip of my pen, I stare at Pedro presenting at the front of the room, but don't hear a word he's saying. I've been in this meeting for almost three hours, and I'm ready for it to end. Every third Friday of the month, we allow our staff to present new tech ideas. Sometimes there are some great ideas that we can use and others... not so much.

I'm not sure if the ideas are boring today or if I just can't concentrate because Everly is the only thing on my mind these days. Who am I kidding? It's both. Thankfully, Ben is here today, and it looks like he's jotting down notes because I haven't written a single thing on my paper. It's pointless for me to be here any longer, so once Pedro finishes his presentation, I excuse myself and go back to my office.

Once I sit in the chair at my desk, I take off my glasses and rub the palms of my hands over my face. I need to figure things out with Everly because she's all I can think about day and night, and it's affecting my work.

A knock sounds on my door, and I tell whoever it is to enter. Ben walks in and sits in front of my desk as I put my glasses back on.

"What's with the glasses?" Ben asks.

"My contacts have been bothering me," I state casually.

"Not getting much sleep?" Ben asks.

I don't answer his question because he already knows the answer.

"What do you need?" I ask curtly.

Ben places his notepad in front of me on the desk. "I figured you would like to look over my notes from the meeting. There were a couple of good ideas I think you should look into."

I grab the notebook and relax in my chair. Of course, Ben would've noticed I wasn't paying attention during the meeting. I scan his notes to find details on the ones he marked I should look into. He always takes notes, but these are extra detailed.

"Thanks," I say while putting the pad in my briefcase.

I'm not getting any work done today as it is, so I might as well go home. We still have almost two weeks until the Halloween party. I need to get my crap together, so I don't continue to be useless, and my father gets wind of it. That's the last thing I need.

Just like Ben always reads my mind, he says, "You should message her, James. See her before the party and just tell her how you feel. You're both adults. Start acting like it and communicate with each other."

I let out a laugh at Ben's words. My younger brother is trying to be so wise, and yet he's not wrong. Communication is the key to a good relationship, which is where Everly and I lack currently and always have.

Ben leaves my office, and I follow behind him, but decide to head home. I hop in the passenger seat of the car while Ryder drives through the city, in the evening, on a Friday night. I love living in the city, but I don't think anyone can ever get used to this traffic.

I think about what Ben said, and he's right. I'm willing to be patient and wait for Everly, but I need her to fully understand what I want. And that's her. I feel like I've made it clear with my actions, but maybe that's not enough.

Before I can talk myself out of it, I pull out my phone and text her.

Have any free time this weekend? Would you like to hang out?

I stare at my phone the whole time, waiting for a response. We are almost back at the apartment when she surprises me by responding.

Everly

No plans. What are you thinking?

I tap my phone nervously with my finger as I think about how to respond. She just basically told me she's free all weekend and willing to hang out. Should I start it off tonight and maybe we can fit in a couple of things through the weekend? Would she go for that?

If I ask her out tonight, what should we do? Ben is right, and I really need to tell her how I'm feeling. It'll be hard because I don't talk much about my feelings, but I need to. We could go out for dinner, and I could see what she's thinking about us. It's clear that she's still attracted to me. I've also noticed she still wears the promise ring I gave her back when she was in high school.

I finally decide and send her a text back.

> Would you like to have dinner with me tonight?

Everly

> Where?

> Your choice. We can eat at my place or go out.

She's taking a while to respond, so I look up from my phone to find Ryder parked in the parking garage and staring at me, smiling.

"What?" I ask like a grumpy old man.

Ryder shakes his head. "We've been sitting here for about five minutes with you staring at your phone. Everly?"

I think about lying, but I know Ryder will just go check my messages to see who I'm talking to. It's his job to keep track of who I'm talking to, who I'm with, and what I'm doing at all times, but sometimes he takes it too far, and I know it's for his own entertainment purposes.

"She agreed to hang out tonight, and I'm waiting for her response on what to do," I say, knowing I sound like a teenager waiting for his crush to respond.

Before he can say anything, my phone vibrates with a text.

Everly

> Your place. I don't feel like being out tonight.

> 7 pm? I'll get dinner.

Everly

> Sounds good. See you then.

My heart races at the thought of her coming over to my place for dinner. I know I'm going to have to talk to her about how I feel and what I'm wanting, but the possibility of something more happening makes another part of my body come to life.

I finally exit Ryder's car and head toward the elevator, with him following behind me.

"She's coming over at seven," I say.

Ryder's face lights up. "Wow, I didn't expect that. I will grab my popcorn for the show."

I roll my eyes but don't respond to him. I know he watches the cameras constantly when I have someone over, but saying things like that where he's clearly enjoying the show... If he wasn't so good at his job and the only person I trust completely, I'd fire him. Disregarding his excitement, I quickly enter my apartment. I order a bunch of Chinese takeout that will deliver and get changed into the clothes I know she finds me attractive in. Sitting on the couch, I scroll through some work emails to distract myself before it's time for her to get here.

CHAPTER ELEVEN

EVERLY

I stand outside James' apartment door and tug the hem of my dress down. I'm wearing a short, spaghetti-strapped maroon dress with a V-neck that shows a good amount of cleavage, especially with my push-up bra. With frustration, I hit myself on the forehead and shake my head. What was I thinking? It was so stupid to wear this dress to a casual dinner at his place.

It's cold outside, so I have a cardigan on over it, but clearly any guy would misread a girl's intentions of wearing this dress. Not only was it stupid to wear this dress, but it was stupid to come over to his place. Again, what was I thinking? Clearly, my brain is on vacation, and my vagina has taken over in that department.

I'm about to turn around and text Declan that we're heading home when the door to James' apartment opens. My eyes meet James, who's wearing a tight gray button-down shirt with the sleeves rolled up and dark-washed jeans. I see his smiling face, and dear God, is he wearing glasses? Sexy black rectangular glasses that I've never seen him wear before. I take a deep breath and slowly let it out. Fuck me, I'm screwed.

"Hey," he says, holding the door open for me.

Everything this man does and says is sexy.

"Hey," I smile and say back, entering his apartment.

The scent of Chinese food assaults me the moment I walk in. I look around his apartment, and it's like Ben's. The only difference is that Ben's was a little cluttered with things, whereas James hardly has anything. It's an open floor plan with a large kitchen on the right as you walk in and then the living area straight back to the left. The dining room is to the right off the kitchen with a large table to fit eight, possibly twelve people if needed. Everything has a place, and even the Chinese food is set up neatly on the island. There's a large spread of food, enough for ten people.

James leads me to the island, where he gets out some plates and utensils for us. "I wasn't sure what you still liked for Chinese food, so I just ordered a little of everything."

I can't help but smile as I notice James seems nervous. When we were younger, he always seemed confident in everything he did. I also notice he's been trying to avoid looking at me other than when I first entered his apartment, where he looked me up and down. I know I look good in this dress, and it does something to me to know he's trying to be a gentleman.

"It's perfect, thank you," I say while making my plate of food and sitting down on the island next to him.

We're both silent for a few moments as we eat, but it doesn't take long before I can't take it anymore. I'm not good at sitting in silence, though James always seems perfectly content with it.

"I've never seen you in glasses before," I say, and it comes out breathier than I wanted it to.

"My contacts have been bothering me," he replies.

If I were seventeen again and we were in his college apartment, I would throw myself at him right now. I'd tell him how sexy he is in his glasses, climb on his lap, and make out with him.

I shove a whole sweet and sour chicken in my mouth to distract myself and cross my legs. I cannot be having these thoughts right now.

James studies me with heat in his gaze. Can he read my mind about what I'm thinking? I feel myself blush and look away, shoving more food into my mouth. I feel like a chipmunk, and this is so unladylike.

James clears his throat and pushes his plate away. "I wanted to talk to you about something."

I swallow my mouth full of food and take a drink to help it go down. I push my plate away as well, as my nerves get the best of my appetite.

"What is it?" I ask.

"Do you want to stay here or get comfortable on the couch?" he asks, looking at the plate I just pushed away.

"The couch sounds good," I answer.

We head to the couch, and both take a seat at opposite ends. I kick off my heels and fold my knees up underneath me with my back against the armrest, facing James. Distance between us is good. My heart is pounding, and maybe the distance will help ease my nerves. I don't know why I'm so nervous. I don't even know what I'm doing or what I want.

As James leans back, relaxing against the couch, his shirt tightens around his perfectly sculpted abs, and I want to just roll my eyes at myself. Yeah, I know exactly what I want, but that doesn't mean it's a good idea.

"I want to give us a try again, Everly. I miss you and I still love you. I meant what I said before you left, and I'm really hoping you'll give us another shot. Give me another chance," he says nervously.

My heart pounds even harder now as he speaks. He's so nervous and so am I. I've never seen him like this before, and I kind of like it. Regardless, I still have my reservations.

"I'm not sure, James. I just..." I trail off, not knowing how to explain what I've been feeling.

"I know there's a lot that's happened in the past six years, but my feelings for you haven't changed." This time he isn't nervous at all and says it with certainty.

"James... Your feelings are for someone completely different. Like you said, a lot has happened in the past six years. I'm different. You're different. We don't really know each other," I say.

"Then let's get to know each other. We'll start tonight. We can take things slowly. Of course, if that's what you want," he says.

My heart squeezes at his words. He's always so willing to be patient with me, even when I know he doesn't want to be. I'm not going to lie, I want this too, but I'm scared. He knows about my past in high school. He's going to want to know my past in college as well, and there are a lot of stupid mistakes in there that even I hate myself for. I don't want to do this and have him find out things about me that change how he feels. If I get attached to him again and he changes his mind... I don't know if I can handle that.

"Just until Halloween. Give me a chance until Halloween. Let's get to know each other and we'll reevaluate then. If you decide you don't want to continue after the party, then we'll stop and be friends. It's less than two weeks," he says.

That's really not the problem, but he's right. What would two weeks hurt? I can't get too attached in two weeks, right? And I can be honest with everything. I hate to bring up my past, but he deserves to know it all, and I'll know his so we can make a decision.

"Alright, deal. We'll get to know each other again. Let's each ask a question and switch off. We have to be honest, but if there's something we're not ready to share, we can pass," I say, hoping he agrees about the passing thing.

"Deal," he says, smiling and shifting closer to me.

As he shifts closer, I try to move further away but can't because the armrest is already against my back. Being close to him always makes me want to make stupid decisions. The amount of chemistry we have is ridiculous. He's the only one who has ever made me feel this way just by being near him. Heck, just by being in the same room as him. Even if I can't see him, I can literally feel him in the same room. Is that normal?

"I'll start, and I have to warn you, I'm going to ask the deep questions," he says seriously.

I suddenly feel nauseous. I know we need to get those questions out of the way, but I'm not ready for them. It might be better to just nod and get them over with.

"What's your favorite TV show?" he asks.

I sigh in relief and laugh. "That's the deep question? I guess the rest will be super easy then. Honestly, I don't really watch TV much anymore, so I'd say it's the same as it was back in high school."

I purposefully didn't tell him what it was because I wanted to see if he remembered. He watched it with me a couple of times, but we always ended up making out halfway through watching TV. It was rare if we made it through a TV show, never mind a movie.

"*Once Upon a Time*?" he asks.

My heart skips a beat. He does remember.

I smile. "Yeah, that's it."

"Your turn," he says, inching just a bit closer.

He barely moves closer that a normal person probably wouldn't have noticed, but I'm very aware of every single move he makes.

"Alright, I guess I have to ask an equally hard question... What is your favorite color?"

He laughs. "It's still the same."

I can't help but smile that he is doing the same thing as me. While we are trying to get to know each other, we also want to see what we remember. I hate to admit it, but I remember everything about James.

"Orange. Got it," I say.

This time, I shift my body so that I'm moving a little closer to him.

We go back and forth with the easy questions, and after each one we inch closer together and are now both sitting directly in the middle of the couch, nearly touching. We're both positioned to face each other, and my heart is racing. I look at his lips, and it takes everything in me not to lean in for a kiss.

I know once we do, it's going to be a mistake. I'm not going to be able to stop myself from going further. We're both silent, like we're thinking the same thing. As he leans forward, my phone vibrates on the coffee table in front of me, pulling me out of my thoughts of wanting to lean in for the kiss.

I quickly pull away and pick up my phone to look at the text. It's Bash.

Bash

It was great seeing you the other night. You looked beautiful and I've missed you. I can't wait for our next night together.

I smile as I quickly text back, trying to keep my eyes off James for a moment to recompose myself.

Thank you handsome. See you soon, love you!

Bash has been texting me ever since the end of my senior year of high school. I started to cut the boys out of my life after Lauren's death due to a series of stupid mistakes that hurt them, but once we all started talking again, Bash has been religious about his text messages. He started out sending me a positive message every morning by telling me how beautiful, strong, and amazing I was. This continued even after I left for Georgia, but over the years it has gotten less frequent. Now he texts about once a week, which still always puts a smile on my face.

I always respond in kind, letting him know how equally amazing he is, matching his texts. If he ever stops, I'll honestly be sad because I always look forward to them. I don't have a brother, but I will always consider him my older brother.

I finally look back at James and see his eyebrows furrowed, watching me.

I put the phone back down now that my heart stopped racing when James asks, "Who was that?"

CHAPTER TWELVE

JAMES

I'm not usually a nosy person and don't care what people do in their personal lives, but I can't help but ask Everly who she's texting. I feel like we were having a moment, and we both wanted to lean into that kiss. But then she quickly grabbed her phone off the table as it buzzed.

Clearly, she used it as a distraction, but then I saw her smiling at her phone as she texted. I need to know who made her smile like that.

"Bash," she responds and shows me the text on the phone.

Well, that's not who I expected, and sigh in relief. I skimmed over the messages and a feeling that I rarely feel overcomes me. Jealousy, maybe? I close my eyes for a moment to regain control of my feelings because I know that text is not what it looks like. Bash has been honest with me about sending her those types of messages to lift her up, which I'm glad he does. He's also made it clear that he views her as a little sister, so I can only assume she feels the same way as him. If they were real siblings, those messages would make sense and mean nothing.

"He still texts you, huh? That's good," I say, not really knowing how to respond to that.

As if she heard my previous thoughts, she says, "Yeah, he texts me weekly. He really is like my big brother."

I nod but say nothing. I trust Bash wouldn't ever do anything, especially after seeing him talk about his new girlfriend. He's mentioned her before, but this is the first time I've been able to see him in person talking about her. He completely lit up the moment she was mentioned and when Everly asked for more information about her.

To break the awkwardness, I ask, "Do you want to continue with the questions, or should we put on a movie?"

She thinks for a moment before saying, "Movie."

"Anything in particular you want to watch?" I ask.

She shakes her head. "I don't really watch much anymore. I'm good for anything."

I scroll through Netflix and pick one of the top ten movies right now. Although we usually never made it much past the first ten minutes without making out, I find a romantic comedy that I know she used to love watching. I'd be lying if I said that wasn't my goal right now.

I get up to grab some drinks and a blanket for her. She thanks me as I place it on her and sit down next to her. On instinct, I put my arm around her, and she immediately leans her head on me. I smile as I try to relax with her and watch the movie.

Twenty minutes into the movie, she bursts out laughing at something that happened, and she looks up at me. I smile but don't laugh because I honestly wasn't paying attention at that moment, which I regret because clearly something hilarious happened.

When her laughter calms, I pull her in closer as she continues to look up at me, and we are in the same position before Bash interrupted us by texting Everly. The way she's looking at me with those hazel eyes and flushed cheeks, I can't hold back anymore. I wanted her to make the first move, but fuck it.

I lean in for the kiss and our mouths collide. We both let out a moan on impact, like we've been thinking about nothing else for the past six years. I grab the back of her head and pull her in more, not easing up on our kiss.

She does the same and shifts closer to me, half on my lap. The kiss intensifies, and I lick her lips to deepen it as our tongues collide. After a few moments, I lean back on the couch to lie on my back and get more comfortable without breaking the kiss. I throw a couple of pillows on the floor to make more room and shift her body directly on top of mine, so she knows she has control to stop or take this further.

I fucking hope she takes it further. The moment I opened the door to my apartment and saw her standing in the hallway in that short maroon dress with her breasts pushed up and looking amazing, I wanted to rip it off. I became instantly hard and had to turn myself away and keep my eyes off her. I didn't think it would be a good start to our first date since she left.

We continue making out on the couch, and I can't keep my hands from wandering up her stomach toward her breasts. Feeling her perfect curves through this dress is a form of torture. I want nothing more than to take this off and explore every inch of her body. I can feel how toned her body is underneath, probably from all the training she's been doing over the years.

I can't help but take a handful of her breasts. She lets out another moan as I squeeze one breast with one hand and my other squeezes her perfect ass. I was trying to hide my erection underneath her, but the way she's grinding against me makes it impossible.

All my self-control is out the window with the noises she's making. I lift the hem of her dress up slowly to see if she protests and, thank God, she doesn't. I remove her dress and throw it to the floor to see her in a black lacy bra and panties. Fuck.

I clumsily flip us over so she's on the bottom and I'm on top of her. I break our kiss for a moment as I help her unbutton my shirt, throw it to the floor, and lift my undershirt over my head, adding that to the pile. She stares at me with lust in her eyes, and I know I'm looking at her the same way. She runs her hands up my stomach and chest while I kiss my way down her neck.

Just as I'm about to unclasp her bra, her phone rings with an annoying alarm sound. We both jump apart from each other as she quickly reaches for it and answers.

"What?" she asks.

I hear a male voice on the other end, but I can't hear what he's saying.

I watch her as she closes her eyes and takes a deep breath. She squeezes her eyes hard, like she's in pain, and then shakes her head.

"Thanks. I'll be out in a minute," she says, and my stomach drops at her words.

"What's wrong?" I ask.

She tries to sit up, so I move off her, giving her room to do so. She leans over and picks up her dress from the floor.

"It was Declan. I have to go," she says in a hurried voice while pulling the dress over her head and down her body.

"Is everything okay?"

She shakes her head and avoids looking at me. "Yeah, it is... I just have to go. I'll talk to you later. Thank you for the dinner and movie, well, some of the movie."

She walks toward the door, and I follow her. Before she can reach for the handle, I grab her arm and turn her to face me. Her cheeks are still flushed, and her expression looks conflicted.

"James... I..." she starts, but I interrupt her.

"It's okay Everly. Everything is okay, though?"

She nods, and I'm not sure if I believe her. Regardless, she is ready to end the night, but I will not let it end like this.

I lean in and kiss her, gently this time. She closes her eyes and melts into me. Good. While I'm desperate to take things further, I'm not going to push her.

We part, and I say, "Good night Everly."

She looks me in the eye and takes a moment before responding.

"Good night, James," she says.

Everly turns to open the door and doesn't look back as she leaves. I close the door once I see her get on the elevator and bang my head against it. Fucking cockblocking Declan. I love the guy, but he has the worst timing ever. Returning to the living room, I grab my shirts but decide against putting them back on. I need a shower to take care of my situation since Everly, in that black lacy lingerie, is currently ingrained in my mind.

CHAPTER THIRTEEN

EVERLY

Declan opens the passenger door for me, and I throw myself angrily into the car. I take a deep breath and lean my head against the door after he closes it. He rounds the car and gets on the driver's side.

Once he's buckled and the car's started, he says, "Buckle."

I look over at him and roll my eyes, taking the seatbelt and whipping it across my body harder than I should have and slamming it into where it clicks in.

"Happy?" I ask in a sarcastic tone.

He shakes his head. "I just did what you asked me to do, Everly."

I sigh, and my anger quickly fades. "I know. I'm sorry, Declan. Thank you."

He doesn't say any more as we drive off. I'm not mad at him, I'm madder at myself, and I'm not even sure why, which makes me even more mad. Declan has access to James' cameras and glances at them every now and then to make sure that everything is okay. James, of course, has given him permission to do so. I asked him to call me if I was taking things too far with James, which he didn't want to do at first, but I made him promise me he would.

So here lies my problem. I'm not sure if I'm pissed off because I told him to call me, and he interrupted us when I wanted nothing more than to let James have his way with me tonight. Or if I'm pissed off because I let it get as far as it did when I shouldn't have. I could have told Declan thanks, it's okay and stayed, but I didn't because a part of me knew it wasn't a good idea. The same part that forced Declan to promise he'd call.

When we park the car in front of my house, Declan places his hand on my arm to stop me from getting out.

"There's a surprise for you waiting inside. Hopefully, it'll make up for tonight," Declan says.

Confused, I look over at him and ask, "What is it?"

He responds, "Not what, who."

I can't wait any longer, so I throw the car door open and walk quickly to my front door. There are only a few people I'd be happy to see surprising me at my house. I'm thankful Declan warned me someone was here because I don't like surprises, and he knows it.

When I open my front door, I hear two girls yell, "Surprise!"

Even though I knew someone was here, I'm still startled and jump. Thank God he warned me. Once I knew my heart wasn't going to jump out of my body, I smile and run over to my two best girlfriends, Ashley and Paige, giving them both hugs.

"What are you guys doing here?" I ask.

I knew Ashley said she'd come visit close to Halloween, but I figured she'd give me a heads up beforehand. I had no idea that Paige would be coming with her. Ashley has been my friend since the summer before senior year of high school. Lauren, Ashley, and I became best friends almost immediately. We all just clicked. After Lauren's death, we had a short falling out, but ultimately became best friends again. Once Ashley and I went to Georgia for college, we stayed to ourselves our freshman year. In our sophomore year, we ended up meeting Paige in one of our classes together and formed a friendship quickly. The three of us were inseparable for the rest of college until Paige moved on to her career and we stayed back to get our master's.

"Well, my interview got moved up, so I came early..." Ashley says, trailing off and looking at Paige to continue.

"And I just got a job promotion, which happens to be based out of New York City," Paige says with a big smile on her face, basically bouncing on her feet.

"What?! Seriously?! When do you start? Where are you living?" I ask excitedly.

"I'm living with my brother until I find an apartment, but I start on Monday!" she replies.

I look back at Ashley. "So, when is your interview?"

She pulls her lips between her teeth like she's trying not to say something, but I can see the gleam in her eyes.

"Well... I may have had the interview this afternoon..." she says, trailing off.

"And?" I ask, trying not to get my hopes up.

"And I was offered the job! I start next Monday!" she says while this time we all bounce up and down, holding hands like teenagers.

"So, we are all going to be in New York? I don't even know what to say..." I say, feeling a little emotional.

I pull out some wine and pour some for everyone. I can't believe my two best girlfriends are both coming to live in New York. Ashley said she's staying at her parents' house until she gets a place, which should be fast because they have a good bit of money, especially since they've been able to save up with my father paying for our house in Georgia.

I offer Paige to stay with me for a while, but she insists on staying with her brother. While Ashley and I come from money, Paige does not. She had to work all the way through college and didn't complain once. I tried offering her some money, but she never accepted it. New York is expensive, so I'm going to have to figure out a way to help her afford something good without her knowing. I can't let her live in a bad part of town.

I convince both of them to stay with me all weekend to have a girls' weekend. I only have one guest bedroom, though. Barry and Declan have the other two bedrooms in the house. My father wanted me to have an excessively huge house in the middle of nowhere to have our entire security team with me and have the property gated, but I refused. I don't want to be locked down like a princess. That's way too much. I know I'm his only child, but sometimes I feel like he takes way too many precautions to protect me.

I was able to convince him to let me get a smaller house with both Declan and Barry living here, along with security cameras in every single room, minus the bathrooms. After I moved in, I went to meet my neighbors, only to find out that my father had also bought that house. He put more security in that house because clearly having two security guards literally living with me isn't enough. I really feel like one day he's going to tell me I am indeed the princess of some random country with the amount of security I have watching me.

"I call taking the couch tonight," Ashley says.

I look at her, confused. "Why on earth would you want to take the couch? I mean, good for Paige for not having to fight for the guest room, but... why?"

Ashley grins. "In case Declan comes out to get some water in the middle of the night in nothing but his boxers. I want to ensure I don't miss that."

Paige and I both laugh, shaking our heads.

"Ashley... When have you ever seen Declan come out in his boxers the entire time we were living together with him in college?" I ask.

She frowns. "That's the point, I haven't! But I was always sleeping in my room, so I would have missed it."

"I'm pretty sure he sleeps in his polo and jeans. I've never seen the man in anything less than that," Paige says.

I mean, it's not a far-fetched conclusion. I have never seen Declan or Barry in their boxers, and we've lived together for many years. I've seen Declan shirtless, but that's only when training and it's hot. Occasionally, I have caught him in gray sweatpants when he comes out to the kitchen in the middle of the night, but I won't be sharing that with Ashley.

"I thought you were over your crush on Declan," I say.

Ashley shrugs her shoulders. "I mean, he's hot. Doesn't hurt to have some eye candy, and I definitely wouldn't say no if he wanted me to jump him."

I shake my head again. Ashley likes looking. She's had a couple of boyfriends in college, but nothing serious. She kept saying she just didn't feel it with any of them, whatever that meant. When it comes to actually doing anything with guys, she's all talk despite her love for looking. She's had the opportunity for a one-night stand before, but that's not her thing.

We spent the night catching up and talking about our future with them moving to New York. I still can't believe they both are moving here. We drank a little too much and stayed up way too late, but we eventually called it a night so we could resume tomorrow.

Once I get into bed, I look at my phone for the first time since leaving James' apartment to find a text from him.

James

> I had a good time tonight. I hope you made it home safely.

I had a great time too, and I'm really glad I hadn't drunk this much while at his apartment because I would've ignored Declan's phone call.

> I did too. Thank you for the dinner and part of the movie.

I'm about to put my phone on the charger when I hear it ding immediately after sending my text.

James

> You're up late.

I look at the clock to find it's just past two a.m. I had no idea that it was so late, or I never would've texted him.

> Sorry! My friends surprised me by coming to town and were waiting at my house.

James

> So that's why you left suddenly?

My heart beats fast, and my mind races with possible responses. It's not why I left his place so suddenly, but it is a good excuse I can use. If I say no, then I will have to explain what really happened. If I say yes... then I will be off the hook, and it may give him the wrong impression that I would have stayed otherwise. Would that be so bad, though? My tipsy self says it wouldn't be.

> Yeah, they are staying for a girls' week-end.

James

> Glad to know they are girls. So I guess that means another date this weekend is out of the question. What about dinner Monday night?

Did he question whether it was a guy who came to stay? I can't help but smile at his message that he could possibly be jealous and that he's asking me on another date.

> Monday night sounds perfect. But first I need to know something.

James

> What?

> What's your favorite pizza topping?

James

Now that is a serious question that I don't know if I can answer.

Are you skipping this question?

James

I suppose not. Pepperoni. What's yours?

Hamburger.

James

I'm glad to know your tastes have changed from plain cheese to adding some flavor. When did that happen?

I swallow hard at his question and shift uncomfortably in bed. How do I tell him it was because of my ex-fiancé?

"Everly, this is the fifth time we've had pizza together and you've gotten cheese every time. I need you to try a bite of mine," Eric said while cutting off a piece of his pizza.

We sat across from each other in my favorite pizza restaurant. Eric was handsome in his staple dark red polo shirt and jeans. His brown hair was short, but always messy in that sexy way. He was clean-shaven and wore those typical accountant-looking glasses over his blue eyes, which fit him since he was majoring in accounting.

"Absolutely not. You got ground beef on your pizza. That sounds awful, and it's hamburger. Why don't they call it hamburger down here?" I said with a frown on my face but couldn't help it turning to a smile.

"I don't know why up north you all call things strange names, but you have to try at least one bite," he said, holding his fork out to me.

To distract him, I continued our conversation. "We do not call things strange names, you do! Like, who doesn't know what a bubbler is? A water fountain is a decoration that spits up water, not something you drink out of. And don't get me started on calling a carriage a buggy! What the heck is a buggy?!"

Eric laughed but continued holding out his fork in front of me. "Don't try to distract me. One bite."

I shook my head and sealed my mouth closed tight. He moved over to my side of the booth, pushing me in further so he could sit. He held it up to my mouth, touching my lips with it, but I wouldn't part them.

"Just one bite. Come on. We'll make a bet. If you do this and don't like it, then I'll do whatever you want. If you do like it, then you do whatever I want," he said with a devious grin.

I rolled my eyes and opened my mouth for him to put the piece in. He knew I couldn't back down from a challenge or bet. I moved it around in my mouth a little bit before chewing it, and I have to say that it was the best-tasting pizza I ever had. The hamburger, or as they called it, ground beef here, tasted amazing. I didn't want to admit it, though.

"It's not that great," I said, trailing off and grabbing a piece of his pizza, taking another bite.

He laughed and traded pizzas with me, so he had the cheese while I had his.

"Looks like you have to do whatever I want," he said with his charming smile.

Another text comes through from James, breaking me out of my memory. I smile at the memory, then my happiness quickly changes to melancholy. I put Eric in the category of the long list of mistakes I made in college, but he wasn't the mistake. Eric was one of the sweetest guys I've ever met, and I broke his heart. I shake my head and read James' text before I can go down that rabbit hole.

James

Have a good night Everly.

Good night James.

I feel bad I didn't respond to his question, but I can't think about this anymore. I put my phone on the charger on my end table and roll over to get some sleep before our fun girls' weekend continues tomorrow.

CHAPTER FOURTEEN

JAMES

My plan to get Everly to hang out with me all weekend backfired once her friends came to town to surprise her. I'm happy she gets to see them because I know she must have been missing them. Ashley is basically her sister since I introduced them back in high school. For the most part, Ashley's a good person with a good head on her shoulders, but I wasn't a huge fan of hers when they were in college together.

I feel Ashley played a role in some of Everly's poor decisions. She's an enabler, and Everly will do almost anything to make others happy. She would do whatever it took to ensure those around her were safe and happy, not caring about how they felt. Then once she left, that quickly turned into just making people happy. She's gotten better now, but during college that was an issue. An issue I sometimes regret not taking advantage of.

I don't know much about Paige, but on paper, she seems perfect. She attended college at Georgia Southern University and got a bachelor's degree in multimedia journalism. She's never gotten a traffic ticket or had any issues with the law. To help pay her way, she worked at a coffee shop on campus and took tutoring gigs. Her current student loan debt is near $20,000, which is great for someone who had no help to pay her way through college. She graduated with a 3.9 GPA and relied on multiple scholarships to help pay tuition and other costs of living.

Her parents live in the same family home in Georgia since the time they got married. She's the oldest child with two brothers and a sister. She never had a boyfriend throughout college, which I assume is due to her lack of time. Of what I heard from Declan, when they went out, she rarely drank, though she would pretend to. She seems like a good friend, but her personality seems a lot different from Ashley and Everly's. I'm honestly surprised the three of them click so well.

Regardless, now my weekend is free, and I plan to make Monday night's dinner memorable. I make my way into a restaurant just outside of New York City with Ryder right behind me. I have an acquaintance who owns the place, and he owes me a favor that I intend to cash in on.

"Good afternoon, do you have a reservation?" the hostess asks with a smile.

"No, I was hoping Mr. Roberts was in today," I say while matching her smile.

"Of course! He just got in a moment ago. I'll be right back." She walks off, swaying her hips.

"So, what's your plan?" Ryder asks while looking around the place.

I ignore him, and he continues walking to the wall with a bunch of pictures hanging. He makes his way to one of me shaking hands with the owner. I shake my head because I asked him not to put that up, but obviously he didn't listen.

"You look very professional, James," Ryder says with a smirk.

"Shut up," I spit back.

Ryder laughs. "Come on, aren't you going to tell me what you're doing here?"

"I need to see something," I respond.

Ryder already knows why we're here, even though I didn't tell him. I swear the guy is a mind reader, or he just has a device in my head so he can hear every single thought that I have before I even have it.

The hostess comes back from around the corner with someone following directly behind her.

"James!! It's good to see you man," he yells and gives me a hug and pat.

I return the hug. "Robert, it's good to see you, too."

Robert isn't his real name, but that's what he goes by. He adopted it with his last name being Roberts. His real name is Cosmo, which he will forever hate his parents for, among many other things.

"What brings you here?" he asks.

"I wanted to check out your famous rooftop spot for a date I have Monday night," I say.

He grins from ear to ear. "Are you planning on proposing?"

Ryder coughs behind me, and I turn to glare at him. Yeah, maybe this is a little extravagant for a date, but Everly deserves it. It would be the perfect proposal spot, and if I didn't already have the proposal planned out, I would do it here.

"It's just a date. An important one," I say.

"Ah, well come on, let's go take a look," he says, waving to follow him.

We walk up to the rooftop, and I stare out at the view. There's nothing around for miles, and it's gorgeous. The sunset would be beautiful from here. If I leave work early and pick Everly up shortly after she gets home from work, we can easily make it here before sunset. I look around the roof at the tables and people eating. There are only a few tables up here, which I can imagine must be reserved well in advance. There are lights strung around for when it gets dark and stylish-looking heaters to keep the patrons warm.

"This is perfect. Can I have it for Monday evening?" I ask, but I know he won't say no.

"Of course, it's all yours. Anything you want to add or change?"

"I'll text you. You know where to bill me," I say, turning around again to look at the view.

She's going to love this, and I know how much she loves looking at the stars. I already checked the weather, and it's supposed to be a perfect night, otherwise, I would've picked somewhere else.

Robert comes over and pats me on the shoulder. "This one's on me, friend. I'll never be able to repay you."

I look at him to see the sincerity in his eyes, and I respond, "Consider it repaid."

He nods and stands beside me, looking out. "You love her?"

I don't look at him as I respond, "Yes."

He nods, but doesn't say anything else. He doesn't know about Everly, not many people do. She wasn't physically part of my life for so many years, so I pretended she didn't exist to those around me, other than those who knew her. That changes now. She's going to be part of my life again, so I want everyone to know, and I'm never letting her go.

After I finish planning my date with Everly, I return home to my office to get a few things done for work so I can leave early on Monday. I glance at the clock as my stomach growls and realize it's already seven pm. Before I get up to start one of the meals, Maria, my personal assistant who does everything, cooked for me in advance, I log into the tracker I have on Everly.

I glance at the screen to find her at a bar not too far from here. My stomach drops a little at her whereabouts, but I ignore it. She's not the same as she used to be years ago, and Declan's got this. As much as I want to go intercept her at the bar, she needs some time to herself with her friends.

I head to the kitchen and hear my phone go off with a text, and I see it's from Declan. My heart races as I read it.

Declan

Adam just walked in.

Declan doesn't need to say anything else, and he knows it. I grab my jacket and keys and race out the door and down the elevator toward my car but remember it's Saturday night in New York City. It would be faster for me to walk and it's not that far. I jog toward the bar and get angrier with every step I take.

Clearly, it's just a coincidence he's there and he would never try anything with Everly, right? Back in high school, he made Everly's life a living hell. He forced himself on her more times than imaginable and threatened her. When she moved to New York, he even had some friends here terrorize her.

If he comes within ten feet of her, I'll kill him. He's had enough warnings. Bash, Ben, Jake, and I had a "talk" with him in high school when we first found out what happened. It wasn't enough to deter him, and neither were her father's warnings, so Declan and I took matters into our own hands. I thought we all got the point across because he hasn't personally bothered her in more than six years.

My mind drifts back to when we first confronted him.

Sitting in the passenger seat, I felt like a bomb that was going to explode at any time. The moment Everly told me that Adam had been raping her, I wanted to go kill him immediately. Of course, I stayed and comforted her instead and told her I wouldn't tell anyone. I didn't sleep that night or the nights after because I failed to protect her as I promised her when she was little.

I was hoping going to the lake house that morning would give me time to process and think through a plan, but that backfired once Jake stuck his dick in Everly. I lost it. All the rage I was holding back I took out on Jake by punching him for sleeping with Everly, and then I spilled her secret to the guys out of anger. I regret it, the yelling out her secret, not the punching Jake part, but ultimately it needed to be told.

The four of us were on our way to have a "talk" with Adam. Everly went back home separately from us from the lake house, so it was the perfect opportunity for us to confront Adam without her knowing. Jake and I put our feud on hold, which meant putting the feud between the four of us on hold. I would have it out with Jake later for sleeping with Everly. Usually when one of us has a beef with another, the other two take sides and it becomes an all-out war. Everly is too important to all of us to screw this up. We'll deal with the aftermath of what Jake did after we deal with Adam.

We waited for Adam to come out of the gym before we got out of the car. We knew he went every night at the same time, thanks to a friend of mine who can find out anything. We surrounded him on the sidewalk and pushed him toward the wall. He dropped his duffel bag, ready for a fight.

"To what do I owe the pleasure, boys?" Adam smirked to hide how scared he was.

He could pretend all he wanted, but eyes never lie.

We crowded him closer so he couldn't move, and I placed my hand on his chest keeping him against the wall. "Did you force yourself on Everly?"

The idiot had the audacity to grin while saying, "Is that what she told you? She's a little whore and begged for it every time."

I didn't even think before punching him directly in the jaw and his head smashed back into the brick wall of the building.

Adam tried to escape my grip and punch me back, but Bash grabbed one arm while Ben grabbed the other, pinning him against the wall.

"Do you want to try that again?" I asked as if I wouldn't be killing him today.

He spat blood out of his mouth onto the ground. "She's a great fuck and a screamer, as I'm sure you know."

I could only see red now, but before I could land another punch, Jake beat me to it. He pressed himself up against Adam and slammed his fist into his stomach. Adam was gasping for air while Jake kneed him in the balls. He would've toppled over if Bash and Ben weren't holding him up.

Jake pushed Adam to straighten up and looked into his face. "If you ever come near Everly again, this beating will be nothing compared to what's going to happen to you. Stay away from her."

Jake started pounding the guy again, and as much as I wanted to let him kill him, I couldn't do that when someone could witness it. I pulled Jake back and forced him to look at me. Once he was calm, I saw the tears forming in his eyes as a stray one fell down his cheek. He looked away and walked toward his car.

I looked back at Adam and grabbed his throat. "Stay. Away. From. Her," I demanded, pronouncing every word clearly through clenched teeth.

I let him go and took one last punch at him before stepping back. Ben and Bash did the same as Adam fell to the ground, groaning. We all got back in the car and drove home silently.

Remembering what happened when the four of us confronted him and the things he said makes me sprint even faster. The beating and threats we made to him weren't even enough that time. The moment he didn't heed our warnings, I never should've let him live. I'm out of breath, but the bar is now in sight, and I'm prepared to kill him this time.

Before I can even open the door to the bar, Declan comes out and pushes me to the side.

"He's gone. Did you not get my texts?" he asks, looking me over with concern.

I shake my head. "No, what happened?"

"He walked in, took a seat with his friends, and then when he spotted Everly, he left. I didn't even have to say anything to him, but I'm watching to make sure he doesn't return. Barry is keeping watch outside, but Adam drove off," he says.

"Did she notice him?" I ask, concerned that she might be upset after seeing him again after all this time and bringing up bad memories.

"No, thankfully. You should go, James," he responds.

I nod. As much as I want to go in there to see for myself that Everly is okay, he's right. I don't want to ruin her night, and then she would ask me why I'm there. I trust Declan has this covered, but I'm not going to leave.

Just as I turn to find some place to keep an eye out on her, Ryder pulls up in a parking spot close to the bar, which has a perfect view of the entrance. How the hell did he manage that? And how did he get here so quickly? I know if I had driven, it would've taken forever to get here. I thank Declan and jump in the passenger seat of Ryder's car before he gets out.

"Talk to me," Ryder says in his business voice.

I'm sure the moment I sprinted out of my apartment, he followed me and read my messages. He knows who Adam is and the details. He was mad I didn't involve him either time I confronted him. Which I suppose this would've been a third.

"He left before I got here, and Everly never saw him," I say, positioning myself inside the car so I can keep a close eye on the bar and surroundings.

He nods and does the same. "I assume we're staying a while?"

"Until she leaves. I want to make sure he doesn't come back," I say, still not convinced it was just a coincidence.

"I think he's taken care of James, but I'll dig some more too just to make sure," he says.

"Thanks."

This isn't a typical bar Everly would go to, but it's one of the cheaper ones around, which I'm sure they did for Paige. Something I've found about Paige is that she will refuse any sort of help or charity. Everly and Ashley could easily cover her, but she's going to be paying her own way, which means they would go to a low-end bar like this.

Adam's family lost a lot of their money and business shortly after he continued bothering Everly. I have a feeling that Asher had a lot to do with that and another reason he's stayed away from her. Though he didn't completely destroy them because someone who has nothing to lose becomes dangerous. He just made a point to show them what could happen and the power he has if they mess with her again. Figuratively speaking, of course, because I have no proof it was him.

Regardless, I know what I'm doing with the rest of my night.

CHAPTER FIFTEEN

EVERLY

I'm having an amazing night with my girls, but I'm not going to lie that I'm missing James. I don't know when he wormed his way completely back into my heart and life, but he has. All the reservations that I had about getting back together with him are currently out the window. Maybe it's also the three margaritas talking. They aren't the best I've had, but they are still alcohol and do their job.

We're currently at a beat-down bar in the city. Really, it's not that bad, but it is one of the cheaper ones. Paige insisted on paying for her own alcohol, so here we are. She's only two margaritas down, and I'm fairly certain she will be nursing that second one for the rest of the night.

Ashley snuck off to the bathroom, and Paige is currently checking her phone, so I take this opportunity to be clingy and text James.

> What are you up to tonight?

James

> Just sat down after a run. What about you?

> At a bar with the girls, missing you.

He doesn't respond immediately, and my heart sinks. Maybe I shouldn't have said that last part about missing him? I don't want to come off as too clingy, but it's what he wants, right? He made it clear he wants to get back together, so you would think that he wants to hear I'm missing him. Ugh, I'm too much in my head, and this alcohol isn't helping. Why am I drinking so much again?

My phone vibrates with a text, but before I can look at it, Ashley sits back down in the seat beside me.

"So, what are we doing tomorrow?" she asks.

"Not drinking. In fact, I think we should stop drinking altogether," I say and mean it.

"Here's to that!" Paige lifts her glass up and we clink them together, laughing.

"You're right, this was fun, but I'm good just hanging out with you guys. Clearly there are no real men to pick up anyway, and you're taken again," Ashley says, looking over at me.

I smile because I suppose I am. I take the break in conversation as an opportunity to look back at my phone.

I smile and text back.

I laugh loudly.

"Are you texting James?" Paige asks.

"Yeah, I can't help it," I say, continuing to keep the grin on my face.

Ashley pats me on the back. "I'm so glad you finally came to your senses about him. Have you guys slept together yet?"

I choke on my margarita. Really, that's what her first question is about us getting back together?

"No, I don't plan on it for a while," I say sincerely.

After all my mistakes in college, I swore off sleeping with guys. I haven't been with anyone since Eric. As much as I want to sleep with James, I want to make sure that we're serious first and we're going to make it work this time. I made a mistake sleeping with Jake and I'm not doing the same with James.

I respond to his message.

> As tempting as that sounds, I'm a wine and dine type of girl now.

James

> I can work with that.

As much as I want to continue texting James all night, I put my phone down and concentrate on my girls, who have somehow made their way over to karaoke without me noticing. I laugh as I watch them up on stage singing and dancing to Carrie Underwood's "Before He Cheats." Once they notice they have my attention, they pull me up to finish out the song with them.

I sing and dance like no one's watching and we're all back in college together. It's a good night, one that I've needed. I've missed my girls, and I'm thankful that they are coming to live in New York with me where we can do life together. Eventually, we'll all get married and have kids to raise together. I couldn't imagine a better life, and it's the first time in a while that I can see a future so clearly. One that involves James and me having a happily ever after, which I never thought would happen.

I startle awake at a loud banging sound beside my bed. I grab my knife from under my pillow and roll to the floor to get my bearings. My head is pounding from the noise and probably the margaritas since I went to bed without drinking any water last night. I flip the knife open and peek my head above my bed to see what is happening.

Jake stands there, staring at me with a wide grin as he continues to bang the pot, surely waking the entire neighborhood.

I stand up straight, with the knife still at the ready in my hands. "What the hell, Jake?"

Jake eyes the knife in my hand and throws the pot and spoon he was using to bang it on the floor.

He holds up his hands and says, "Well, it's not as fun as back in high school. You didn't try to kill me when I did this sort of thing."

I laugh and put the knife back under my pillow. Now that he mentions it, I do vaguely remember the first morning I returned to the Crawford's house for the summer before my senior year of high school. Jake woke me up with his old marching band drums. I smile at the memory.

"Sorry, I'm not used to you playing pranks like this on me in my own house," I say seriously, but still have a smile on my face.

Jake has always been a prankster, and we've done a lot together. I still think my favorite was the last Thanksgiving we all had together at the Crawford's house. We put a farting machine down at the adult side of the table and made everyone think one of them was farting. It was hilarious. I wonder if we should pull another one this Thanksgiving.

I go to my dresser and grab out a t-shirt and leggings. I head to the bathroom and close the door behind me to change. Usually, I would stay in my pajamas for a while on a Sunday morning, but the pajamas I'm wearing aren't something I want to be wearing in front of Jake. He's my best friend, but with our history, it feels wrong, especially since James and I are getting back together.

As I'm changing, I yell through the door, "What are you doing in my room?"

"I tried calling, but you didn't answer. When I came to the door, Declan let me in," he says.

I finish getting dressed and come out of the bathroom while brushing my hair. "You have a key. You didn't need to bother Declan."

Jake smirks. "Oh, but I wanted to mess with people today."

I shake my head. "Okay, but seriously, why are you here?"

He doesn't respond and walks out of my bedroom door. So, did he come all this way just to randomly wake me up with a lot of noise? I know he likes to play pranks on people, but that's random. It's not April Fools, which I have an alarm on my phone to ensure I avoid Jake all that day. That's his favorite holiday, and while I like to play pranks, I could never beat him at it.

I follow him downstairs to the kitchen, where there's a bag sitting on the island. He grabs it and hands it to me. I open it up and squeal when I see a hardback copy of the new release of a book series that I've been obsessed with. I bounce up and down for a moment before wrapping my arms around Jake's neck and suffocating him in a hug.

When I finally let go of him, I realize that today is Sunday. "Wait, this doesn't come out until Tuesday. How did you get it?"

He grins and says, "Open to the first page."

I do what he said and find a handwritten note inside addressed to me with the author's signature. I read it three times before believing it's real.

I look back up at Jake, and I know tears are forming in my eyes. "Jake... How did you do this? Thank you."

"I have a friend who knows her personally and called in a favor."

I shake my head in disbelief and hug him again, a lot gentler this time. I hear a throat clear and turn around to find Paige and Ashley entering the room, still in their pajamas.

"Hey Jake, didn't expect to see you here," Ashley says in a suspicious tone.

"Hey Ashley, didn't know you were in town," he responds. He looks over toward Paige, tipping his head, and says, "Good morning, Paige, it's good to see you."

Paige blushes and shyly says, "Good morning."

What on earth is happening here? Why is Ashley treating Jake like he shouldn't be here, and Paige is acting like a teenage girl with a crush? Am I dreaming? I'd be really upset to wake up now when I just got this amazing gift from Jake.

"Well, I won't keep you from your girls. I just wanted to drop by and give that to you as soon as I got it," he says while walking toward the door.

I follow him over and open it for him. "Thank you again, Jake. This was so thoughtful."

He leans down and kisses me on the forehead before saying goodbye to everyone and walking out the door.

"What was that?" Ashley eyes me cautiously.

"I'm wondering the same. What was that? You treated him like he was up to something," I reply.

Ashley shakes her head and sighs. "Everly... I just don't trust him, and you're getting back together with James."

"What does that mean?" I ask, getting a little angry at where this is going.

"It means that you should be concentrating on James and maybe spending a little less time with Jake."

"He's one of my best friends," I state defensively.

Ashley puts up her hands in surrender. "I'm not trying to start something. You know I'm always on your side."

I can tell she wants to say more, but she doesn't. I was so happy a moment ago when Jake gave me this book, and now I'm angry.

"Do you have anything to say?" I look over at Paige, and she just responds with her hands up in surrender as well.

I let out a deep breath and shake my bad mood away. "I'm sorry. I get what you're saying, Ashley, and I really don't see him much. I'll figure it all out..." I pause and hold out the book to her. "Want to see what he gave me?"

Ashley takes the book, and her eyes go wide. "What?! How?!"

My smile comes back. "He said he had a friend who knew her and called in a favor. Open it."

Ashley opens the book to the page that was signed with the little note. Paige reads over her shoulder, and they both squeal just like I did when Jake first gave it to me.

"Wow, this is amazing Everly. Jake really is a great guy," Paige says.

Okay, now's my opportunity to ask. I never thought Paige had feelings for Jake all the times we hung out together, but I feel like that's the case right now.

"Do you like him?" I ask her.

"Who?" Paige asks.

I laugh. "Jake, of course."

She sucks her lips into a flat line, and that's the only response I need to know the answer.

"Oh my God, you like Jake?!" Ashley steps back in shock.

"What? No!" Paige denies, but it doesn't sound convincing.

"No, just no. Paige, you haven't even had a real boyfriend in for like ever. You need someone... that's not like Jake," Ashley says.

"Hey, Jake is amazing," I state, defending him.

"I'm not saying he's not, it's just... I don't want to be rude..." she stops herself from saying what she wants to.

"He's a man whore," Paige finishes for her.

Ashley laughs. "Yeah, that."

I shake my head. "I can't deny that, but I think that once he finds someone he truly loves, it'll be different."

"I agree," Ashley responds.

"You just don't think that's me," Paige says.

Ashley cringes. "Ah, I don't know what's wrong with me. I'm PMSing. If you really want him, Paige, I'm not saying don't. He really is a good guy."

That makes me feel better. I was getting a little upset that Ashley was hating on Jake. He's done nothing wrong and has always been so good to me. I'm the one who hurt him, along with many others, sadly. I hope I can put all these mistakes in the past and not remake them this time with James.

I pour myself some coffee because all these conversations are getting too deep for me in the morning after a night of drinking.

"Nah, I don't want him. It's like Ashley's attraction to Declan and Ben," Paige states.

I choke on the first sip of my coffee and cough for a moment in surprise at what Paige just said.

Once I regain my composure, I ask, "Say what? I know about Declan, but what about Ben?"

Ashley blushes and walks away. "Nothing about Ben. No idea who Ben is. I'm going to get changed."

Paige and I laugh as Ashley walks away. I remember Ashley having a little crush on him back in high school, but nothing came of it. I'm surprised she still likes him. He doesn't have a girlfriend as far as I know. I feel like she should give that a shot. We all know that Declan isn't ever going to work out for her.

After finishing my coffee, I tell Paige I'm going to head back to my room for a little bit to rest to get rid of my headache. While I do have a headache, I just want a few moments to read this book. I don't plan to read long since they are both leaving me this afternoon, but it doesn't hurt to take a few moments to myself, especially since I probably would've still been sleeping if Jake hadn't woken me in such a dramatic way.

CHAPTER SIXTEEN

JAMES

I tap my fingers on my desk and stare at the clock. Two more hours until I pick Everly up for our date. I haven't been able to concentrate much thinking about tonight. I feel like it's going to be a big night for us, and I don't want to do anything to screw it up. I fully intend to pick her up, have a great evening, and drop her off at home, but there's a part of me that has hope she'll want to come back to my place or invite me to hers afterward.

My cell rings, and I pick up immediately as I notice Ryder is calling.

"What's up?" I ask.

"I'm heading up to your office now. We need to talk," he states urgently.

"I'm here, come in," I respond, hanging up my phone.

I pull up Everly's tracker to find that she's still at work. I don't have anything from Declan, so I'm assuming she's not what Ryder needs to talk about. He doesn't come to my office often to talk, so something's up.

I pace my office until he comes into the room and closes the door behind him.

He doesn't bother sitting before he starts to speak. "I got a call from Hank as a heads up someone's been looking into Everly."

"Who?" I ask while sitting back behind my desk as he sits in the seat in front of it.

"Not sure, but they want to know everything and anything about her. I have him trying to feed false information their way. He's digging further to see if we can get a name," he states seriously.

"I want extra security on her until we figure it out."

"Already done. I've spoken to her father's security team on the way over. I think you should tell her," he says.

"Not yet. I don't want to scare her," I reply.

She's not a fan of being back in New York, and if she knows someone is looking into her, she may get spooked enough to leave again, and I can't have that. I trust her and my security team. Without an actual threat, I'm not too worried yet.

"I think it's a good idea to lie low until we get more information," he starts, but I interrupt.

"No, it'll be fine. I'm not canceling our date tonight. If they are looking into her, they will see that she rarely goes out, especially on the weekdays. She's safer going out with me where they wouldn't know where she is," I say.

Ryder sighs, "Alright, if that's what you want. I'm going to insist on coming with you. If someone is after her and you're with her, then you're a target, too."

I think about it for a moment. Everly hasn't met Ryder yet and doesn't know about him at all. I don't even think she knows that I have a security team. I never had a problem with her knowing, but I have sent Ryder to spy on her many times, and if she's noticed him, I don't want her to put two and two together. She did meet him at that bar one day and didn't say anything, so maybe it'll be fine.

"Can you just follow behind discreetly?" I ask instead of telling him to because he is my head of security for a reason, and I trust his judgment when it comes to things like this.

"No, I'm driving. If something goes down and we're being followed, I want to be in control."

"Okay, fine. I guess you get to officially meet Everly in less than two hours," I sigh.

He has a huge grin on his face as he says, "Finally!"

I can't help but laugh. He's been dying to officially meet her, but I haven't let him. He lets himself out, and I immediately call Declan.

"I've already talked to Ryder," Declan answers.

"Good. What are the extra precautions being taken?" I ask.

"Barry and I are still on our normal shifts, and we have another following at a safe distance. She's being tracked 24/7 and there are eyes on her at all times."

"Alright. I'm still picking Everly up tonight, but Ryder is coming with us," I state.

"You sure you still want to go out?" he asks, just like Ryder did.

"Yes. You're not going to tell her, are you?"

He's silent for a moment. "Not yet. I don't want to scare her without knowing more facts first. It could be nothing."

"Agreed," I state.

Declan hangs up without another word. He's always to the point with me, no small talk, and I appreciate that.

When I finally get back to work, I only have thirty minutes before I need to leave to head home and get ready for tonight. I do a quick scan of my emails and don't notice anything of importance, so I log out and head home for the day.

As I ring Everly's doorbell, Ryder stands next to me wearing a professional black suit with an earpiece, looking like the personal security detail for the president.

"Is all this really necessary?" I ask, gesturing toward his outfit.

"Yes. I'm here to make sure everyone stays safe," he says, just as professionally as he's dressed.

I shake my head. "What about the earpiece?"

He doesn't answer and just stares at me.

Everly opens the door with a smile as she looks at me, and then her face turns to confusion when she sees Ryder. I watch her brows squeeze together as she tries to place where she recognizes him from and why he's here.

"Everly. This is Ryder..." I start to say, but she quickly interrupts me.

"Ryder... Weren't you the guy I met at the bar?" she asks, looking even more confused.

I look over at him, and he puts on his charming smile for her before answering. "Yes, I am. It's nice to officially meet you, Everly."

Ryder holds out his hand for Everly to shake and she takes it, still looking confused.

"So, what are you doing here?" she asks.

We both look at each other for a moment, and I gesture for him to go ahead and tell her. She aimed the question at him, so it's his to answer.

He clears his throat. "I'm James' head of security. I'll be escorting you both, and I thought it was finally time that I meet you."

She opens the door wider and gestures for us to come in. "I'll just be another minute and then we can go. Please make yourself comfortable."

I watch her head up the stairs, which I assume is to her room. The house is big with an open concept, like my apartment. When you walk in, there's a large foyer, and to the left is a dining room sectioned off that houses a table that could fit 12 guests. If you keep going straight past the dining room, you run into the kitchen on the left and the living room to the right. It's a beautiful house with a farmhouse decor. I honestly didn't expect that to be her style. As I look around, I notice that it's clean, but there are quite a few things out of place or cluttered.

As I make my way to the couch, I notice some photo frames on the fireplace. I start from the left and make my way to the right. The first one is of her, Ashley, and Lauren in high school. It looks like this was taken Homecoming night. The next photo is of her, Ashley, and Paige in college. They are all holding beers, and it looks like they are at a frat party. The next one is of her and her father. It's a recent photo of them, but it was taken in Georgia since it was at her house down there.

There's one photo left, and it's of her, Jake, Bash, Ben, and me. I smile at the memory of this photo. We're in Ben's bathroom with a kiddie pool of water and sand surrounding it. Everly and I are lounging in the pool while the others are trying to build sandcastles. This was the first item we completed on our bucket list the summer before Everly, Ben, and Jake's senior year of high school.

When my mom barged in on us, I thought for sure she was going to scold us. We always wanted to do that as kids, but she refused to let us. I was surprised she just took a picture and left us to it. Of course, her condition was that we had to clean up the mess, and we did for the most part. A couple of nights later, Ben came to my room at two in the morning, fed up and waking me to help him scrub the floors because he couldn't stand stepping on the leftover sand every time he used the bathroom.

I look toward the steps to see she's not coming back down-stairs yet, so I head to the couch and sit down next to Ryder, who has already made himself comfortable. I notice a book on the coffee table and pick it up.

The cover has a man and a woman holding hands on a beach. It must be one of those romance novels she loves to read. I open it to find a handwritten note inside made out to Everly, and it's signed by the author. That's neat.

I flip through and don't see a bookmark on any pages, so I wonder if she's already finished the book. When I reach the last page, I notice another handwritten note, but this time it's not from the author.

Everly,

True love never gives up. Against all odds, it finds a way to prevail.

Jake

I read the short message over and over again as my anger rises. Jake gave her this book, and clearly, he loves her, thinking they had true love. When did he give her this?

Ryder must have noticed my reaction because he asks, "What's wrong?"

I close the book and pass it over to him. He immediately turns to the last page where he saw me have a reaction, reads it, and closes it gently, placing it back where we found it.

"It might not be what it looks like," he states.

"It's always what it fucking looks like with Jake," I say, standing up and pacing the room because I can't sit any longer.

"James, don't get mad now. You're about to go on the most extravagant date you've ever been on and planned. Take a deep breath and forget about it," he says, standing with me.

I close my eyes and take a deep breath. He's right. I can't get mad right now, but I fully intend to get mad later. I'm going to find out when she got this book from him, and I'm going to have to confront him. Everly is mine, and I'm not going to have Jake swoop in again trying to steal her away.

I turn back toward the stairs as I hear footsteps. Everly makes her way down the stairs wearing a long hunter green dress that's fitted and shows every curve of her body. The dress has a deep v-neck, showing the perfect amount of cleavage where her breasts are pressed together and begging for me to stick my face between them.

I close my eyes and take another deep breath to stop those thoughts before I have a situation I need to cover up. I'm trying hard not to think about having sex with her and just enjoy her company, but she's making it difficult. Her hair has gotten longer than in high school, and she curled it, putting part of it up. The red in her hair seems to be more pronounced like this, and I love it.

When she makes it down the stairs, I finally speak. "You look gorgeous."

She smiles and says, "You look handsome yourself. After seeing you both dressed up nicely, I figured I should, too."

"Shall we?" I ask as I hold out my arm for her to put hers in.

She does, and we walk out the door with Ryder in front and Declan behind us.

Chapter Seventeen

EVERLY

James opens the door to the back seat of the car and closes it once I get in. He joins me in the back on the other side. Ryder slips into the driver's seat after we're both settled and drives off. I sit still, feeling awkward and nervous. Both because James and I are going out on a real date when it's been years, and because I'm meeting Ryder for the first time.

I knew James had a security team, but I've never met any of them. Well, I didn't think I had. I met Ryder at the bar, and it seemed like he was flirting with me. Obviously, that wasn't the case, and it makes sense that he jumped in because there was another guy trying to talk with me when James left the bar for a moment. He seems more familiar than that though, and did at the bar too. Maybe I have seen him in the background before during high school or something, if he was with him back then.

"What are you thinking about?" James asks.

"Just thinking that Ryder looks familiar and not just from the bar," I reply.

I watch as both of them make eye contact in the mirror. I knew it. He's definitely been around. I can't believe I hadn't noticed or paid attention. I've worked hard with Declan during training on how to be aware of my surroundings and the people in it, but clearly, I need more work.

"How long have you been with James?" I ask.

Ryder glances back at me in the mirror and says, "Since he was in high school."

What? That long? So, it makes sense that I must have seen him a time or two back then. At least that explains why he looks so familiar.

"How old are you? You look way too young to have been with him since then," I state.

He doesn't answer my question. "Well, thank you. I take that as a compliment."

I don't push it because it's really none of my business how old he is. "Why are you here?" I ask bluntly.

James laughs, and Ryder clears his throat.

"I'm almost always around," he replies.

"Well, yeah, I get that, but I mean, why are you here today? Driving us? You never have before."

"I told James that I wanted to officially meet you since he mentioned you two are becoming serious again," he says with a smirk.

I look over at James to see him shaking his head at Ryder.

I smile. "Oh, did he now?"

James put his hand on my thigh. "I said that I was hoping we were getting serious again."

I have so many more questions for Ryder, but I don't feel like now is the appropriate time. James and I are supposed to be on a date, and I've really been looking forward to tonight. I am nervous though because I know we need to have some hard conversations if we're going to make this work. I think it's better that we get it over with sooner rather than later.

We pull up at a nice restaurant that's a bit out of the city. It's the only thing around for miles, and I've never been to a place like this before. The sun is about to set, and I bet it's beautiful from out here.

Once we park, James quickly exits the car and opens my door. He holds out his hand for me, and I take it. Every time I touch him, I feel a spark that radiates through my entire body. I lean closer to him as we walk inside.

Once we make it in, we're greeted by the hostess, who acts like she knows James well and gives him a flirty smile. I can't help but feel the jealousy rise. I want to shout at her, "Don't look at my man like that," but I don't because that would be stupid. And technically he's not mine, as we haven't put a label on us yet.

She leads us up some stairs, and I notice the sway in her hips as she walks in front of us. I roll my eyes.

We're brought to the rooftop, and I take a deep breath as I look around. It's beautiful. There's one table in the middle of the roof and a couple of couches toward the edges. There are lights dangling around the whole roof that are turned on, since it's going to be dark soon, and there are some heaters to keep us warm.

We're led to the table, and James pulls out the seat for me as I sit. I love that he's always the perfect gentleman. The hostess lets us know our server will be with us shortly. Thank God it's a male because I wouldn't be able to stand someone else hitting on him all night during our date.

"Where did you find this place? It's gorgeous," I ask.

He smiles. "My friend owns it."

Of course. He must have called in a favor because there's no way this rooftop doesn't rent out months or even a year in advance. I look over toward where the sun is setting, debating if I should get up to look at it or not. I really want to watch it, but we haven't even looked at the menu yet.

James stands up and holds his hand out to me. "Let's go watch the sunset. We can order later."

I take his hand and head over to the edge of the roof, leaning on the wall. You can't see anything for miles, just the beautiful sunset. It's amazing that this is just outside of the city because it looks like we're deep in the countryside. This must have cost a fortune for the land alone.

James moves behind me and wraps his arms around my waist as I place mine on top of his. I lean back into him and love feeling his warmth surrounding me. I feel so at ease with him holding me like nothing else in the world matters. I've always felt so safe in his arms. Nothing compares to this feeling. How have I lived without him for so many years? Better question, why have I lived without him for so many years?

Once the sun has basically set, we make our way back to the table, and the server arrives shortly after.

"Good evening Mr. and Mrs. Crawford. Would you like me to go over anything on the menu with you?" he asks, mistaking me for James' wife.

James doesn't correct him, and neither do I. I'd be lying if I said I didn't like the sound of it. Mrs. Crawford. Everly Crawford. I used to write that in my notebooks all the time in high school. I always felt so childish, but I loved the sound of it.

James orders some type of wine for us, but I'm not paying attention. I just realized that I hadn't even looked at the menu yet. James must have noticed because he ends up ordering for both of us. He orders some appetizers and each of us some sort of fancy chicken dish. While I've eaten my fair share of fancy foods, he knows that I much prefer the basics. It got bad when I was in college because I ate a lot of pizzas and burgers. And sweet tea. How I miss sweet tea.

Once the server leaves, I look up at the sky to notice it's clear and you can see the stars perfectly.

"Wow, James... The view is beautiful. Thank you for bringing me here."

I look at him, and he smiles at me. "It is."

I blush and take a sip of the wine I didn't even notice the server bring. How long was I staring at the stars?

"So how was your day?" he asks.

"It was long, honestly. I have a student who's really struggling, and it's hard to leave that at work and not think about it at home," I say, feeling a little depressed thinking about it.

"I'm sorry. Those students are lucky to have you. If anyone can help, I know it'll be you," he says sincerely.

"What about you? How was work?" I change the topic to him.

"Long. I didn't get much done. I was thinking a lot about tonight."

"This must have taken some time to plan," I say.

He shrugs his shoulders. "It's worth it to see you smile."

Why is he so perfect? Would it be acceptable to jump him right here at the table? Or there are a couple of couches to choose from that I could drag him to. I shake my head to ignore those thoughts. That's not why we're here, even if that's exactly what I want and I'm sure he wouldn't object.

"I wanted to talk about a few things," he turns the conversation more serious.

"Okay, shoot," I reply, wanting to get it over with.

"I wanted to talk about us... What we are. I want you to be my girlfriend Everly."

I smile and nod. "I want that too."

"Good. Then it's official and we're exclusive," he states possessively, and sits back in his chair with a serious expression.

I would think being his girlfriend would show that without saying, but clearly, he thinks it needs to be said, and I'm pretty sure I know why.

"Of course that would mean we're exclusive," I state, wanting him to tell me what he's thinking versus me bringing it up.

"Then I have to ask... about Jake," he states.

I could play it off and ask what about Jake, but I don't. I don't want to play games. I want us to be honest with each other, and I want him to know that I'm being honest and not hiding anything.

"Jake and I are just friends. We've always been friends, but I won't lie to you that we had a friends with benefits situation for a summer back in college. We have no feelings like that for each other," I say, noticing how he's tensing up.

"Are you sure?" he asks.

"Sure about what?"

"That there are no feelings," he elaborates.

"No, there's not. I mean, I love Jake, but as a friend."

"What about him?"

I sigh. "I'm pretty sure he feels the same way."

James is now fisting the table. "I don't think he does Everly. I think he's in love with you."

Really? Even so, what is he wanting to come out of this? I'm not going to stop being friends with Jake, and I really hope that one day they will be friends again, too. I hate that I'm the reason their friendship is ruined.

"What do you want me to do, James?" I ask.

He doesn't respond, and then the server brings out the appetizers. We're both tense, and neither of us wants to continue the conversation first. Me being me, I can't handle the silence, so he wins, and I lose.

"He's my friend James, and he always will be. I'm not going to jump into bed with him again. Ever," I state.

He nods, but still doesn't say anything. We both take some of the food from the appetizer and place it on our plates.

After a few more moments of silence, he finally speaks. "I saw the book he gave you. When did he give that to you?"

My heart stops. Shit. Of course he saw that. It was on the table for anyone to see. I haven't finished the book yet, but I did look at the back and saw Jake's note. It looks bad, even I know that.

"Yesterday."

"Everly..."

I interrupt him. "No, it's not what it looks like. It was a quote from the book, James."

Once again, he doesn't say anything, and neither do I. I want nothing more than to sit here and defend Jake, but I don't think he is in the mood to listen to anything I have to say. What James doesn't know is that Jake wrote that quote for James and me. Not for Jake and me. Jake has always pushed me toward James and told me that we belong together. The only time that stopped was after I found out about James' girlfriend and the interview. That's when I was stupid and jumped into bed with Jake. I know I made these mistakes, but I'm not like that anymore.

"What about you? I know you had a girlfriend for a while. Stacey, I believe?" If he wants to play the ex-game, I'll play it.

"She wasn't my girlfriend," he growls.

I laugh. "I saw the photos and articles, James. You were with her for a while."

"Not everything is what it looks like in the papers. You should know that," he states calmly.

"I do, but are you going to tell me that you never slept with her?" I accuse.

He doesn't answer, which is answer enough.

"See. I know that her family is connected to yours, so I'm not stupid enough to think that you don't talk to her," I state.

Again, he doesn't respond. Ugh, honestly, this is something that really annoys me about James. He shuts down and just doesn't talk when he doesn't want to. Our communication lacks greatly, and it always has. This is such a beautiful night and date. I hate that it's turning out like this. I knew we needed to have these discussions, but I didn't want this.

"I don't want to argue," he states.

"Me neither. Let's just agree that we're exclusive and trust each other. Okay? It's a start," I say, trying to form a truce.

"Agreed," he replies.

Once our food comes, we're silent for a bit, just enjoying each other's company, the good food, and amazing view of the night sky. The tension between us has faded as we both finish our meals and head to the couch to relax for a bit before leaving.

He lies back on the couch, and I lie between his legs against him while he holds me. This will never get old.

James whispers in my ear, "Everly, you are so beautiful. Thank you for giving us another chance. I love you. I've always loved you."

My heart skips a beat and then beats faster. He has no idea how true that is for me, too. I need to just tell him the truth. I need to stop guarding my heart and do what feels right.

I turn to face him and put my hand on his cheek as I say, "James... The moment I left for Georgia, I left a piece of my heart with you. No matter how hard I tried, I've never stopped loving you. I will never stop loving you."

He looks at me like he's processing my words and that he's shocked to hear them. It doesn't take long before his mouth lands on mine. He pushes me back onto the couch and continues to kiss me. After a few minutes, he pulls away, looking me in the eye.

"You have no idea how much I've wanted to hear you say that. Jesus Everly, I love you so much. Please let me take you right here on this couch."

I laugh. "James! I'm not going to have sex on a couch on your friend's rooftop!"

He groans and leans his forehead against mine.

"Come home with me. In fact, come stay with me. I don't want to be without you for another day," he says seriously.

As tempting as it is to say yes, I know that I shouldn't. It's only been a few weeks since we've been seeing each other again. We just officially became a couple again. I know it feels like no time has passed between us, but it has. A lot has happened in those years that I know will need to be figured out first.

"James... I can't. I want to, but you know I can't," I say breathlessly.

"You can, but I understand. We'll take this as slow as you need to, I promise," he says like he's hurting.

I kiss him again, but we quickly part as our server comes back up to see if we want dessert. If I'm being honest, the only dessert that I want is sitting right beside me.

Chapter Eighteen
•••••••••

JAMES

Since she won't come back to my place tonight, I drag out the night on the couch on the rooftop. She lays back on me, and we go between talking about random things, getting to know each other again, saying nothing at all, and just enjoying each other's company under the stars.

I absentmindedly run my fingers up and down her arm and make my way to her hand and twist the promise ring I gave her.

"You still wear this," I state.

I've noticed her wearing it every time I see her, but I haven't brought it up until now. I also know that she's never taken it off, even during college.

"I never take it off," she whispers.

As much as I don't want to, I need to bring up more about her past. I need for us to get it all out of the way so we can move on together.

"Even when you were engaged to Eric?" I ask.

She freezes, and I can feel her stop breathing for a moment.

"You know about Eric?" she continues to whisper.

I nod, even though she can't see it. I know she can feel it.

She sighs. "Even when I was with Eric, I never took it off."

"Why?" I ask, hoping the answer is what I think it is.

She shrugs her shoulders. "Well, for one, it's beautiful. For two... I guess I just always had hope that maybe one day if I kept it on, that meant your promise still stood and you'd come back for me."

Shit. I feel like my heart is being ripped out by her words. She was waiting for me all that time? I was so stupid to stay away for as long as I did. Could everything have been avoided if I had just gone to visit her in college that first year? If I had fought harder for her?

"It still stands Everly. The promise I made to you still stands," I say while brushing back her hair with my fingers.

She snuggles into me closer but doesn't say anything else. I let us sit in silence before I continue the conversation. I try to think it over a little, so I don't say the wrong thing again to make her angry. The conversation about Jake didn't go well, though I don't know how it could have, anyway.

"If you still felt that way, why did you get engaged to Eric?" I ask.

She sits up and positions her body to face me so she can see me as she speaks. "James... I made a lot of mistakes in college. A lot of stupid mistakes that I regret. I was drowning back then, and I didn't know how to cope with it. I turned to alcohol and drugs, which made things worse. I thought you were over me and in love with someone else. I tried to forget about you by being with Jake. He was never anything more than my friend, and Eric came along when I needed someone the most. He was there for me when I needed it, and I went along with dating him and saying yes to the engagement because I thought I was supposed to. I thought it would make me forget about you…"

She looks like she wants to say more, but she doesn't. It takes a lot for someone to admit their mistakes, and I hate that she's saying Eric was there for her when she needed it the most. That should've been me. I know exactly what she's referring to, and I'm not going to push the subject tonight.

"I made a lot of mistakes too. Did you love him?" I ask, hoping her answer is no.

She shakes her head no. "I want to say I did, but I didn't. Not the way I love you and always have. I wanted to. On paper, we were the perfect couple, but there just wasn't love. At least, not on my side."

She sounds like she really regrets everything she did back then and especially when it comes to Eric. I hate the fact she let another man touch her, and she was even engaged to him. I remember finding out and taking the first flight out to Georgia to stop it from happening. By the time I got there, I decided against it and took the first flight back to New York. She may have a lot of regrets, but I'm pretty sure I can match them with my regrets.

"If I would have come to see you when you got engaged and told you not to, what would you have done?" I'm not one who likes to play what-ifs, but I need to know how deep her feelings go for me.

She looks back and forth between my eyes and thinks before responding. "Do you want the truth?"

"I always want the truth."

She doesn't look me in the eye as she responds. "I spent many nights hoping you would come to Georgia and tell me you still loved me and wanted to be with me. I said yes, thinking that if you loved me, you wouldn't let me get engaged to him, never mind marry him."

Fuck me. Why the hell didn't I just go see her when I flew all the way to Georgia? I'm an idiot.

"I thought you were happy. I thought that's what you wanted. All I've ever wanted was for you to be happy," I say.

She stares at me and tries to hide the tears she's been holding back from me. I pull her in closer and wipe under each eye and hold her close. She doesn't say anything back, but she doesn't need to. We both made mistakes that kept us apart, but what matters is that I have her back now, and I'm not going to be making the same mistakes again. I'm not letting her go. I will follow her to the ends of the earth if I have to.

I drop Everly off at her house after our date and decide to make a pit stop before heading back to mine. I want Everly to come back to my place, but I know she isn't ready yet. I just want her to move in with me, especially with this new threat against her, that we aren't sure how serious it is or not.

After escorting her to her door, I get back in the car with Ryder to see he has taken off his suit jacket and that stupid earpiece, which I know was just for show.

"Home?" Ryder asks as I hop into the passenger seat.

"Not quite yet. I'd like to pay Jake a visit," I state ominously.

Ryder studies me before responding. "Are you sure that's a good idea? It's late James, maybe we should plan this visit out better."

"No. I want to do it tonight," I state.

Ryder nods and drives off toward Jake's apartment.

Jake doesn't live too far from Everly, which I'm assuming was planned on his part. It's almost 11 at night when we make it to his place, and I don't care if he's already sleeping or not. It's time I confront him and make him aware that Everly is mine.

I bang on his door and wait for him to open it. Ryder stands beside me, refusing to let me do this on my own. I don't know if he thinks I'm about to get in a fight and will need his help, or that he is going to keep me from killing him.

Jake doesn't take long before answering the door. I didn't expect him to be fully dressed at this time of night, but he is.

Jake has a wide grin on his face that I already want to punch off him.

"James, what a pleasant surprise. To what do I owe the pleasure so late at night?" he asks sarcastically.

"We need to talk," I state to the point.

Jake steps back and opens the door wider for both me and Ryder to enter. We take a few steps in, but don't leave the entryway. I don't think this is going to take long. Usually Ryder steps back, giving me space, but this time he's right next to me.

"Should I be calling my security for backup?" Jake asks jokingly, looking at Ryder.

I don't want jokes or small talk, so I get to the point.

"We need to talk about Everly," I state.

"Ah, I knew this was coming. Alright, lay it on me," he once again says mockingly.

I step closer to him, getting angry. "This isn't a joke, Jake. Everly is mine, and I want you to stay away from her."

His smile fades as he says, "Everly is one of my best friends. I'm not going to stay away from her."

"I don't think you understand what I'm saying, Jake," I threaten.

Jake sighs and puts his hands up in defeat. "James... I'm not going to get in the way of you and Everly. I had my shot with her and she didn't want me. It's always been you, James. Nobody stands a chance against you."

I take a step back and breathe. I'm still angry, but I'm confused. I didn't expect Jake to back off so easily, if he really means it.

"What about that book you gave her?" I ask accusingly.

"It's just a book that she loves. I had a friend that knew the author, and I couldn't pass up the opportunity to get it for her," he states, shrugging his shoulders.

"And the note in the back?" I question.

"Was a quote from the book, which I thought fit perfectly for you and her," he says.

That's what Everly said, except for the last part. This is way too easy.

As if he can read my mind, he continues, "James, you've been my brother my entire life. I don't want to fight with you anymore, especially over a girl. Everly is special, but she's yours and you're hers, no matter how much distance or time passes. I get that now. I didn't back then, and I'm sorry. I never meant to hurt you, and I hope one day you can forgive me."

Well shit. He wasn't supposed to be standing here apologizing to me and telling me that he understands Everly is mine. He was supposed to be defending himself or telling me he's not going to be backing off Everly so I could punch him again. He deserves to be punched, but he's right. We've basically been brothers our whole lives. I don't want to fight with him anymore either, but I'm not sure I'm ready to let it all go yet.

"I don't trust you," I say.

"Yeah, I know," he responds.

We're both quiet for a few moments, not knowing what to say to the other. This isn't how I expected this conversation to go, so I need time to comprehend it. I back away from him and head toward the door.

"There's no second chance if you mess this up, Jake," I warn.

"I won't," he says as he watches me head out the door with Ryder right behind me.

Ryder and I don't talk all the way back to the car, but the moment we get in, he says, "I didn't expect that."

"Yeah, me neither," I say as I contemplate what Jake said.

"For what it's worth, I think he means it."

"You're probably right," I say.

I've been angry at Jake for so many years. It's hard to just let that anger go, but at the same time, I'm ready to let it go. If he's going to be part of Everly's life, then I need to. He was always like a brother to me, and maybe it is time to forgive him since he's asking for it.

CHAPTER NINETEEN

EVERLY

Halloween is finally here. I've been looking forward to this party because I haven't been able to see all the boys since our last get together. We've been group messaging, and apparently James convinced everyone to dress up as a character from *Once Upon a Time*. No one will tell me who they are going as, but James requested that I dress up as Emma Swan. She wouldn't have been my first pick, but I'm really hoping there's a reason he chose this character for me.

After getting dressed, I look in the mirror to see myself wearing dark blue skinny jeans with knee-high brown boots. I found a gray cami to go under the red leather jacket she normally wears. I throw on a blonde, wavy wig that looks exactly like her hair in the show. It's not a sexy outfit by any means, but I'm not trying to impress anyone but James. Plus, it almost covers every piece of my skin, so I'll be warm on this chilly October night.

There's a knock on my bedroom door, and I open it to find Ashley and Paige standing on the other side.

I look over their outfits and say, "Oh my gosh, you both look hot!"

Ashley is wearing a pirate costume, and by pirate costume, I mean basically a few rags. She's wearing a super short black and red ragged skirt with black fishnet leggings and a white sports bra with a black and gold strap underneath, then white poofy sleeves, but her shoulders are showing. She has her hair put up cute with a dew rag.

Paige is wearing a witch's costume. It's a long-sleeved, low-cut black dress that is so short it hardly reaches past her butt. She has black fishnet leggings as well and black high heels. Of course, it's topped with a witch's hat. I can't say I've ever seen her dress up this sexy before, but she looks amazing.

"Thank you. I didn't really have anything, so Ashley let me borrow her dress, and I had the rest," she says shyly.

"Well, I think it's perfect, and you look amazing," I say, trying to boost her confidence a little.

"I'm trying to tell her there's no way she's not getting hit on tonight, but she doesn't believe me," Ashley says as they come to sit in my room.

As they wait for me, I put the finishing touches on my make-up.

"I'm not really looking for anyone right now," Paige says, averting her eyes from both of us.

I look her over, trying to figure out what's going on. She's usually shy when it comes to guys, but this is different.

"What's going on, Paige? Have you found someone?" I ask, hoping that's what it is.

I see her blush, and she shakes her head. "No! Not really... Maybe..."

Ashley's eyes go round before she says, "Okay, details, now!"

"Well... Okay, don't kill me for not telling you sooner, but I quit my job like two weeks ago..." she trails off.

"What?!" I yell in surprise and sit right in front of her as she's speaking.

"My boss was awful, and I knew it wasn't going to be worth it, so I just quit. So, I got a new job that day, and now I may have a thing for my new boss," she says, cringing.

"Okay, wait. Multiple things here. What did your old boss do?" I ask, hoping it's nothing too horrible.

Paige is a good girl who plays by the rules. She went to college, got her degree, and got perfect grades. She does everything right, so for her to just quit out of the blue, it had to be something big.

"I really don't want to talk about it right now. It's over, and I want to move on," she says.

Ashley and I exchange looks but agree to move on.

"Okay, tell us about your new job and new boss," Ashley says, wagging her eyebrows.

"I'm waitressing right now. It pays good money, and the tips are great. It's just supposed to be temporary until I find another job in my field," she reassures us.

I can't be mad at her for doing what she needs to do. Her family doesn't come from money, so she has always worked hard to get what she needs and save. I want to offer her some help, but I know she will refuse. I'm working with a friend to pay off her student loans and make it look like it didn't come from me. I'll expedite this, so it happens next week. One less payment will help ease her burden.

We can tell she doesn't want to continue talking about the job, so Ashley and I both silently agree to drop that. I will find out where it is though later.

Paige continues about her boss, "I went in for a drink after I quit, and I met my boss. After a few drinks and spilling everything that happened, he hired me. He's kind of closed off, but he's sweet when he wants to be. He's so hot and cold though that I don't know. I really like him, but I'm not sure how he feels about me."

I nod. "Maybe he's trying not to like you because he's your boss."

Ashley agrees, and Paige mentions she thought it might be the same thing. Regardless, it's only been a couple of weeks since she started there, so I'm sure they will figure it out.

Declan drives the three of us to the Hale's house. I told James that I would meet him there since I'd be going with Ashley and Paige. I'm excited to see him because I haven't been able to see him much since our big date. We've been able to sneak in some coffee breaks and a lot of phone calls, but that's about it.

I feel like a teenager again, wanting to spend all my time with James, but not being able to because of school. This time it's because of work and other random life commitments, like training with Declan. For some reason, he's been adamant about training more and harder lately. I've also noticed that security has been increased, even though they haven't said anything. Something is up, but I trust them to tell me if it's something serious.

Declan pulls up to the house, and the party looks to be in full swing. Cars are lined down the whole street. There's a spot in the driveway of the Crawford's house next door that Declan pulls into, which I'm sure was dedicated specifically for us. Once we all get out of the car, I can't help but stop and stare for a moment.

There are so many memories of this house, and it has been many years since I've been back. I spent every summer when I was in school here since my mother passed away. I look over toward the Hale house and smile at the memories there too. We all used to sneak out to each other's houses when we were younger. Looking back, I'm pretty sure that our parents knew because there's no way security wouldn't have seen or heard us. Regardless, it's hard not to stand here and get sentimental.

"Ready?" Ashley asks as she loops her arm around mine and Paige's. We walk through the yard toward the front door of the Hale's house.

The house looks so different decorated with Halloween decor. The layout is similar to the Crawford's house. As you walk in, there's black garland lining the staircase and spider webs reaching from every corner of the house. The large chandelier even has webs and a giant spider all over it. Random gargoyles and bloody creatures are everywhere.

"Everly!" Mrs. Crawford comes running from the back of the house, with Mrs. Hale following behind her.

She pulls me into a hug and then holds me at arm's length, looking me over.

"You look so beautiful and grown. It's been too long. We need to update your photo on the wall. We will remedy that this Thanksgiving, yes?" she asks, but I know it's not a request.

When you walk into the Crawford's house, you will find portraits of their family plus Bash, Jake, and me. I'm sure the boys' portraits are all updated, so it was only a matter of time before she asked for a new one of me.

Mrs. Crawford barely looks like she's aged a day. She has shoulder-length blonde hair and piercing blue eyes. She's gorgeous, and Ben has always looked just like her. It's funny because James hardly looks like his mother or brother.

After I agree to pose for a new portrait on the wall during Thanksgiving, Mrs. Crawford moves on to talking with my friends and I say a quick hello to Mrs. Hale, thanking her for inviting us. I continue walking around, looking at the décor and pushing through the good amount of people hanging out right past the foyer.

I immediately find the boys standing in the corner of the room with beers in their hands talking, though James is missing. I scan the room and don't see him anywhere. I decide to walk over and see if they know where he is. Though I also want a closer look at their outfits because, oh my God, they make amazing *Once Upon a Time* characters.

"You guys look amazing!" I talk loudly over the loud, scary music that's playing.

They all look at me and smile, looking me over. I know they have all seen the show because I forced them to watch it back in high school, but I doubt they really wanted to dress up like these characters.

"You're a perfect Emma Swan, Everly," Ben says, gesturing toward my outfit.

"You all are perfect too, like wow. You guys went all out," I say, admiring their outfits.

Ben is dressed as Robin Hood. Like full-on Robin Hood with the dark green cape, leather outfit and dark brown boots. Plus, the enormous bow and arrow. He even has dark hair and scruff, which I'm not sure if he dyed it or if it's a wig. With that hair color, I can see the resemblance to James.

Bash is dressed as Prince Charming, with his dark red velvet cape draped over his dark brown pants and vest. He also wears knee-high black boots. Of course, he is wielding a sword which looks completely real and heavy. I'm kind of scared to ask.

Then there's Jake. Jake's dressed as Rumpelstiltskin, and he eerily looks just like him. He must have painted his skin color and added some wrinkles, which all look so real. He wears tight brown leather pants and knee-high black boots as well. Over a silky long-sleeved shirt, he is wearing a brown vest. He also holds the blade, which looks real. Being Jake, I wouldn't doubt that it is.

I turn back to Bash and ask, "So, where's Amelia? Is she dressed as Snow White?"

Bash frowns and shakes his head. "She couldn't make it tonight."

Oh, that stinks. I was really looking forward to meeting his girlfriend. He made her sound so amazing. It would've been nice to have another girl in the group.

"What he means to say is that he screwed up and they are in a fight," Jake interrupts.

Ouch. Hopefully, they'll fix that soon.

I'm quickly distracted when Ashley and Paige come up to the group. Ashley places herself next to Ben and starts talking with him. They smile at each other, and she laughs, putting her arm on his. At least she's not being shy tonight like she usually is around him. They would make a cute couple.

Jake is checking out Paige from a distance and leans to whisper in my ear, "When did she get so hot?"

I smack Jake's arm and say sternly, "She's always been hot, but no, Jake."

He puts up his hands in front of him and says, "I'm not going there."

I shake my head at him. Jake will probably spend the night flirting with her, but I know he's true to his word that he won't go there. He doesn't want to mess with my friends.

I randomly shiver and feel goosebumps forming on my skin. I can feel someone watching me, and I know exactly who it is. I can feel his presence as he enters the room, even though I'm not looking at him. I turn around to find James standing in the doorway, staring at me.

Holy fuck, he's Hook, and he looks hot. My chest tightens with him in those black leather pants and a vest with the long black leather coat that fits around him perfectly. I close my eyes and take a deep breath to compose myself. I have never wanted to jump a man so badly in my life, but with the way he looks, I know I'm fucked tonight. Literally.

CHAPTER TWENTY

JAMES

I walk back into the room after a stupid business call took me away from my friends. I stop in my tracks as I see Everly standing with the group, with her back facing me. I can't help but stare at her perfect ass in those tight skinny jeans. As if she can feel me staring, she turns around to face me, and fuck does the look she's giving me give me an instant hard-on.

I watch as she looks me up and down and her mouth parts in surprise. Hook has always been her favorite character on the show, which is why I specifically requested her to be Emma Swan. Her outfit might not be revealing, but it's still sexy as hell, and all I want to do is go over there and rip it off her. By the way she's looking at me, she feels the same.

I give her a smile and head in her direction. The moment I make my way to her, I wrap my arm around her waist and pull her in for a kiss. I feel her knees bend as she holds onto me and moans in my mouth. Yeah, I'm not going to be able to hold back tonight.

We kiss for longer than what's appropriate for a social gathering like this, but fuck if I care. I want my mouth on her for as long as she'll let me. I also may have noticed that Jake was standing right next to her, so that's a bonus to this display of affection.

She finally pulls away from me and says, "I was looking for you."

I push her hair behind her ear, well her wig, as I study her beautiful face.

"I had an important business call come through that I had to take," I reply.

Ben drags us back into the conversation with the group, and we spend some time reminiscing about the past. I laugh harder than I have in a while. It feels good having us all back together again, like no time has passed.

"Do you still have a scar from when you caught me on fire?" Bash asks Everly.

"Oh my gosh, yes! Look!" Everly quickly lifts her shirt, showing that she does still have a burn mark from one of the best weekends of my life.

Almost as quickly as she tugs it up to show everyone, I tug it back down. She gives me a wicked smile.

I lean in to whisper in her ear, "Don't you dare show others what's mine again. You're playing a dangerous game, lifting your shirt up like that."

I hear her breath hitch, and a little moan comes out of her. She's already so turned on. It's not going to take much convincing tonight. We've already been teasing each other through texts the past week, and she's been a willing participant.

Bash lifts his sleeve to show his burn mark, which still sits on his wrist as well.

"You know, I'm pretty sure Everly just shouldn't be near fire," Ben says while pushing a candle that sits on a table next to us further away from her.

"What? I'm not dangerous when it comes to fire. It's fine," Everly says, feigning to be hurt.

"Um, no. If you remember correctly, you almost burnt my face off with a propane heater. Thankfully, it was just my bangs. I still feel like they haven't grown back correctly though," Ben says while playing with his hair, which he dyed tonight to match the character he's wearing.

"Okay, fine. That's only two instances. That's not enough to say I shouldn't be around fire," she states.

"Everly..." Jake starts. "You remember that time in college?"

"No! Jake, you promised that would stay between us!" She puts her hand over his mouth to stop him from speaking.

He pulls her hand away and continues, "Sorry Everly, but Ben's right. You shouldn't be around fire, and I think everyone needs to know how dangerous you are with it."

I haven't heard this story, so I'm curious. Clearly, the others haven't either because they are invested as well.

"So, the power went out one day at the house, and it was pitch black. As you all know, Everly is afraid of the dark, so she went to find some candles, which she dragged me with her every step of the way..." Jake trails off to look at Everly's reaction.

She has wide eyes and is shaking her head. "Jake, please. You don't have to do this..."

Oh, this is going to be good.

Jake smiles and continues, "So she found some and lit them. She was carrying one around with her and somehow, I'm not sure how, she lit the curtain on fire. That thing went up in flames so fast it was crazy!"

Everyone has wide eyes and is laughing, but we all know that isn't the end of the story.

He continues, "So she thought it would help to tear the curtain down and throw it at me. My pants caught on fire, so I did the whole stop, drop, and roll thing while she decided to pick up the curtain again and start flinging it around for whatever reason."

Everly interrupted, "I thought it would put the fire out! Full disclosure, I was drunk and probably had just done drugs, so none of this can be held against me."

Everyone laughs as Jake continues, "So, Declan and Barry both came running in, but by that time she had the other curtain somehow on fire and was tearing that one off and threw it at Declan as he entered. He tried to dodge it but didn't have enough time, so his shirt caught on fire and Everly's dress was on fire. We were all on fire on the ground rolling around, trying to take off our clothes, when Barry saved the day."

At this point, everyone is dying of laughter picturing the three of them rolling around on the floor on fire. Even Everly can't contain her laughter and there are tears in her eyes.

"What did Barry do?" Bash asks.

"He brought in a fire extinguisher and put out the fire. We were all completely covered in that white foam stuff, along with the entire room. It took hours to get it cleaned up, and that's with the help of professional cleaners. Needless to say, Declan doesn't allow Everly around fire anymore either," Jake says while shrugging his shoulders at Everly, who is glaring at him.

"Good to know. Sounds like Everly has set everyone on fire but me. I'll have to be extra cautious when she's around fire," I say with a smirk.

She just shakes her head and leans into me. I can feel her laughing still. I know those aren't her finest moments, but they are still great memories. Even if it was Jake that was with her and not me.

Her friends, Ashley and Paige, come back after the story is finished, missing out on a good laugh. I watch Ashley as she's all up on my brother and flirting with him. Ben is one of the smartest guys I know, but he is dense when it comes to girls. I don't think he realizes she's flirting with him.

Everly leans in and whispers in my ear, "What do you say we take a walk and reminisce more about the old days?"

She doesn't have to ask me twice. I grab her hand and lead her out the back door, where there are a few people hanging out on the porch. It's much quieter out here without the music blaring.

It's cold out today, so I wrap my arms around her, holding her tight as we look out into their backyard.

"Do you remember how Bash and Jake set up that ridiculous paintball course?" she asks while smiling.

"Yes, and you looked ridiculous," I state back, laughing.

"No, I didn't!" she defends herself.

"You were completely decked out with full body armor and a helmet. We couldn't even tell it was you. Though I have to say you surprised us all with how well you did and how much you improved," I say.

"And yet I still lost and had to be your slave for the rest of the day. You know, I don't think I ever thanked you for that," she says, squeezing my arms tighter.

I chuckle. "For having you as my slave? Baby, I'll gladly have you as my slave any day."

She smacks my hand that's around her and says, "No! For using that to make me feel better. You could have taken advantage and made me do whatever you wanted, but you didn't. You spent the rest of the day with me, doing what you knew I needed. Thank you."

Of course I did that. Why wouldn't I have? She was still upset with everyone knowing what happened with Adam, and that was my fault. And of course, with what actually happened with him. I wanted to give her a good day and just be there for her. I love that I'm always the one who can comfort her. That I've always been the one she comes to for comfort, even when we were little.

"So, did your parents keep our rooms the same, or did they change them into some random art studio?" she asks.

"I'm pretty sure they left them alone, so they are exactly the same as we left them. Want to go sneak over and check them out?" I ask, hoping she'll say yes.

"Yes!" she responds.

We walk off the back porch and through the side yard to get to the house. We enter through the back door, which is unlocked, and make our way through the dark kitchen and up to the foyer, where I turn on some lights.

"I don't want you to be scared and try to find a candle for light," I say.

Everly laughs. "You're a jerk!"

I lead her up the stairs and stop at the top, asking, "Which room do you want to see first? Yours, Ben's or mine?"

She doesn't hesitate before saying, "Yours."

I'm excited as I step in front of her and lead the way. I want to be a gentleman and open the door for her, but I also don't want her to see the hard-on I'm already sporting.

We walk into the room, and it's exactly as I left it. There isn't anything on the walls as I never put much there to begin with, but I took it off before I moved out to go to college. My old computer and desk still sit to the side of the room, and my bed looks perfectly made. There's no dust in here, so clearly the cleaners still come through to make sure it stays clean.

Everly sits on the edge of my bed, and I'm having a hard time not going over there, pushing her down and fucking her right now.

She rubs the comforter on the bed and says, "There's some great memories right here too."

She looks up at me, and all I can respond with is, "Mmm."

I'm still standing by the door and without taking my eyes off her, I close and lock it behind me. She gets up off the bed and slowly walks toward me. She places her hands on my chest and rubs it up and down. It takes every effort in me not to just grab her and have my way with her.

"You remembered Hook was my favorite character," she whispers.

"I did."

"You look just like him in this. It's perfect. Do you remember the last time we both dressed up together?" she asks, as if I could ever forget.

"How could I forget?" I say, pulling her in closer.

She continues to caress my chest and moves her hands slowly to take off the long leather coat I'm wearing. I slowly shrug it off and throw it on the chair next to me. I want her to lead, and I want to take my time with her.

She looks up at me, and I can tell she wants this as badly as I do. I turn us around, push her up against the wall and my mouth crashes onto hers.

CHAPTER TWENTY-ONE

EVERLY

I knew the moment we walked into James' old room, it was all over. Any self-control I had left was gone when my foot stepped through that doorway. Who have I been kidding that I could resist him?

His mouth crashes on mine as he pins me to the wall by the door. His hands roam down my back and cups my ass. He lifts me up as I wrap my legs around him and my fingers are tangled in his hair.

He slowly kisses down my chin, and I arch my neck as he begins his descent down it. Goosebumps rise on my skin with how good his lips feel on my neck. Carrying me over to his desk, he sits me on it beside his computer. Objects crash to the floor loudly with one swipe of his arm, and it sounds like something breaks. Neither of us cares, as his mouth never leaves mine.

He unbuttons my pants and unzips the zipper. I lift my hips as he slowly drags my jeans down my thighs and follows their path with kisses. He stops for a moment, pulling each of my boots off slowly.

Before he pulls my jeans off the rest of the way, he straightens and leans forward so his face is inches from mine.

"It's time to remind you how good we are together," he says, leaning his forehead against mine.

It's his way of asking for permission, and I know once I give it, that's it. I nod my head because I can't speak right now. My breathing is so erratic, and I just need him.

"If we do this, you're mine. You understand?" he demands.

"I've always been yours," I whisper.

"No more games. I'm going to fuck you so hard you won't ever forget you're mine again," he growls, and his expression is intense.

"Please," I beg, needing him already.

He pulls my jeans off and throws them to the floor. My leather jacket and tank top get torn off shortly after, leaving me in my bra and underwear.

James steps back and admires me for a moment. "You're so fucking hot."

I feel myself blush under his stare and at his words. He quickly claims my mouth again as I peel off his clothes. His chest is finally bare, showing those perfect abs, and he's down to just the leather pants and boots. Jesus, I think I'm going to come just from staring at the man.

He pushes me to lie back on the desk as his fingers trace up my legs and thighs, stopping just short of where I need him. I groan in protest.

He continues tracing up my stomach to my breasts, circling around and then to my back, unclasping my bra. He kisses up my neck and to my mouth while still not touching where I need him.

"James..." I breathe out, hoping he understands my need.

"Baby, I'm getting there. You've made me wait this long to touch you again. I'm going to take my time and explore every inch of you," he responds while still kissing me everywhere on my body.

I am so wound up I don't think I can take it anymore. I need him, and dear God, if I have to look at him in these leather pants any longer, I'm going to lose it.

"Please take your pants off and fuck me," I beg, writhing beneath his touch.

He smirks, steps back, and slowly takes off his boots and pants.

"Better?" he asks.

"It won't be until you're inside me," I say, grabbing his thick erection through his boxers.

He groans as I stroke him, and he closes his eyes. I'm hoping this will get rid of whatever self-control he has left, so he'll fuck me.

Finally, he leans forward, pulls off my panties, and kisses me again as his thumb finds its way to my clit. He rubs circles around it, and I swear I'm about to explode, but he stops just as I'm about to come.

"James..." I protest again.

He drags a finger across me and says, "Oh baby, you're so ready for me."

He lifts me off the desk and takes off his boxers as he bends me over it.

"So many times I have imagined fucking you bent over my desk," he says, while not waiting any longer.

He positions himself right at my entrance, teasing me even more. I try to push my hips back to force him to enter, but he holds me steady.

He leans over me and whispers in my ear, "Who do you belong to?"

"You," I whisper back.

At that, he thrusts inside me, hard. I wince at the slight pain for a moment, and he doesn't move, allowing me to get used to him inside me, stretching me. I hold on to the edge of the desk as he thrusts in and out, harder each time.

Our breathing becomes erratic, and so do his movements.

"James... I'm... going to come," I say, tensing, holding onto the desk for dear life.

"Come for me, Everly," he demands.

And I do. I finally find my release, and it's so intense my knees buckle, but thankfully I'm holding onto the desk.

James slows his rhythm for a moment and then pulls out of me. He flips me around, lifts me, and carries me to the bed.

He lays me down on my back and positions his body on top of mine. I'm still dazed and worn from my orgasm, but the way he's looking at me makes me want to have him all over again.

He kisses down my neck again and slowly makes his way to my breasts. He cups them and plays with them for a moment before taking a nipple in his mouth. I moan and arch my back, my body acting like five seconds ago didn't just happen.

He uses his finger to circle my clit again as he puts his mouth near my ear and whispers into it.

"Did you enjoy that, Everly?" he asks cockily.

I moan, "Yes."

He smirks and puts his face inches from mine. "Good. I'm going to fuck you in my old bed, and then you're coming home with me tonight so I can fuck you in my bed now. Do you agree?"

Fuck me if I wouldn't agree to just about anything at this moment, and he knows it.

"Yes. Please James," I state as he enters two fingers inside me.

He curls his fingers, hitting just the right spot, and I want nothing more than to have him inside me to come again. He knows what I'm thinking because he pulls them out and positions himself to thrust inside me again, and he does.

I hold on to him tightly as our mouths and tongues tangle together with the rest of our limbs. He stills for a moment, and I know he's close, trying to make this last. He picks up the pace again, and our breathing becomes more and more erratic.

I tense, and he breathes out, "I'm going to come. Come with me, Everly."

As if my body will do anything he demands, we come together and neither of us can stay quiet. Thankfully, we're in another house away from the party, so no one can hear us. Once we both recover, he slowly pulls out and lies beside me, kissing my temple.

I look over at him and rub my hand through his hair as we stare at each other. I can't believe we're here. It's like no time has passed at all, and we've always been together. I love this man so much, and I've fallen madly in love with him again. There's no going back now.

Chapter Twenty-Two

EVERLY

I wake up stretching and feeling the soft comforter above me. I roll over and faceplant into a wall. No, that's not a wall... that's a body. I close my eyes and think for a moment to get my bearings. I snuggle into his chest, realizing it's James. We left the Halloween party shortly after our time in his old bedroom, and he made good on his promise to continue back at his place. I blush, thinking about everything that occurred last night.

I glance at the clock to find it's five-thirty in the morning and we both have to get up for work in a few minutes. I hate that Halloween fell on a Thursday this year. It would've been nice to spend the weekend in James' bed and not get up for real life.

"Good morning," James says in his raspy morning voice.

Jesus, I forgot how sexy this man is, even in the morning. My body reacts to him as if we didn't just spend the night sleeping together in every possible position.

I smile at him. "Good morning."

"Skip work today," he says while kissing down my neck.

Apparently, I'm not the only one who feels like I need another round of what happened last night.

I groan. "Ugh, I wish I could, but I have to go to work today."

He continues to kiss me and asks, "Are you sure there's nothing I can do to make you skip?"

I allow him to continue kissing me for a few moments because it feels so good. I've missed this.

"I wish, but I really have to go to work. I can't miss the day after a holiday. Something always happens with the students, and I need to be there for them," I state while reluctantly pushing him off and rolling out of bed.

As I stand up, I find James looking at me in a way I've never seen before.

"What is it?" I ask, concerned about why he's looking at me like that.

He shakes his head and smiles. "You're just amazing. What you do for those kids is amazing."

He gets out of bed and kisses me again. Ugh, I need to get out of here before he convinces me to stay. That was so sweet of him to say, but I don't feel amazing half the time. I feel like I'm failing some of those kids and can't get through to them. I remember the emotions well at that age and how they take over your reasoning.

"Let me make you breakfast before you go," he says while putting on his gray sweatpants.

Yeah, gray sweatpants on a guy is everything girls say. I can't help but stare.

"No, I have to get back to get some clothes. As fun as being Emma Swan was last night, I can't show up to work looking like her," I say, grabbing my clothes off the floor.

"No need. I have clothes for you in the closet," he states nonchalantly.

Huh? I walk into his closet and look on the opposite side of his clothes. Sure enough, there are a ton of women's clothes in here. Everything from fancy, casual, and work. They all look brand new.

"James... What is this?" I ask.

"I ordered some clothes for you because I wanted to have them here in case you decided to spend a night or forever. You don't have to go back to your place to get changed," he says, as if all of this is normal.

I grab some clothes that would be perfect for work and try not to think about when he did this. I know James has always known what he wants in life, and he goes for it, but this is too much, right? I feel like he knows we're just going to be together, and that's it, so he's preparing for it. Part of me feels like running, and the other part thinks that's the sweetest thing he could do.

He must have realized I'm in my head because he stands in front of me and lifts my chin to look up at him.

"Hey, don't overthink it. I love you Everly, and I want to be with you. If you're not comfortable with anything, that's fine, just let me know. I wanted to make sure you have everything you need wherever you are," he states.

I close my eyes for a moment and take a deep breath. Can this man be any sweeter? His love for me is just so unconditional, and I don't know why. What does he even see in me? I'm a mess.

"I love you, James," I say while standing on my toes to lean up and kiss him.

We stay like that for a moment before he parts and says he's going to make breakfast. I head to the bathroom and change. Once I look in the mirror, I realize how awful I look. My make-up is smudged. I completely forgot to take it off last night.

I scrub off the remaining makeup and brush my teeth with the new toothbrush set out for me. That's when I realize there's a pink makeup bag sitting out on the counter. I open it to find makeup that I always use, all brand new.

Okay, if I didn't know James so well, I would definitely be running. This is stalkerish, right? He must have had someone talk with my staff or Declan or something to figure out what I use for makeup and my clothing size. He even got the bra size right. Unlike someone who might try to kidnap me and make me feel comfortable, he did it for the right reasons.

I laugh at myself for those thoughts. Yeah, I read too many books sometimes. My life is pretty crazy as it is with all the security and stuff, but this isn't crazy. I think. Right?

I finish getting ready and head downstairs, where James has a plate of eggs, bacon, and pancakes out for me with coffee.

"This looks amazing, James, thank you," I say, taking a sip of my coffee.

Of course, he has the perfect amount of caramel macchiato creamer mixed in with my coffee.

He sits down with a plate next to me, and we eat.

"Thank you for everything, James. It was nice of you to get everything I need here," I state in a wary voice. I really mean it. I appreciate it all, but it definitely isn't normal.

He laughs. "Everly, I've known you since you were little. I know everything about you, so it's easy to get all the things you like and use. Not much has changed, but it also helps that Maria does anything I ask her to. It was easy for her to get in touch with your staff to get the information needed."

I was right. He got the information from everyone I know.

"Why though? Why go through all the trouble to have everything here just in case I stay over one night?"

"I've never doubted that you'd stay over quite often." He pauses, grabbing my hand and toying with the promise ring on it. "I made a promise, and I'm going to keep it. After last night, you're mine, Everly. I'm not letting you get away again."

My heart beats rapidly, and I want to jump him again. I cannot live without him. He's right. I am his, and nothing is going to change that.

After a long day of work, I'm meeting Asher over at his club to hang out. We still meet weekly, but our visits seem to be getting shorter and shorter. Ashley is coming to meet me as well. We might have a drink or two, but we're just hanging out to talk. Our days of drinking too much are over. We all agreed we're getting too old for it.

After ordering a margarita and a burger, Asher comes to sit next to me.

"How was your day?" he asks, just like he always does.

I sigh. "It was good, but long. The usual after a holiday with students. There's always drama, especially with rich kids. How was your day?"

He nods like he understands, then responds, "It was good. I've been keeping busy."

He has been keeping busy, and I don't even know with what. I know he has a lot of businesses, but I feel like I barely know anything about him, and it bothers me. He's my friend, not actually my therapist. I should know more.

"Tell me about it. What's been keeping you busy?" I ask, hoping he'll give up something.

I often ask him about his personal life, but usually he just changes the subject, so I'm surprised when he answers.

"I've got some people who don't like me after me and what's mine, so I'm having to deal with that," he says, looking tired.

I can imagine a man as powerful as him would make quite a few enemies, even though he's one of the nicest people I know. People are going to want what he has, and he's going to have to work hard to keep it. Thankfully, he has a lot of great people surrounding him to help.

"If there's anything I can ever do, let me know. I want to help," I state.

He gives me a genuine smile. "Thank you. If there is, I'll let you know."

He quickly switches the subject back to me. "So, how are you and James?"

I tell him everything. I tell him about last night and this morning. I even tell him how I'm feeling, like maybe it was a little weird with everything this morning.

"I think James knows what he wants, and he's ready to take it. And that's you. I don't think it's weird. I think you might be trying to find something wrong," he says, switching to his therapist role.

Am I? "Why would I do that?"

"Are you scared?" he asks.

"No. I don't think so." I pause to think for a moment. "Maybe I am. It's going too well at the moment, and nothing good lasts. We both know that."

He doesn't deny it. "Well, it's good right now, so you should enjoy it. Life is short. Don't make the mistake of wasting the time you have with him."

He's absolutely right, as always. We continue talking for about twenty more minutes, just hanging out mostly, when Ashley shows up and sits next to me.

"Hey!" she says, giving me a hug from her seat and then glancing over at Asher.

"Hey! How are you?" I ask.

"Good, I need to get a margarita," she says while flagging down the bartender.

I notice the strangeness between Asher and Ashley. Neither of them has said a word to each other or even acknowledged the other's existence. Weird. Why is everything weird today?

Asher stands up from his seat and doesn't take his eyes off Ashley. "It was good seeing you, Everly. Let me know if you need anything."

I stand and give him a hug before he walks off, then sit back down watching Ashley stare straight ahead.

"What was that?" I ask.

"What was what?" she asks innocently.

"You and Asher," I state.

"Who's Asher?"

Okay, yeah, there's something going on between them.

"Ashley..." I state while giving her the "I know something's going on" look.

She sighs. "It's nothing. He just..." she stops for a moment and glances over toward where Asher walked off to. "Really, it's nothing."

"Did something happen between you two?"

"No, not really. I don't know. Just whenever he's around, I get this odd feeling, like I need to be with him. I thought it was just another crush, but it doesn't feel like when I look at Ben and Declan. It feels like... I don't know, more?" she murmurs, grasping for the right words.

I didn't realize that she even knew Asher like that. He was barely around when she was, and they never really spoke to each other. Did I miss something?

"Have you two talked more than I know about?" I ask.

She shrugs her shoulders. "I came in one day alone, and we did talk for a bit. Honestly, I feel stupid. I flirted with him, but he shot me down. It's been awkward since and we both silently agreed to pretend the other doesn't exist."

Well, that doesn't sound like Asher either. Strange. Either way, we really need to find Ashley a boyfriend. She hasn't had very much luck. Too bad she won't let me try to hook her up with Ben, since she clearly likes him at least a little. Though she admitted not as much as Asher.

Speaking of boyfriends, I watch a cute guy sit next to Ashley. He looks about our age, and he immediately starts talking to her. He's attractive, and she seems okay, so I decide to excuse myself to head to the bathroom, which I don't really need to use.

Instead of going to hang out in a gross bathroom, which Asher's staff really does take great care of, I decide to head toward Declan. I don't feel like dealing with random drunk guys tonight, but also want to give Ashley a little space for a moment.

I lean against the wall that Declan's leaning against. "How's it going?" I ask him.

He raises his eyebrows in question at me.

"Oh, come on, hang out with me for five minutes," I say, nudging him with my elbow.

A smirk lifts on his face. "Don't feel like getting hit on tonight?"

"No, I really don't." I sigh.

I should've invited James, but I needed to talk to Asher alone, and Ashley seemed like she needed a night out with a friend. If Paige wasn't working, she'd be here too, and it would make things much easier.

Declan and I both act like creepers staring at Ashley talking to the guy. She laughs at something he says, and he puts his hand on her thigh. Oddly enough, she doesn't push it away like she normally would.

He scoots a little closer and whispers something in her ear. I can't tell her response, but I'm surprised at what I witness next. Asher comes barging up to the guy and places his hand on his shoulder. He leans down and says something in his ear, and the guy's face turns pale. The guy immediately leaves without saying anything to Ashley.

I have no idea what that was about, but now Ashley is standing and yelling at Asher. She's poking him in the chest and throwing her arms up and shrugging her shoulders. Asher doesn't say anything back and is just taking it.

"Do I leave it alone, or should I go over there?" I ask Declan.

Declan is watching closely with a smile on his face. "Up to you, but I'm pretty sure Ashley is five seconds away from punching Asher in the throat."

With that, I push off the wall and head over there. "This is ridiculous!" I hear Ashley shout as I get closer.

"What's going on?" I look at Asher, and he doesn't say anything.

"I was hitting it off with Sante, and Asher decided to scare him off," she says.

I raise my eyebrows, looking at Asher.

He sighs. "He was a creep. I did you a favor."

Before anything more can happen, I stand in front of Ashley and turn her around, facing away from Asher. "Let's go back to my place and hang out."

I look back at Asher, and he has a pained look on his face. I mouth, "You okay?" He nods in return. I walk Ashley out the door, and Declan follows. She's still so angry.

I force her to jump in the car with Declan and me, saying we'll have someone get her car later. I don't want her driving while she's so mad. She continues to go off most of the drive home just saying she doesn't understand why Asher would interrupt like that, but I have a feeling. I'm not going to say it because she won't believe me. My eyes meet Declan's in the rearview mirror, and we're both thinking the same thing. Asher likes Ashley.

CHAPTER TWENTY-THREE

JAMES

I tap my fingers on my desk, waiting for this phone call to be over. It's Saturday night, and there's nothing more that I want than to hop into bed and stay there all night with Everly. She came back over this morning, and we've hung out all day, having lunch and taking a walk through Central Park. It's cold outside, but it has always been her favorite thing to do.

"I think we're going to have to meet in person to continue discussing this, James," Mr. Moore says over the phone.

Really? Because I started this conversation saying we should discuss this in person. I couldn't be rude, though. Mr. Moore is one of our biggest business partners and a good friend of my father's. I've already turned his daughter down and apparently broke her heart, so I'm walking on thin ice with him.

"How about Monday morning at my office?" I ask, hoping he accepts and ends this call.

"I'll be there at ten," he states, hanging up the phone.

One thing I appreciate about the man is that he's to the point. There's nothing I can't stand more than a bunch of small talk during a business meeting. We're here for one reason. Let's figure it out and move on. Small talk is saved for events and kissing ass, which I both despise.

I sigh and clean up my desk, realizing that the call took over an hour. When I come out of my office and head to the living room, Everly is on the phone and she's talking in a hushed voice. I walk louder than I normally would to announce my presence. Her head turns in my direction, and she quickly says goodbye to whoever she was talking to, hangs up, and gives me a small smile.

Everly has been distracted with her phone since coming back from our walk in Central Park. Something is bothering her, but she hasn't said anything about it. When I asked, she said it's nothing and changed the subject.

I want nothing more than to look at her phone and see who it was that texted her. I also want to go check the cameras and listen in on the conversation that she was just having, but I'm not going to do that. She seemed weirded out yesterday about me having all the things she needs here that I don't want to add invasion of privacy to that list when we're just getting back together. Not that I'm opposed to doing it because I've been doing it for a while when it comes to her.

"Everything good?" she asks me as I sit down next to her on the couch and put my arm around her.

"Yeah, we're going to finish up the conversation on Monday. What about you?" I ask again, hoping she will reveal what's on her mind.

"Everything's good," she replies, but I know that's not true.

She looks distant, almost sad. I can feel her emotions like they're my own, and she's anything but fine. I fight the urge to find out who she was talking to. If she wanted me to know, she would tell me. She's not the same as she used to be, and I need to trust her.

Well, if talking about it isn't going to help her, then I know how I can make her feel better at this moment.

I lean in to kiss her, and she immediately responds, kissing me back. I smile against her lips. She was fighting us so hard before, and now she's giving in.

I pull back for a moment, just taking her in. Her smell, her touch, her appearance, and how responsive she is to me. I fucking love every part of this woman. She came to my apartment wearing those tight skinny jeans that show off her ass perfectly and a long-sleeve crop top sweater to ensure I could see it. When we were walking through Central Park, I made her wear a long coat so no one else could be checking out what's mine because every man with eyes would be staring at her.

I kiss down her neck and pull her sweater and shirt over her head, so she is only in a bra. I stare at her as my dick strains against my pants. She knew exactly what she was doing when she put on this red lacy bra. I kiss between her breasts and all the way down her stomach, unbuttoning her pants. She lifts her hips so I can pull her pants off, and I throw them across the room.

I'm on my knees in front of her on the couch and damn if it isn't exactly where I should be. Worshipping her and her body is what I was made to do, and I intend to do it. I rub my hands up her legs and push her thighs apart. I press my nose right against her center with her underwear still on and take her in.

"James..." she moans while tugging on my hair.

God, I love when she pulls on my hair and says my name like that. I don't waste any time before pulling down her underwear, and they join her pants on the floor. I lift my hand to drag my finger across her to feel how wet she is for me. As much as I want to rip my pants off and fuck her this second, I want to make her feel good first and forget whatever was bothering her a few minutes ago.

I move back to kissing up her thighs until I reach exactly where she wants me. I feel her tense as my face is between her legs, inches from her. I look up at her, and she's already writhing below me with her eyes closed and head back.

"Eyes on me, baby. I want to see you when you come," I say, and her eyes instantly find mine.

I smirk, watching her watch me in anticipation. I don't keep her waiting any longer as I slide my tongue over her and feast on her like she's my last meal. God, she tastes so good. Her hand is still in my hair, pulling me closer to her, while the other clenches the couch.

I rub my hand up her thigh and push two fingers inside her, and she moans, which in turn makes me moan. I continue licking and sucking as I curve my fingers to hit the spot that drives her crazy. She's so close I can feel her tensing, so I suck hard one last time as she comes undone.

I watch her head fly back as she lets out her release and screams my name. I groan and adjust myself with my free hand because, fuck if her coming undone doesn't almost make me come in my pants like a teenager.

Once her eyes find me again, I pull my fingers out of her and put them in my mouth, licking her off them as she watches.

I move on top of her and kiss from her neck to her ear. "Want to move to the bed?"

She debates for a moment before saying, "No, it's my turn to taste you."

Fuck. It's only been two days since I've had her, but it feels like years with how just her words can set me off.

She wastes no time undoing my pants and allowing them to join hers on the floor. I lift my shirt over my head, and I love the way she looks at me, admiring me. She rubs her hands over my chest, down my stomach, and to my hard cock.

She strokes me slowly, driving me crazy, and gets down on her knees in front of me. She wastes no time wrapping her pretty mouth around my dick and sucking. Jesus, I try to think about something unsexy to keep myself from blowing my load immediately.

The way she takes me all the way in her mouth down her throat brings me back to the present as I grab her hair, pulling on it. I begin fucking her mouth and moaning as she continues.

"Fuck baby, I'm going to come," I state as a warning.

She doesn't pull away, so I let myself go and release inside her mouth. She swallows every last drop, and if that isn't the sexiest thing I've ever seen, I don't know what is. She pulls away from me and licks at a drop that fell on her bottom lip. Never mind, that is.

I pull her up and into a deep kiss. "Let's go to the bedroom."

She smiles back lazily and says, "Okay, but I'm staying there for the rest of the night."

"Good, because I had no intention of letting you leave the bed for the rest of the night," I say, smiling.

As I pick her up and carry her bridal style to the bedroom, she laughs. I'll never get sick of hearing that sound or the sounds she makes when I'm making her feel good. I place her gently on the bed and remove her bra. It's the last layer between us, and I need it gone.

I settle in bed beside her and hold her close, whispering in her ear, "I love you, Everly."

She looks up at me with those beautiful hazel eyes, replying, "I love you too, James. Forever."

Chapter Twenty-Four

EVERLY

Last night with James was perfect. I don't know how, but I'm falling in love with the man even more. Every reservation I had about him is going out the window. The hurt from the past seems to be a distant memory that doesn't matter anymore. He loves me and I love him, so why fight this?

I look over at the clock to see it's eleven in the morning. We spent all night exploring each other's bodies again, cuddling, and just talking through the night. I don't want to get up and leave, but I have to.

I gently move his arm off me and roll out of bed, trying not to wake him up, but, as always, I fail.

"Stay in bed," he rasps, capturing my arm.

I sigh. "I can't. I have somewhere to be," I state, hoping he won't ask where that is.

"Where do you have to be besides in my bed?" He looks up pleadingly.

I close my eyes and take a deep breath. How do I answer this? I don't want to leave him, and I especially don't want to go where I'm headed, but I have to.

"I'm meeting an old friend who's in town for lunch. I won't be long. I'll be back soon," I state, pleading with my eyes not to ask any more questions.

Of course he does. "Who?"

My heart pounds as I debate how to answer this. How do I tell him I'm going to see my ex-fiancé, who I haven't spoken to since we broke up? That he texted me yesterday, wanting to meet up while he's in town. I don't want to, but I owe it to him to show up. It's the right thing to do.

I squeeze my eyebrows together, looking at James, hoping he understands to drop it. I don't want to tell him right now, not that I won't eventually tell him. I just don't want to at this moment. We had a perfect night last night and I don't want to walk out of here like this.

"Can we just talk about it when I get back?" I ask.

I can tell he's concerned and possibly hurt. That's not my intention, but I don't want him to worry the entire time I'm out with Eric. Then again, he looks like he's going to worry, regardless.

I sigh. "Eric texted me yesterday. He wants to meet for lunch, and I owe it to him to meet him."

James' expression is tense. "Why do you owe it to him?"

I close my eyes. "James, please. Can we just talk about this later? I promise I won't be long."

"Fine," he says, getting out of bed and pulling on some boxers from his dresser.

This is what I didn't want. He's mad, and now I'm going to be leaving mad, upset, and feeling guilty. Why is it that my past always comes back to haunt me?

I go into the closet and blindly grab a shirt, sweater, and jeans. I take about twenty minutes getting ready in the bathroom, hoping that it'll be enough time for James to calm down from the initial shock of me telling him I'm meeting Eric. I get it. If he told me he was meeting with Stacey, I would probably act the same way.

When I come out, I find James in the kitchen putting together some lunch for himself. He put on some sweatpants, but still doesn't have a shirt on. I can't help but stare. Damn it, James.

He looks over at me, smirking, knowing exactly what he's doing to me. I walk over and rub my hands up his chest and wrap my arms around his neck. I kiss him for longer than I intended to.

I lean back and say, "I love you, James. I'll be back soon, and we'll talk about it, okay? No secrets. I only want you."

He doesn't look convinced but lets me go without saying anything further. I sigh as I walk toward the door and take a quick glance back at him. He doesn't look at me, so I leave and hope that whatever it is that Eric wants, it'll be quick.

I sit across the table from Eric at the restaurant in his hotel. Declan's sitting at a seat at the bar, which so happens to be right next to our table. He will be able to hear and see everything. Usually, he would give me more privacy, but he clearly wants to ensure I know I don't have privacy with Eric. I'm fine with that because I don't intend anything to happen here that would hurt James.

"You look beautiful," Eric says nervously.

"Thank you," I state, not knowing how else to respond to that.

"I've missed you," he states.

I close my eyes for a moment to compose myself. "Eric..."

He stops me. "Everly, I know we broke up a year ago, but I can't do this anymore. I've tried to move on, but I can't. I'm ready to fight for us."

Shit. I had a feeling this was what it was going to be about, but I was hoping it wasn't. I was hoping this would be a closure thing. A, "Hey, we're good, and I'd love to still be friends that pass each other occasionally if I'm in town." I broke his heart, and I never expected him to forgive me for that.

"Eric... I'm sorry..." I state, not knowing how to word this.

I take a glance over at Declan, who's taking a drink of his soda watching intently, but not showing on his face what he's thinking.

"Just hear me out. I understand why we broke up, but Everly... Don't you miss us at all? We had a lot of fun, we never fought, we were perfect together," he states, pained.

He's right. From the perspective of an outsider, we were the perfect couple. We went to parties and had a blast. We stayed in and were comfortable. We never fought about anything. He loved me and would do anything for me. There was only one problem with our relationship. I never loved him in that way.

I feel the tears burning behind my eyes. It's not fair to him, and he's one of my biggest regrets.

"Eric, I'm so sorry. You're right. We were perfect at that time. You are perfect," I state, not knowing what else to say.

"I'm moving to New York, Everly," he says.

No, oh Eric, please no.

"No, please. Don't move here. Eric... We can't..." I start to say, but the words die in my throat. How do I break his heart again?

"It's already done, Everly. I have a job lined up that I start tomorrow."

My heart stops, and I feel those tears trying to break through. How did I not realize he wasn't over me? How did I not realize he was trying to move to New York for me? I just moved here myself two months ago.

"Eric, I'm sorry. We can't be together," I say.

"Is it because of him?" he asks with a growl.

I nod my head, not wanting to say anything more.

"Everly, please give me another shot. I'll show you that we're meant to be. He's not right for you. He doesn't deserve you," he continues to try to change my mind.

"You're wrong. I don't deserve either of you. I never did," I say truthfully.

He shakes his head. "Yes, you do. We deserve a shot. He wasn't there when you needed it the most, don't you see that? I'll always be there for you. I'll never let you down. I tried to give you space this past year, and the moment I heard you were back in New York, I did everything I could to get here."

That's what hurts the most about this. Eric has worked so hard to get where he is today, and he doesn't have that much money. He would have had to sacrifice so much to get here. He did it all for me and what will never be between us. I wish he would've talked to me sooner.

"I love him, Eric." I don't want to hurt him, but he has to know.

He looks hurt and angry. "How can you love him? He wasn't there for you when you needed him, Everly."

I close my eyes and think about how to respond. He's right. I can't deny that. The memories come flooding back to me.

"Shhh. You're going to get us caught," I said to Ashley.

She couldn't stop giggling as I grabbed the keys to Declan's car off the hook. It was one in the morning and Declan was fast asleep. Barry, who was on watch, went to the bathroom so we had two minutes tops to get out of there.

We made it to Declan's car and turned on the engine. Ashley blasted the music as I pulled out of the driveway. We had a little too much to drink and were completely high. We were invited to a party to celebrate the end of our junior year in college, but Declan banned us from going. He was doing that a lot lately. We pretended we were happy spending the night at home but planned to sneak out. They would eventually catch us, but it should be well after the party. Barry shouldn't notice our absence since we made it look like we went to bed.

We sang loudly and danced to the music as I drove. Before I could see it coming, another car swerved into my lane, and I swerved to avoid it. I over-corrected as the car dipped into a ditch, flipped over, and smashed into a tree. Everything went black.

I woke up with my head pounding and everything dark. I groaned as I put my hand to my forehead, where it hurt and felt something wet and sticky. I felt weird and like I was trapped. I moved my hand toward my shoulder to find I had a seatbelt on. That's right, we were in a car.

It took me a moment to remember we were driving and then swerved off the road. I reached for my phone in my pocket but couldn't find it.

"Ashley, I can't see. Are you there?" I asked, trying to look in her direction, but it was too dark.

"Ashley?" I asked again, but there was no response.

I reached my arm up to feel the roof of the car. We were upside down. That's why I felt weird. I reached over toward where she was sitting and felt her body next to mine. Why wasn't she responding?

"Ashley!" I yelled out, and she still wasn't answering.

I started to panic. My eyes were adjusting to the darkness, and I could see her figure. She was buckled in her seat like I was hanging upside down. I needed to get us out of there. I reached for my seatbelt and unbuckled it, which gravity forced me to the ground, or technically to the ceiling. I groaned at the sharp pain in my neck and shoulder as I fell. I didn't think that through.

I tried to open the car door, but it wouldn't budge. I couldn't roll the window down because the car was off. Crap. I started crying out in panic and banging on the car. No one could hear me.

I felt dizzy as the pain from my injuries surfaced. I was more hurt than I thought, but I couldn't concentrate on that. I needed to get Ashley help.

"Everly!" I heard a voice call. It was Declan!

"Declan!" I screamed and heard him coming closer to the car.

He somehow ripped the door open and pulled me out. "Everly, Jesus. Sit here. The ambulance is coming."

"Declan... Ashley..." I couldn't get the words out, but he understood.

He went to the passenger seat and somehow pried that door open, too. I didn't even notice Barry with him until I saw them both taking her gently out of the car. She wasn't responding. She wasn't moving.

I crawled my way over toward her, and Declan yelled at me to stay still, but I couldn't. Not when my friend was hurt.

"Ashley!" I yelled out again, but she still wasn't responding.

No... Ashley... You can't... I can't lose you too. What have I done?

I started panicking and hyperventilating. I couldn't breathe. Declan came over trying to get me to sit back, but the moment his arms were around me, I blacked out.

That was one of the worst nights of my life. Ashley almost died, and it was because of me. I remember waking up two days later in the hospital feeling like crap, with casts and bandages everywhere. I had a horrible concussion and stitches on my forehead. I still have a scar there. My left arm and leg were broken, along with one of my ribs.

My first thought was of Ashley, and I tried getting out of bed, but I was too dizzy. Declan and Eric were both in the room with me the moment I woke up. Thankfully, Ashley was alive, just in worse shape than me. Asher was there as well, who was conveniently in Georgia on business. I was in the hospital for over a week. All of my friends came to visit, including Bash, Jake, and Ben. Eric never left my side in the hospital room, only when Paige insisted she get a moment alone with me so he could go eat.

After that, Eric stayed at my place, helping me recover. He took off work for me and ended up losing his job over it. We met in class the previous semester and hit it off, becoming good friends, but after everything we ended up dating and the rest was history. He proposed a year later. I accepted, and we were a week from getting married before I broke it off with him. He was there for me when I needed someone, and James wasn't. James never once contacted me while I was in the hospital or showed that he cared.

I can't show Eric that he's right though, that it bothers me. That's something James and I are going to have to work out.

"I know I keep saying this, but I'm really sorry, Eric. Thank you for being there for me and for being an amazing friend. I couldn't have done it without you, but we can't be together. You deserve so much better than me, and I really hope you find the happiness you deserve," I state with the tears finally falling.

Remembering the past is difficult, and I'm trying hard to move forward. Eric would've been a safe choice. He doesn't know everything about my past, and he was the perfect boyfriend and fiancé. The only problem is I don't love him. I love James. I'll always love James.

CHAPTER TWENTY-FIVE

JAMES

The moment Everly left, I wanted to chase after her and lock her in my apartment. I didn't want her to go talk to Eric. What is it that she needs to talk to him about? I've been keeping tabs on him, and he's been working in Georgia. I didn't even hear about him flying to New York. I'm going to have to talk to Hank about not giving me a heads up or letting this one fly under the radar.

After she left, I immediately put on some clothes and followed her. I get to the garage, and Ryder is waiting for me. He places his hand on my chest to stop me. I swat his arm away, hating when he does that.

"What do you plan to do, James?" he asks like he just wants to know my plan.

"I'm going to follow her, and fuck, I don't know. Interrupt their lunch and threaten him?" I ask because I don't know what my plan is.

I just want to bring her back home and make sure Eric knows she's mine.

"Since you asked, I'll tell you what you should do. Walk back into that apartment and wait for her to come back," he states with a straight face.

Does he not know me by now? That's the furthest thing from what I'll do.

Ryder sighs. "I know you, James, and know that's not what you want to do."

Get out of my head, Ryder. How does he always know what I'm thinking?

"Come on," he says while putting his arm around my shoulder like we're good buddies, as he leads me back to the elevator.

I'm not sure why, but I don't fight him. Honestly, I'm sick of fighting everyone. I'm exhausted. He probably has a point. I should trust Everly. If we're going to make it work this time, I need to trust her. It won't stop me from texting Declan, though.

Ryder leads me back to my apartment and comes in to sit with me. I run my hands through my hair and pull on it as I tense. Everly's going to make me go bald before I'm even thirty.

I text Declan to find out what's going on. His response is almost immediate.

Declan

They're just talking.

What about?

Declan

Talk to Everly when she gets back.

He's not going to give up any information either. Instead of sitting around waiting for her to come home like a dog, I get up and change into some workout clothes.

Before I head to my room, I tell Ryder, "Meet me in the gym in five."

Ryder nods and heads out. There's nothing like sparring and getting in a few hits when I'm angry and not sure what to do with myself.

When I walk back into my apartment from the gym with Ryder, Everly is sitting on the couch. I sigh in relief that she's here. She didn't run away with Eric. She's here.

"Hey," she says with a small smile.

"Hey," I say back and walk over to her.

I know I'm sweaty and probably look like a mess from the few hits that Ryder got in on me while I was distracted thinking about her, but she doesn't push me away as I lean in to kiss her.

"You should go take a shower," she states as we part.

I smile. "Is that your way of telling me I stink?"

She laughs. "No, I like when you're all sweaty like this."

"Yeah?" I ask as I cock an eyebrow.

"Mmm hmm," she replies.

All my worries drain away with the way she's looking at me, like she wants me to take her now and fuck if I don't want to, but I can't. We need to talk about this.

"Did you want to talk about Eric?" I ask.

Her expression completely changes from the flirty girl that was just standing in front of me to a sad one. I hate it when she looks like that.

"Not really..." she whispers.

I look at her like I understand, but we need to. She knows that too. We both head to the kitchen where I get a glass of water, and she sits at the island on a barstool. I stand across from her, downing my water.

"He wanted to get back together," she blurts out.

My body tenses at her words. I knew it! I should've gone with my gut and followed her, making sure he was aware that she's mine.

"And?" I ask her to continue.

"And I told him I'm sorry, but we can't. That I'm in love with you," she states and offers nothing more. I can tell there's more.

"How did he take it?"

"Not well. He's hurt, and I feel bad because it's my fault," she says.

"It's not your fault you don't love him anymore, Everly," I say, but the words burn in my mouth.

The fact that she loved him at all destroys me. I know she said she didn't think she did, but she had to of, at least a little.

"I never loved him, James. I strung him along the entire time, and he was so good to me, but I never loved him. Not the way I've always loved you," she says, looking at the floor like she's about to cry.

I make my way around the island and pull her into me, holding her.

"Why weren't you there?" she asks.

Huh? "Where?"

"Why weren't you there... when I was in the hospital after my accident? After my junior year of college," she states, not looking at me.

My heart clenches at the ache. That's one of my biggest regrets when it comes to her. I knew she needed me, and I wasn't there for her.

"Everly..." I say, not knowing how to answer.

She finally looks up at me. "I need to know, James. I need to know this so we can get past it."

I look up at the ceiling, remembering the day I found out she was in the hospital.

I got off my fourteen-hour flight from New York to Japan, and I was exhausted. I left at 7 pm and could hardly sleep on the flight over. Mr. Moore spent almost the entire flight trying to convince me why I should marry his daughter. While I didn't disagree with him about how beautiful and smart she was, along with it being a good business move, I couldn't pull the trigger. Everly is it for me. She always will be.

We got into the car that was waiting to take us to our hotel. The moment I turned my phone on, I saw a dozen missed calls and messages from Declan, Bash, Ben, Ryder and even Jake. If Jake was calling, something was wrong.

I listened to my first voicemail from Declan, and my heart stopped. Everly was in an accident, and Ashley didn't look like she was going to make it. Everly would recover from her injuries, but the doctors said it would take a miracle for Ashley. She'd been in surgery all night.

I never wanted to attend this business trip to Japan, but my father insisted I do this for the experience.

"I have to fly back," I told Mr. Moore with panic in my voice.

"What happened?" he asked, seeing the concern on my face.

"It's... my family needs me. A friend who's part of the family has been in an accident. I need to be there," I stated, not being able to tell him how much Everly meant to me.

I was pretending to entertain the idea of being with his daughter, per my father's request.

"We have a meeting in only a few hours, James. You're fourteen hours from home. Whatever it is, forget about it for now and attend this meeting. This is a big deal for us both. Don't ruin it," he said.

He was right. If I left, our chances of making a deal with this company would be out the window. I nodded, and we continued toward the hotel room. I'd call Declan and make sure she was doing okay. It was going to take me a day to get home, anyway. A few more hours would be okay, right? All the messages I was receiving indicated she had all her friends and family there.

That meeting took four days to complete, and we came to an agreement on our deal. I kept in contact with Declan and Ryder, who I sent to watch out for her when I left for Japan instead of coming with me, and she was doing okay.

By the time I got back from Japan, she was getting out of the hospital. I flew back to New York and jumped immediately on a plane to Savannah, Georgia. Ryder met me at the airport and drove me two hours through the horrible traffic to get to her. I'll never forget how I felt when I saw her getting out of the car that day.

We sat there waiting for her to arrive home. I needed to see her. I needed to be with her. I knew I was supposed to stay away from her because that's what she wanted, but she almost died.

We watched Declan drive into the driveway, and I put my hand on the car door to get out, but paused when I saw someone else get out of the car and head toward Everly's door. I watched as he helped her out of the car and then lifted her up to carry her inside. Everything in me deflated as they went in, and Declan paused by his car, looking our way.

I got out and leaned against the car as Declan came over to Ryder and me.

"Who's that?" I asked him.

He gave me a pitying look, and I felt sick. I didn't need him to answer to know.

"His name is Eric. They've been getting close all semester. He didn't leave her side the entire time at the hospital," he stated.

"They're together?" I asked, trying to hold in every emotion I was feeling.

"They weren't, but they are now," he said.

Fuck. If only I had come back. If I had come back and stayed with her in the hospital, would it be me carrying her into the house right now? I wasn't, though. I chose work over her. I kept telling myself that's what she wanted. She wanted me to concentrate on work, to get my business in order. That's what all this was supposed to be, right? She was supposed to find herself, and I was supposed to get work in order so we could finally be together and concentrate on each other.

"She gave up on me, didn't she?" I asked.

Declan didn't answer.

"Is he good to her?" My voice cracked.

"He is," he responded.

I took another look toward the house. She was in there with him. He was taking care of her. Ashley was still in the hospital, but they said she'd miraculously make a full recovery. I knew Everly was going to struggle with her role in what happened with Ashley. I wanted to be the one she could talk to about it, but could I? I needed to go back to New York and finish this deal. I couldn't be there for her, but he could.

If I walked in there right now, it would confuse her. She needed someone who could be there for her, and I wanted to. I really wanted to, but I couldn't at the moment.

"It's best if I stay away," I stated and didn't question.

Ryder and Declan looked at each other, but neither of them said anything.

"Tell me otherwise, Declan. Tell me it's better for her if I go in there right now," I pleaded.

"How long can you stay?" he asked.

We both knew the answer to that. Not long enough.

"I love her, Declan. You know that."

He nodded. "I can't tell you what to do, James, but right now, she needs someone. And that's not me or Asher."

Fuck. He was right, and I knew it. I just said it myself. What should I do? I could give up my role in the company. I could give it to Ben, but at what cost? Would I resent her later for it? Would we even be together ten years from now? I'd be left with nothing. No job and no Everly. She'd be worth the risk, though. I couldn't make this decision on no sleep and running empty.

I got back in the car and told Ryder to drive me back to the airport.

"That's one of my biggest regrets, Everly," I state, and I can see she believes me.

"Tell me what happened," she says.

I take a deep breath before answering, "I had just left for a flight to Japan the night the accident happened. I didn't find out until I got there. Everyone convinced me we needed this deal, and I listened to them. Declan said you were going to be okay, so I stayed. I flew immediately to Georgia when I returned and waited outside your house the day you were released from the hospital..."

She interrupts me. "You were there? The day I got out, you were right there?"

I nod. "I watched as Eric carried you inside. I talked to Declan and decided it was best if I left without you knowing I was there."

Tears were forming in her eyes. "Why'd you leave? Why didn't you come to me?"

Fuck, her tears kill me. "You needed someone who could be there for you, and that wasn't me at the time. I was an idiot, so I left. I left you for Eric to take care of. I knew he could be there for you, and I couldn't. It wouldn't have been fair to you."

"But you came? You cared enough to come?" she asks, looking at me with tears in her eyes.

"Of course I did, baby. I love you. I've always loved you. It took everything in me not to go to you that day," I say truthfully.

I was a mess. I told Ryder to turn around and go back at least twenty times before finally getting to the airport and getting on that plane. Ryder flew back with me to ensure I did nothing stupid. He didn't protest and did everything I asked of him. Yes,

I pay him, but he didn't have to. He didn't have to do any of that.

Neither of us says anything more. We don't talk more about her conversation with Eric, and she doesn't ask me more about the time I didn't go to her when she needed me the most. She just gets up and kisses me, pulling me toward the bedroom where we would spend the rest of the day together, just us.

Chapter Twenty-Six

EVERLY

Thanksgiving is finally here. It's one of my favorite holidays. I love getting together with the Crawfords, Hales, and my father. I've skipped it for too many years, and I intend to never miss another.

James and I have kept busy the past few weeks, but I've spent almost every night at his apartment. As much as I didn't want to be back in New York, it's been nice. I have all my friends here now. Ashley, Paige, and I get together every other weekend for a girls' night, and all the boys and I have been getting together when we can too. Ben spends a good bit of time at James' apartment as well, so we've seen a lot of him. It's like my life is finally getting to where I've always dreamt it to be. James and I together with our friends close by. I wish I could see my father more, but he said he's working hard to retire soon, so that'll change.

James and I arrive early because I'd promised Mrs. Crawford to update the portrait of me when I saw her on Halloween. The artist is coming to take some detailed photos of me so he can bring them home to paint later. I'm thankful we don't have to do a few sessions and sit forever while they paint me live. I'm certain Mrs. Crawford would prefer that though. I feel like it all turns out the same, anyway.

James and I are in the sitting room with Ben and his parents. The doorbell rings, and one of their workers gets the door. I know who it is before he enters the room. I haven't told James about any of the pranks that we're going to pull today. It's not that I don't want him to know, but I want him to experience them. Well, one of them I'm not fully aware of either, but Jake said he will let me know when I need to about how it's going to go down, so I don't ruin it.

Jake walks into the room, and I can tell everyone is surprised to see him here so early.

"Jake! You're early." Mrs. Crawford gets up to give him a big hug.

I look toward James to see his reaction, and surprisingly, he doesn't give one. They have been working to repair their friendship, and I'm thankful for that. It looks like it's going well, and I hope it stays that way.

"I had to run an errand, and it ended early, so I figured I would just come by," Jake says with an enormous grin on his face staring at me.

I notice the little bag he has at his side. It looks like a man's version of a crossbody purse. He must have the supplies in there that we need.

"What's up with the purse?" Ben asks Jake.

Jake's mouth falls open as he gasps dramatically. "This is not a purse. It's a satchel, and it's very popular right now."

I almost laugh but contain myself. To avoid further questions and get caught, I get up and grab Jake's arm, pulling him to the edge of the sitting room.

Before leaving I say, "We'll be right back. I just need to talk to Jake for a moment."

James cocks his eyebrow at me in question, and everyone else just stares. We leave the room and stand against the wall so we can still hear in the room, but not be seen.

Jake whispers to me, "You're too obvious, Everly."

I sigh. "I'm sorry. You know I'm terrible at this. Do you think they're onto us?"

Jake has a huge grin. "I'd bet they are, listen."

We're both quiet as we listen in on their conversation. We immediately hear them talking about us.

"Do you think they are up to something?" Ben asks.

"They aren't children anymore. I doubt they would pull a prank like last time," Mrs. Crawford confidently states.

James laughs, and I feel it in my very soul. I love hearing his laugh.

"They are definitely planning something," James says.

I facepalm my head and look at Jake. "Sorry."

Jake shrugs and pulls me up the stairs and into my old room. I was just in here for Halloween and it still looks exactly the same.

I can't believe they keep these rooms like this, and no one uses them. He locks the door behind us.

"How long do we have before the artist gets here?" Jake asks.

"I think like twenty minutes," I reply.

Jake starts pulling out a bunch of random supplies and laying them on the bed. It looks like there's paint, a thin paintbrush, some rubbing alcohol, clay-looking stuff, and some metal tools. I'm not entirely sure how this is going to work, but we'll see.

"Alright, sit here and I'll start. Where do you want it on your face?" he asks while pouring the rubbing alcohol into the paint palette.

I point to my right temple and say, "I guess somewhere around here?"

He grins and says, "That'll be perfect."

Jake starts putting the clay on my face and sculpting it. I hope he knows what he's doing. Otherwise, this isn't going to work. We thought it would be funny to put a giant boil on my face for them to take pictures of me and insist that they don't remove it from the painting. Then when Mrs. Crawford gets the painting, she's going to be in for a huge shock. I can only imagine her reaction and wish I could see it.

I know she pays a lot of money for these and uses the same guy, named Jessie, every year, so of course I'll be sending him money for his time and to replace it with the real one when she asks him to redo it.

While Jake is putting on the final touches, my phone vibrates with a text from James.

James

Everything okay?

Yeah, I'm just getting ready for the photos.

James

I thought you were talking with Jake?

Crap! I'm really horrible at this sometimes. I don't know how we ever succeed at pranks when I'm involved, but we always seem to.

Yeah, of course. I figured to not waste time so we're talking while I get changed.

James

You're changing with Jake in the room?

Oh, come on! My heart races. I'm panicking, and my hand is shaking.

"What's wrong?" Jake stops what he's doing and asks.

"I suck at this Jake." I show him the texts on my phone.

Jake lets out a deep belly laugh and holds onto his stomach with the paintbrush still in his hand.

"Yeah, you do," he says while continuing to laugh.

"That's not helpful. Help me," I say, handing him the phone.

He puts down the paintbrush and grabs my phone. He takes a few moments to type something out and hands it back.

When I look at it, he's already hit send.

> Of course not. I can't let him see the lacy black undergarments I have on. Oops never mind I forgot I'm not wearing any underwear.

"Jake! Did you just sext my boyfriend?" I slap his arm but can't help but laugh.

"It'll distract him from your mistake," he shrugs.

He's not wrong because a moment later, another text comes through from James.

James

> You can't put that image in my head while I'm sitting with my family.

> Sorry.

James

> After photos I expect you to stay in your room until I get there.

> I'll be waiting.

The excitement builds inside me, and it's hard for me to sit still. Today is going to be a great day. We have this prank for the photos, James coming up to my room, and a Thanksgiving meal all together.

"Alright, finished," Jake says while turning my head from side to side to inspect it.

I stand up and walk into the bathroom to look in the mirror. My mouth drops open in surprise at how large it is and how real it looks. There's a giant boil, about the size of my fist, on my right temple.

I go to touch it, but Jake stops me. "No! Don't touch it. It just has to last through the photos."

We hear a doorbell ring and know that it's picture time.

"Alright, I'll go distract everyone while you go meet him where you're supposed to. I'll make sure no one comes in. Don't come out though until I text you," Jake says while leaving the room.

It only takes a few moments before Jake's texting me that everything is ready. He's supposed to be distracting everyone, especially Mrs. Crawford, while I go into the room to meet Jessie.

As I walk into the room, Jessie turns around and says, "Ah! Everly!" He comes closer to give me a hug but stops in his tracks. "Oh, dear!! Everly, what on earth is that on your face?"

I give a small laugh before saying, "Oh, well... It popped up a while ago and it's just a big thing. I'm trying to embrace having it and not needing to look perfect."

Jessie steps back further and cringes. "Alright... Well... No worries, I'll remove it during the painting. You're going to be beautiful."

I'm trying hard to hold back my laughter and continue acting. "What? No! Don't do that. I insist that it stay. It's part of who I am right now."

Jessie sighs. "It's big enough to be a whole other you, but if you insist... then I won't remove it. You're gorgeous no matter what."

I feel a little guilty for lying to him, but this picture is going to turn out amazing and completely shock Mrs. Crawford. It'll be worth it.

We spent about twenty minutes while he took pictures from every angle humanly possible. I feel even worse about pranking him since he's being so nice about the fake boil. He was definitely surprised at first, but now he's just trying to make me feel beautiful.

"That's it, my sweet girl. It was so good seeing you again," he says while giving me a hug.

"You too Jessie, I missed you. I'm sure I'll see you again next year," I respond as he walks out the doorway.

I text Jake to let him know that he's gone and I'm heading back to my room. Hopefully, he can keep everyone away, except James.

Once I make it back to my room, I don't have time to sit down before the door opens. My back is facing the door, but I can feel that it's James. I hear the door click closed and lock. Heavy footsteps lead from the door toward me, and then I feel strong arms wrap around my waist.

"Now let me take a look at what you're wearing under this dress," he whispers in my left ear.

He lifts my dress and runs his hand up my thigh and to where my underwear should be. He moans when he finds that there isn't anything there. After Jake sent the text message about me not wearing underwear, I had to take it off. What's creepy is Jake was accurate when sending what type of undergarments I was wearing. I'm going to put that as it was just a good guess.

As James kisses down the back of my neck, I stop him. "James, wait."

He stills and asks, "What is it?"

I smile, thinking about the giant boil he hasn't seen yet on my face.

"I have to freshen up and take care of something before heading back downstairs," I say, trying to remove myself from his arms.

"It can wait," he replies while kissing down my neck further.

"No, you don't understand," I say, turning around to face him.

He looks me over for a moment and asks, "What is that on your face?"

I laugh. Hard. I have to sit on the bed because I'm laughing so hard, which makes James laugh with me.

Once I control my laughter, I explain to James the prank Jake and I just did.

James shakes his head. "I knew it. I knew you were plotting a prank. My mom is going to have a heart attack when she sees your portrait."

I go to the bathroom to take it off, and James helps me. I reapply my makeup in that spot, so no one can see where it once was. After taking care of that, James and I enjoy our time together in my old room and bed. By the time we're done, everyone has arrived.

CHAPTER TWENTY-SEVEN

JAMES

We make it through dinner completely unscathed from a prank. When I saw that fake boil on Everly's face, I knew that couldn't be the only prank they had planned, but so far it is. Everyone kept looking over in their direction throughout the meal, just waiting for the other shoe to drop. I thought for sure they would pull something else because Everly looked like she was having a hard time eating. Maybe that's the prank, not pulling a prank at all, but making us think they were working on one.

After lunch, all the men sit on one side of the room with our drinks while the women sit on the other. I want nothing more than to have Everly sitting on my lap right now and being close to her, but we'll be heading home shortly, so I can survive a little longer without her. She's talking with my mom and Mrs. Hale. I know she wishes there were more girls, so the others better step it up soon to get girlfriends to join us during the holidays.

"What happened with Amelia?" I ask Bash.

He's staring over at Everly as well, probably thinking about how Amelia should be here.

He shrugs his shoulders and says, "We're working through some things. She has her own family to spend time with during the holidays, anyway."

I don't push Bash to say more, but I can tell he's upset. Whatever it is, I really hope they can work it out. I've never seen him like this because of a girl before.

We all spend the next thirty minutes talking when our cook comes into the room and says something to my mom.

My mom laughs out loud. "Oh dear. Sorry everyone, as Susan was about to put the dessert in, she realized she left the buns in the oven."

Everyone laughs, and Jake stands up, heading toward Everly.

She stands up next to him as he clears his throat and places his arm around her. "Well, since we're talking about buns in the oven..."

Everyone stops talking, staring at them. My heart begins pounding hard against my chest as I see Everly's eyes grow wide, looking at him. Surely that's not what he means.

He continues, "Everly and I have some news..."

The pause is too long, and Everly says, "Jake, this is horrible timing to tell everyone."

Tell everyone what? I try to keep my cool, but rage builds as I fist my hands, ready to kill Jake once and for all.

Bash grabs my arm but doesn't say anything, as he's also intently watching them.

"As you all know, Everly and I have been friends since we were babies. We had a few moments where we thought we'd be more... anyway, speaking of babies..." Jake gets interrupted by Everly's father.

"Son, don't you dare tell us you knocked up my daughter," Mr. Monroe threatens.

Jake laughs nervously and takes his arm away from Everly. "What? No! What gave you that idea?"

Everly starts dying of laughter beside Jake, and everyone else joins. I let out a small laugh, not because I find it funny, but because I'm relieved. I can't believe that Jake would pull this type of prank in front of me, with our history.

Jake looks over at me and winks. Now I laugh. As mad as I was a moment ago, it makes me happy to know that he is comfortable doing that. I miss it. I miss us all being friends and trusting each other to do stuff like this.

Jake goes on to explain that they are starting a charity for babies and their mothers. I didn't hear all the details because I was too busy still thinking about the fact that Jake could have possibly knocked up Everly, but I think it's great. The charity, not him possibly knocking her up. Everly told me about one of her students being pregnant and at a loss for what to do with no support from her family. She was really invested in this student and passionate about helping her and others. It sounds like this would help teenage mothers, but also other mothers with no support or ability to take care of a baby.

As everything winds down and people leave, my father pulls me aside in his office to talk. We work together, but I rarely see him or talk to him alone in person. He's trying to retire, so he's pretty hands-off or working in other areas to get everything ready for my takeover.

"What's up?" I ask him as he gestures for me to take a seat in front of his desk.

He sits behind it and says, "I wanted to talk to you about your future."

I'm not fond of talking about business on holidays, but I'm not about to tell my father we can't talk. I'll give him a few minutes and then tell him I need to get going.

"What about it?" I ask.

He looks me over for a moment and smiles. "Tell me about you and Everly."

I smile back. "I love her."

I'm not going to hide it from him, and I don't think I need to. I know he was pushing for me to be with Stacey, but we both know that won't happen, now or ever.

He nods. "Are you going to marry her?"

"Yes," I state with no hesitation.

"Good. It's about time. You need to settle down and start a family. I'm retiring soon and I want grandkids," he states with the smile still on his face.

It's nice seeing my dad be... a dad. Rarely do we have these moments.

I laugh. "Did Jake's prank put babies in your head?"

He grins. "You know, if he had knocked her up and you didn't kill him, I would've."

I don't doubt for a second in my mind that's not true.

My dad turns serious. "Look James, I'm going to tell you a few things, and I hope you listen. There's not much that I regret in life, but I do regret not being there for you and Ben more as you were growing up."

I stop him. "Dad, you were there when you could be. You've built this business to be where it is today."

He holds up his hand so he can continue, "Yes, and I did it for both of you, but I still regret not being able to be with you more. The business is in a good place, and when I retire, it'll be in an even better place. Take the time to be with your future wife and children. Enjoy it, because it goes by faster than you can imagine."

It's rare I get emotional talking to my dad, but I can feel everything he's saying. He's a good father, but I can see his regret.

I nod. "I will."

"Good. Now, to the second part. I've worked hard to make this company legitimate. Your grandfather was a good man, but he got roped in with some shady people with the business. It's really difficult to get out of once you're in, but I think we're finally there. Thomas has taken the brunt of that on for me. Once we both retire, everything should be as it should. You'll always have offers from the wrong places, and I suggest you don't take them or get involved. It's not worth it, son," he states with concern.

I know what he's talking about because I've also helped him occasionally with some of this work. Many people who want to provide something illegal to us for something in return have approached me. I've been able to deny it, and most of that is with my father's help. Staying clean and keeping the company legitimate is my ultimate goal for my future wife and children.

"I understand," I say.

"Good. Now, when are you going to ask her to marry you?"

My smile widens as I tell him my plans for the proposal that hopefully will be perfect, and she'll say yes.

Chapter Twenty-Eight

EVERLY

I wake up nauseous and run to the bathroom. I barely make it to the toilet before throwing up everything I ate the night before. After a few moments, I walk away with the nausea barely subsiding. What did I do last night?

While brushing my teeth and getting my bearings, I think about what I did last night and where I am. I slept at home for the first time in a while because I wasn't feeling great. In case I was getting sick, I wanted to stay away from James, and I needed to get a good night's rest. It's Monday morning, and I have to work today, after being off the previous week for Thanksgiving break.

I go downstairs and get some ginger ale to help settle my stomach. I wonder if it's because of something I ate. I haven't felt like this since the last time I had a hangover, which has been a while. I debate eating breakfast for a moment and finally decide that maybe a piece of plain toast will help. Hopefully, I'm not getting the stomach bug. I'll know in a few minutes if so.

Declan comes into the kitchen and looks me over. "You look terrible. Are you okay?"

Well, that was rude. "Thanks Declan."

"Not what I meant. You look pale, and I heard you vomiting. You should stay home today if you're sick," he states.

"I think it's something I ate last night. I'll be okay," I say, and he walks off, taking my word for it.

When my toast is ready, I sit down at the counter and take a couple of bites. My stomach protests, so I throw the rest away. I go upstairs to take a quick shower, but after a few moments I feel weak and nauseous again, so I get out and lie in bed.

I still have an hour before needing to leave for work, so I'll just get dressed quickly and rest before going. If I throw up again, I'll stay home.

I don't throw up again, so Declan drives me to work. I'm feeling a little better, but the nausea is still there. I haven't had any other issues, though I prefer that it would be coming out the other end because I can handle that much better than throwing up.

When I walk into the office, Kendra, the front desk receptionist, welcomes me back from the break. I smile at her weakly, and she notices.

"Are you okay?" she asks with concern.

Do I really look that terrible like Declan said?

"I'm fine. I've just been nauseous lately," I state, and it's true.

Something has been off with my stomach since Thanksgiving. I didn't eat much during that meal because I felt nauseous, but it wasn't horrible. Last night it hit worse and then, obviously, this morning.

"Are you pregnant?" Kendra asks nonchalantly.

I laugh. "Of course not."

As I head into my office, I close the door and stop laughing. I'm not pregnant, right? I look at the calendar to see when my last period was. It was October 17. My heart stops beating for a moment as I realize that was almost six and a half weeks ago.

Okay, don't panic. I'm on the pill and I sometimes don't have my period. This is nothing out of the normal for me, so odds are I'm not pregnant. Though I missed a few pills while adjusting to life back in New York. Okay, I missed more than just a few pills.

Oh my God, I'm pregnant. I can't be pregnant. I'm not married. James and I just got back together and we're in a good place. I close my eyes for a moment and take a deep breath to calm down. I breathe fast, almost to the point of a panic attack. It's fine. I'm not pregnant. I'll take a test and then laugh about this later, thinking that I could've been.

My phone dings with a text from Declan.

Declan

Are you okay?

What? How does he know I'm not okay?

> Why?

Declan

> I got a notification your heart rate has spiked and it's not going down.

> Seriously?! You track my heart rate? How?

Declan

> Your watch.

Oh duh. The watch Declan gave me back in high school. It tracks my heart rate and has a tracker in it. I can hit the button on the side too if I need help and can't reach my phone and Declan isn't nearby.

> I'm fine, still not feeling well.

Declan

> Ready to go home?

I debate for a few moments but decide it's probably best if I do. I hate to leave, especially after a week of no school because these kids need me, but I'll be no use to them if I can't concentrate on anything but the what-ifs. I need to take a pregnancy test to see that I'm not and I'll be fine coming back to work tomorrow.

I leave work and get in the car with Declan.

"Can you take me to the pharmacy?" I ask, and he nods.

Once we get there, he gets out of the car to escort me in, but I don't want him to see what I'm buying.

"Can you just... stay here?" I ask.

Declan stares at me without responding.

"Please? It'll take me like two minutes," I state, hoping he will let me go alone.

"No," he says.

Ugh. It's probably my fault for giving him reasons in the past not to trust me alone, but I feel like we're past that now.

"What's going on Everly?" he asks, looking at me, concerned.

I look around me like I'm looking to make sure no one I know is around before whispering, "I think I'm pregnant."

He doesn't react at all to what I just said and leads me inside the pharmacy. Usually he would keep his distance, but he walks right beside me the whole time while I get the test, checkout, and get back in the car.

The drive home feels like forever as I hold the pharmacy bag in my hand with the test. I can't help but think about what if I am pregnant?

As if Declan can read my mind, he says, "Don't think about the what-ifs, Kid. Just wait until you take the test."

I nod and try to do what he says, but I fail. How will James take the news if I am? We haven't talked about kids yet, but I can't imagine he's ready for a baby. We're not even married. I'm going to derail his life all over again.

The memories come back from my sophomore year in college.

I debated opening the article sitting on my laptop screen. I always tried to avoid everything about James, but this one caught my attention. My heart sank into my stomach as I opened it and saw his arm around a gorgeous woman. They were at some type of event and smiling at the cameras. He looked... happy. The second picture was of him looking down at her lovingly. I took a couple of deep breaths to keep the nausea at bay. It hurt seeing this. To torture myself more, I continued reading the article. There was an interview with him, and I skimmed most of it until I found a part that made tears stream down my face.

Interviewer asked, "So are you and Stacey serious? This isn't the first event we've seen you at together. Might there be an engagement soon?"

James answered, "We've been together for a while, yes, but none of that in the near future. Sorry to disappoint."

Interviewer asked, "Why not? You two look so happy together."

James answered, "I'm really busy with work and can't be distracted right now."

Interviewer asked, "Oh? Is that what happened a couple of years ago when things were going under when you were starting to work with your father? Were you distracted then?"

James answered, "Yeah, girls can derail everything."

I stopped reading there, exited the website and closed my laptop. Was that how he really felt about me? I derailed everything in his life and distracted him from his work? I felt even more sick. I went to the bathroom and took a shower to clear my mind.

The moment we get home, I run up to my bathroom to take the test. I set the timer and pace in the bathroom because there is nothing better to do. I don't even last a minute before looking at the test and my heart stops.

It's positive.

I'm pregnant.

I walk out of my bathroom and run into a large body. I don't need to look up to know it's Declan. He looks at me and instantly knows.

"It's going to be okay, Everly," he says while wrapping his arms around me in a hug.

Fuck. How am I going to tell James? I can't keep this to myself. I need to tell him, and the sooner the better.

"Can you take me to James' office?" I ask Declan.

He nods and keeps his hand on my lower back as he leads me out the door and back to the car to tell my boyfriend that I'm carrying a baby that he probably doesn't want.

Chapter Twenty-Nine

JAMES

After the conversation with my father about marrying Everly, I knew I had some loose ends to tie up. One of those being Stacey.

I asked her to come in for a meeting this morning. I thought about taking her to lunch, but I feel like this is better done in a professional setting. For me, not for her.

There's a knock on the door, and Stacey enters. She's wearing high heels, a short black pencil skirt, and a red ruffle blouse that shows off her cleavage. She's wearing her famous red lipstick that somehow never smears. A year ago, I would've been all over that, and she knows it.

"It's so good to see you, James," she says, coming up to me and giving me a hug and kiss on the cheek.

"You too," I say to be polite.

I gesture for her to sit, and she does. I sit behind my desk, trying to put as much distance as possible between us.

"What can I do for you?" she asks with a flirty smile.

I've turned down all her advances since Everly broke her engagement with her fiancé. She has always initiated meetings with me, this being the first I have with her since then.

"I'll cut to the chase. I want to be sure you understand that there is no possibility between us anymore," I state dryly.

Her smile fades for a second before returning. "Oh?"

"I will be getting engaged soon, and I didn't want to blindside you with it," I say.

She looks me in the eye to see if I'm serious before responding, "Well, that's wonderful for you, James. I appreciate you giving me a heads up."

I look her over and can't tell if she's serious or not. Is she really okay with this, or is it going to be a problem?

"I'm sorry we didn't work out. I really love her Stacey," I state sincerely.

Stacey lets out a sigh and lets her posture slouch a little, putting a smile back on her face. "I really am happy for you, James. My father will be disappointed, but I've always known there was someone else you loved. I won't say that I'm not disappointed because I could see a wonderful future with you, but as long as you're happy..."

"I am," I interrupt.

She stands up. "Good. I won't be in your way. I'll warn my father, so you don't have to have that awkward conversation."

I go over to give her a hug, and she kisses me on the cheek, which also catches half my mouth. She pulls away and walks out the door like everything is fine. No matter the type of news, she always handles it with grace, and her true feelings remain a mystery to me. She'll make a great wife in the type of business world we live in. Just not for me.

As I go to close the door behind her, I see Everly standing a few feet away watching as Stacey passes her and then looking over at me. My heart stops as I see her face drop and she runs toward the stairs, with Declan quickly following behind her.

The elevator doors close with Stacey in it, and I run after Everly to catch her. "Everly, wait!"

She doesn't stop and, reaching the door, opens it. Declan stands in front of me, putting his hand on my chest to stop me.

He then points to the side of his mouth and says, "Clean yourself up first, James, and figure out what you're doing."

I'm not sure what he means, but I let her go, and Declan follows her. I head back to my office and look in the mirror to find a red lipstick stain on my face where Stacey just kissed me.

FUCK!

The one fucking time her lipstick smears and Everly is standing right there. I quickly rub it off and grab my phone from my desk, dialing Everly. I can't screw this up with her. I just got her back.

I dial her phone, and she doesn't answer. I look at the time, and it's eleven in the morning. What was she doing here? It's not lunchtime, and she never skips work, especially after a holiday. Something is wrong. I can feel it.

I have my assistant cancel my meetings for the rest of the day and drive immediately to Everly's house. I know she's there because I tracked her through all three devices. I wanted to make sure she didn't take her ring off at home and go elsewhere.

I ring the doorbell and Declan immediately answers. Instead of letting me inside, he steps out and closes the door behind him.

"I need to talk to her, Declan," I state seriously.

"What the hell was that?" Declan asks, looking angry.

I've never been on the receiving end of Declan's anger. We've always been on the same page when it comes to Everly.

"It wasn't what it looked like," I say and regret it because that always sounds wrong.

"It looked bad, James."

I run my hand through my hair and shake my head. "I called her in for a meeting to ensure she knew we were over. I'm proposing to Everly, and I thought I owed it to Stacey to let her know before she found out in the tabloids. She said she was happy for me and kissed me goodbye. It meant nothing."

Declan looks me over, and his expression softens. "Go talk to her, but give her time. Imagine if the roles were reversed."

I don't want to imagine if the roles were reversed. If I saw Eric coming out of her office and evidence that he kissed her, I'd kill him. It might not be what it looks like, but it doesn't mean it doesn't hurt.

I nod, and he lets me in. I go upstairs to find her sitting in her chair writing something in her notebook.

I knock on the doorframe, and she turns around and quickly closes her notebook.

"Can we talk?" I ask, hoping she says yes.

I can tell she's torn. Her eyes are puffy from crying. I hate that I made her cry. My heart squeezes at the sight.

"Sure, why not," she says while moving over to sit comfortably on her bed.

I head over to sit in her desk chair when I glance at the notebook that she was just writing in. It says "Dear Lauren" on the front. My heart sinks. Does she write letters to her deceased friend Lauren?

"It's not what you think," I state, not knowing how else to start.

"You mean that wasn't her lipstick on your lips?" she asks angrily.

"No, I mean, it was, but we didn't kiss. I called her in for a meeting to ensure she knew we would never happen and we're purely business. I didn't want any complications with you and me in the future and just wanted to make sure we were good there. She accepted and kissed me goodbye. That's it," I say, pleading with my eyes that she believes me.

"Oh, just a kiss goodbye, that's it?" She let out a small laugh.

I don't say anything. I'm at a loss for what to say.

"I mean, a hug wouldn't have been good enough, right? Like when I told Eric that I love you and it would never happen between us. I gave him a hug goodbye, but I should've kissed him, right?" she asks sarcastically.

"No. I didn't expect it, Everly. I gave her a hug, and she just kissed me. She does that to everyone. It's just how she is," I state, hoping she believes me.

She clearly doesn't because she rolls her eyes. "It's fine, James."

"It's not fine. You're mad, and I understand why," I say.

We're both quiet for a moment, but I can see the gears turning in her head and the anger that's surfacing on her face.

"I'm not just mad, James. I'm hurt! This isn't the first time I found her coming out of your office with you two all over each other!" she yells and throws her hands up.

"Wow, what are you talking about, Everly?" I ask, taken aback.

She drops her head and shakes it. When she lifts it, I see the tears coming from her eyes. I stand up and start toward her, embracing her in a hug to comfort her, but she pushes me away. She never pushes me away.

"A week before my wedding with Eric, I came back to New York to see you. I wanted to talk to you before I married him to make sure we were really over. It was late, and most of your staff was gone. I waited outside your office, and your receptionist had just left. I thought you were just working late, but when you came out, she was with you. I hid behind a stupid plant and watched you two make out in front of me, and you told her you'd meet her at her place that night..." she trails off, crying even more.

She came back to see me before the wedding? She saw that? I remember that night clearly. When I thought she was going to get married the following week, I was in a bad place. I was stupid and would take out my frustrations with Stacey, using her for sex to get my mind off Everly. It meant nothing to me.

"Baby... You should've told me... Damn it Everly, all I've ever wanted was you. I have so many regrets in life, but my biggest one is letting you go. I never stopped loving you. I was only trying to cope with losing you," I say while walking toward her again.

She's crying and shaking her head while it hangs low. I pull her into my arms again, but this time she doesn't push me away. She cries into my chest, and I put my head on hers.

"Baby, my life means nothing without you. Please don't leave me. Please believe me that nothing happened today. I can't lose you. I love you so much," I plead with my voice breaking.

After a few minutes, she looks up at me. "Do you promise nothing happened between you two? That you're done with her?"

I don't hesitate before saying, "I promise. I only want you Everly. I only have ever wanted you. I can't live without you anymore."

She looks at me for a moment, and whatever she sees on my face makes her trust me because she leans forward and kisses me.

I take hold of the sides of her face and kiss her back, neither of us breaking the kiss even when we both need to come up for air.

CHAPTER THIRTY

EVERLY

When I leave work, I text Paige that I'm on my way to the coffee shop to meet with her. She texted me earlier that she has something she wants to talk to me about after work, which is perfect because I could really use a friend to talk about this pregnancy with and how to tell James.

Declan is still the only one who knows about my pregnancy. He promised he wouldn't tell anyone and would let me do it when I'm ready. It has been three days since I found out I'm pregnant. I fully intended to tell James the day I went to his office, but then everything happened with Stacey, and I lost the courage to tell him. I've avoided him for the past few days to figure things out.

I haven't been able to sleep much since that day. A lot of it has to do with still comprehending my pregnancy and telling James. But also, what happened that day with Stacey brought back memories of how Eric and I ended, and I've been struggling with hating myself all over again.

Eric came over right after work. We had one week until we were married. One week until Eric and I were forever. Eric is an amazing guy, and he would be a perfect husband. Seeing Stacey yesterday with James at his office destroyed me, though. I realized just how much I wasn't over James, but I had to be. Marrying Eric would help that.

"Hey baby, one more week," Eric stated as he walked in the door and kissed me.

I smiled, but I knew it didn't reach my eyes. I went to the kitchen and started warming up dinner. Eric came over every night. We ate together, and he usually stayed the night, but we didn't live together. I insisted we wait until marriage for that, and he had no problem respecting my decision.

"What's wrong?" he asked, always aware of how I was feeling.

I felt even guiltier now for going behind his back to see James. I couldn't tell him, though. It would hurt him.

"You went to see him, didn't you?" he asked quietly.

My head shot up to look at him. "What?"

"Your ex. You went to see him," he stated, because he already knew the answer.

"I'm sorry, I did," I replied, giving him a guilty look.

"What did he say?"

I shook my head. "I didn't talk to him. He's with someone else, so I left it alone. It was stupid."

Eric let out a breath and looked relieved. "That's good."

Was it, though? It was for him, yes. For me, I wasn't sure. Maybe it was. It was time to let this go. James was my first love. It didn't mean he needed to be my last.

Eric got up and came over to hug me. He held me at arm's length and said, "Everly, it's okay. I know you loved him. It's normal to want closure before a new beginning."

Why was Eric so perfect and understanding?

"Eric... I'm just so sorry. You're amazing. I don't want to lie to you. I think I'm still in love with him. I just can't lie to you anymore," I stated, while feeling the tears burn the back of my eyes.

"It's okay. I'll wait. I love you Everly, and I know that in time you'll love me back without loving him too," he said, so sure about everything.

No... No, that wasn't right. My heart sank, and I felt awful. Jake said something similar to me back in high school and again when he was heading back to college after the summer we spent together. That wasn't fair. It wasn't fair to Jake, and it wasn't fair to Eric. Both are amazing guys, and I kept hurting them. What was wrong with me?

"Eric... I'm so sorry. I thought I could do this. I thought I loved you. You're amazing, and you deserve someone who loves you unconditionally and as much as you love them. I can't do this to you..." I said while pulling away from him.

"What are you saying Everly?" he asked, looking hurt.

It broke my heart to do this, but I took off the engagement ring he gave me. I held it out for him to take, but he shook his head no and stepped back.

"Everly... Please, let's just talk this through. I don't want to lose you. I love you," he said, and I could tell how much pain he was in.

"I know, and that's why I can't do this. Please Eric. Please take the ring and leave. Find someone who will love you. You deserve so much more than me," I said while grabbing his hand and putting the ring in it.

"Everly... I need you," he pleaded.

"Please Eric. Please go. I'm so sorry," I said, still trying to hold back the tears.

"Is this really what you want?" he asked with hope in his eyes that it's not.

"Yes," I stated with certainty.

This time, I was certain it was what I wanted. I didn't have to lie. With James, I lied, but with Eric, it was the truth. He deserved so much better, and I hate myself for stringing him along for so long. I was a horrible person, and I deserved to never be loved again.

As I gather things from my desk, I shake off that memory. There's nothing I can do to change the past, and if I keep thinking about all the pain I caused everyone, then I'm just going to spiral into another depression. I need to move on and try to make the right decisions in the future.

I walk out of the school to find Declan waiting for me on the stairs as he usually does. I look at the street and see the traffic, which means it will take forever to get to the coffee shop to meet Paige by car.

"Let's just walk to the coffee shop. It'll be faster," I say when meeting up with Declan.

"Sure," he says and takes my workbag from me.

We stop at the car so he can throw it in before we walk there. There's no need to bring it with me. We take a couple of shortcuts through some alleys and halfway through the walk, I remember I left my phone in my bag.

"Crap, I left my phone in my workbag," I say while feeling inside my pockets to be sure.

"Do you want to go back and get it?" he stops and asks.

"No, that's okay. I'll have you text James if I'm going to be late, so he doesn't worry. I'm not sure how long Paige wants to meet for."

When we start walking again, a shiver runs down my spine. The alley is eerily quiet today. This area is typically safe, so I brush it off, thinking it's just the chill in the air. Declan picks up the pace in front of me and puts an arm out for me to stop. He must feel something, too. Before Declan can reach for his gun, some men jump out from between the buildings and grab both of us. Declan begins fighting, but I'm turned away from him and the two men who have me are dragging me away.

I knee one of them in the balls, hard, and he falls to the ground, holding himself. My heart is racing as the other gets a better grip on me with one arm around my throat and the other around my waist. I try to kick him as well, but I can't reach him with my legs. I take his arm with mine and loosen his grip from my neck just enough to bite down on him as hard as I can. It must have shocked him, because he lets out a growl and throws me to the ground. I catch myself and quickly turn to face Declan.

There are six men surrounding him. Just as I go to lunge forward to help Declan, I hear a gunshot. I freeze, and my ears ring. The two men I injured must have recovered themselves, because they grab me again, but I hardly comprehend it. The men surrounding Declan back away enough for me to see the blood gushing from his stomach. Declan's eyes are fixed on me. He's determined to save me. He continues stepping forward to reach me as the two men holding me pick me up and walk away.

Another gunshot rings out and this time Declan falls to the ground. I hear the thump of his body hitting the concrete and see the blood quickly seeping out around him. I scream, thrash, and kick to get away from the men so I can get to Declan.

"Declan!!!" I scream, but he doesn't move.

No. No, this can't be happening. The two men who have me have now turned the corner, and I hear one more gunshot. A loud sob escapes my throat, and I stop fighting. I feel like I'm having a nightmare. This is all just a dream, right? Declan can't be dead.

I'm thrown into the trunk of a car, and I try to kick my legs up to stop it from closing, but they are too strong. I'm thrashing around, kicking, and screaming, but the car starts moving, and I know no one can hear me.

I take a deep breath to calm myself and bring myself back to reality. I breathe and count to ten. I can hear Declan's voice in my head and try to push back all the emotions I'm currently feeling.

Breathe Kid, calm yourself. Take inventory of your injuries.

I start with my feet and work my way up my body. I have a little pain in my knee and around my waist, but no injuries.

Good, now look at your surroundings. Where are you?

I'm in a trunk. A small car's trunk and we're driving.

Alright, is there anything in the trunk with you that you can use as a weapon?

I slowly feel around with my arms and legs. There's nothing at all in the trunk. I also don't have my knife on me because I was at work. I never feel comfortable carrying it while working. I'm so stupid. I should've always kept one on me. I throw my hand to my wrist to feel for my watch. I can't believe I forgot about it, but it's not there. They must have taken it off me. How did I not realize they did that? If only I had paid more attention to my surroundings before all this happened.

Stop thinking about what-ifs, Kid. Think about what's happening now. No weapons, that's okay. Use your body as the weapon when they get you out of the trunk. Now kick the taillight out and see where you're at.

I kick hard at the taillight, but it's not budging. I kick and kick, but nothing is happening. My heart rate picks up again, and I panic.

Breathe, Kid. Turn yourself around and try the other one.

I take a few moments to spin myself around in the cramped trunk and kick at the other taillight. It pops out in only a couple of kicks. I let out the breath I was holding in. I spin myself around again and try to peek out. I see the road, but don't see any cars around. It seems like we're on a dirt road now, off the main road. I try to duck down more to look out further, but I can't see any signs or anything. This is useless.

The car comes to a stop, and my head hits against the trunk. I feel nauseous thinking about what's coming. They are going to take me out of this trunk, and I'm going to have to fight my way through. I have no idea where I am or how many men there are. How am I supposed to escape?

Don't panic. You don't know what you're up against, so just wait and see.

The trunk opens, and the sunlight blinds me for a moment. One of the men who threw me in here grabs me by my arms and pulls me out. I don't bother fighting because I don't know my surroundings yet. I look around to find two other cars pulling up and seven men total piling out of the cars and following behind us. There are too many, and I can see they have guns. There's no use in fighting right now and getting hurt. I need a plan.

Good. Keep your eyes open and pay attention to your surroundings.

They push me through the door of what looks like a small, abandoned house. It's beaten down and looks like it's falling apart. I'm pushed past the kitchen, living room, and into a bedroom. There's a bed in the corner and a chair. There's wood nailed over the window, so only a sliver of light is being let through.

The man pushing me through the house plops me down into the chair and ties my feet to the legs and my hands behind my back. Three other men stand and watch. Once the man finishes tying me up, he stands in front of me and looks me over.

"You're not going to fight?" he asks with a grin.

"Why would I? I'm clearly outnumbered. I'd never win," I say angrily.

"Smart girl," he says.

The guy who tied me up steps back and leans against the wall with his arms folded.

One of the men beside him speaks up. "What do we do now?"

He responds, "We wait for instructions."

They continue to stare at me, and I just stare back. There's no point in talking to them because they aren't going to tell me anything that I want to know. I could provoke them, but again, there's no point. I need to keep myself in good shape to escape. I don't want needless injuries to impede my escape attempt.

Another man walks up to the door and says, "Boss wants to talk to you."

He nods and they all leave the room. The door closes, and I hear the click of the lock. Do they really think that lock is going to do much? This house is falling apart. I'm pretty sure even I could kick down that door. Though, I wouldn't be stupid enough to attempt it without knowing exactly who and how many men are on the other side of it.

The moment they are gone, I immediately examine the ties on my wrists and ankles. I play with it, trying to slip my hands out, but it's too tight. I'm going to have to try to untie it. As I'm messing with the ties on my wrists, the rope cuts into them more and burns. I take a break for a moment, and the guy walks back in not even a few minutes after he left.

"The boss is running a little late, but he'll be here soon. He was nice enough to say you could take a nap while you wait," he says while pulling something out of his pocket.

Crap, it's a syringe. They want to knock me out.

"No thanks, I'll just sit here patiently," I say, keeping my voice calm.

"Sorry, that wasn't an option," he says while jabbing me in the neck with the needle.

It doesn't take long before everything gets fuzzy. I try to keep my eyes from closing, but I end up squeezing them shut as the memory from earlier floods my brain. All I hear are the gunshots and thump from Declan's body hitting the ground before I go under.

CHAPTER THIRTY-ONE

JAMES

I'm late getting out of work and haven't heard from Everly all day. She usually texts me if I'm late, but she didn't this time and I'm a little worried. She's supposed to come over tonight. It seems like she's not feeling well, as she's been acting off and avoiding me this past week. I don't blame her after what happened with Stacey, but I was hoping she would have forgiven me by now. I pick up my phone to call her, but see I'm receiving a call from Barry. Barry never calls me unless it's an emergency.

"Barry?" I answer on the first ring.

"Someone took Everly," he says, and my heart literally stops.

I swallow the lump in my throat and say, "Details, now."

"Declan didn't check in and my call went to voicemail. I found him shot three times in the alley close to that coffee shop Everly frequents. She wasn't anywhere around, and her stuff, including her cell phone, was in the car at the school. Her watch was found a few feet from Declan."

What was she doing in the alley? She usually tells me if she's going to get coffee after school. Regardless, someone took her, and we need to find her.

I try not to think too much about Declan being shot three times and found on the ground. Few could walk away from that, and it really depends on where he was shot. My stomach is in knots thinking about him being dead, but I can't think about it right now because we have to find Everly. He would want us to concentrate on finding Everly.

"If she doesn't have her phone or watch, then we can't track her that way. She should be wearing the ring. Track it," I say and hang up.

I put a tracker in the promise ring that I gave her back when she was in high school. That one was a prototype we were working on with the company, and now all the bugs have been worked out of it. It's one of our bestsellers. She has no idea about it, and I figured it was best that way, especially since she continued to wear it while she was away from me for six years.

The moment I get in my car, I pull up the tracker and start heading to where she is. I call Ryder through my car, and he picks up on the first ring.

"Already on it, boss," he says, not needing me to explain the situation.

"How far out are you?" I ask, grinding my teeth together, trying to keep my cool.

"Ten minutes," he says.

I'm twenty minutes out. He'll make it there first. Somehow, traffic is on my side today, which makes everyone lucky because I would have to murder some people on the way if it wasn't. The moment I get out of the city, I press the pedal down and go well over a hundred miles per hour.

My phone rings, and it's Thomas, Everly's dad.

"Thomas," I state, trying to concentrate on the road.

"I assume you heard. Are you on your way?" he asks.

"I'm twelve minutes out. Ryder will be there any minute," I state while dodging cars and hear them honking at me.

"Any ideas who has her?" he asks.

Do I have any fucking ideas? No, I don't know who would want to steal my girlfriend, but I have a guess why they would.

"I'm assuming you pissed someone off," I try to state calmly.

I can hear Thomas sigh and then yell something inaudible to the person next to him.

"Call me if you have any updates," he says and hangs up.

I slam the steering wheel with my right palm three times and let out an angry groan. I'm trying my best to keep my cool, but the more time that passes, the less I can control myself.

Ryder calls, and once again I answer immediately. "Tell me you have her."

There's a slight pause, which tells me everything I need to know.

"She's not here," he states.

"What the fuck do you mean, she's not there?" I slam on my brakes, going from a hundred miles per hour to zero in five seconds.

Cars swerve around me honking, and I pull off to the side of the road.

"Her ring was left on a chair. It looks like she was tied up here for a bit then moved," he says, but his voice indicates there is something else.

"And?"

"They left all of her clothes too," he states professionally.

I close my eyes and put my forehead on the steering wheel, taking a deep breath. Fuck, Everly. They stripped her. Whoever did this is going to pay when we find them.

"We have to find her. What are our leads?" I ask.

There's silence again.

"Nothing? We have nothing? Between you, Barry, and Thomas, you're telling me there's nothing?"

"James, we'll find her."

I don't have time for this. I end the call and try to calm myself. Who would have taken her? I doubt it was anyone I knew. It had to be because of her father, but he didn't seem to know either. There's no way to track her now.

I think about who I can turn to. Who knows this city inside and out? Asher!

I call Asher, but his damn phone goes to voicemail. I leave a not so friendly message, but I don't care at this point. I shoot him a text too, just in case.

The only other person I can think of is someone I don't want to get involved with, and we've never gotten involved with before, but what choice do I have? I'd sell my fucking soul if it means getting Everly back alive.

My heart races as the phone rings. He answers on the third ring.

"To what do I owe the pleasure, James?" he asks.

I take a deep breath and say, "I need a favor, Lorenzo."

I can basically hear his smirk over the phone, but I don't give a crap right now.

"And what is this favor?"

"My girlfriend was taken, and I don't know by who. They've stripped her, so no tracking is available, but I can send you all the details of where they were. I need her found. Right now," I say, trying not to sound desperate but knowing I'm failing.

"Everly?" he asks.

"Yes," I respond through gritted teeth.

"Send me where you tracked her stuff to and whatever else is important. I'm on it," he says, hanging up the phone.

I quickly send him the location of where the ring was found and where she was taken from. I lean back in the driver's seat and stare at the ceiling. There's no point in going to where we thought she was because she's not there, but where do I go now? As much as I want to scour this whole city, that would be a waste of time. I decide to head home and meet Barry there with Everly's stuff. Maybe I can see if there's anything on her phone that will give us a hint of where she is.

After reading through her texts, I've found nothing. I called her friend Paige, who she was supposed to meet at the coffee shop, but she gave me nothing useful as she said that she never showed up.

I called Bash to get his hacker friend working on the street cameras to see if he could find anything. If we could just find the car that took her or see the face of one of the men, then we'd be better off than where we are now. Which is nowhere. Bash is currently on his way over as support.

After almost five hours from when she was noticed to be taken, which is way too long, Lorenzo calls me back.

"We know who has her," he states.

"And?"

"They are a powerful enemy of ours. I'll lose men in this battle," he states, like this is all just a strategic play.

I know exactly what he's doing and saying, and I don't give a fuck. He's saying this is a huge favor to ask, with lives lost. That means I'll owe him later, for a favor of equal size.

"If you get her out alive, you can have my damn empire Lorenzo," I state, dead serious. I'll give anything to get her back.

"I know. I've already sent my guys in. They will find her. That's not why I'm calling," he says, and I notice something not right in his voice.

"What is it?" I ask, and the fear that is already splitting through my body intensifies.

"The guys who took her are ruthless. They don't treat prisoners well, especially women. I just wanted you to know that if we get her back..."

I interrupt him. "When we get her back."

He clears his throat. "When we get her back, she may not be the same."

My hand clenches my phone hard, and I'm surprised it doesn't break. "Do whatever you have to do to get her back. I'll give you whatever you want."

Lorenzo sighs. "We'll get her, James."

I hang up the phone and throw it on the floor. As I swipe everything off my desk in anger, Bash walks in.

Chapter Thirty-Two

Everly

I slowly open my eyes to find it dark. My head is pounding, and as I try to lift it, my neck hurts like I've been sleeping on it wrong all night. When I try to lift my arms, I realize they are stuck on something.

The pain in my head is quickly forgotten as my heart begins to race and the memories of what happened come flooding back. I was taken in the alleyway and Declan... My stomach turns with nausea, and it takes every bit of willpower to keep the contents in my stomach. I can't help the tears that escape and the sobs as I think about Declan lying dead on the ground in that alley. I let myself cry it out for a few minutes. I don't know if it's because of the drugs they gave me or my pregnancy, but it's impossible to stop it. So, I let myself feel it so I can move on and concentrate on trying to escape.

By the time I finally control my emotions, my eyes have adjusted to the darkness. I look around the room, which is a lot smaller than I remember. Also, there's no window. The only light coming in is from underneath the door. It's almost as if I'm now in a closet. They must have moved me to another location.

I look down at myself to find that I'm no longer wearing my own clothes. I'm in a short dress, so that means they must have stripped me to ensure I didn't have a tracker, then moved me to be safe.

As I continue working the ropes on my wrists, I hear footsteps come closer to my door and stop. I hear a voice outside that I haven't heard before. I stop what I'm doing to listen.

"Ah, Thomas, so good to talk to you. I'm glad you answered my call. I have a little bit of a request for you."

There's a long pause and then the man laughs.

"Yes, yes. So, you know why I'm calling then. Your daughter has grown into quite the beauty, you know. I'm going to make you a deal. You have twenty-four hours to give me back my guy or I'll use your daughter to make you pay."

There's another long pause.

"I see. Well, should I just take care of her now, then?"

Another pause.

"Ah, okay. I knew you were a smart and resourceful man. I'll be in touch."

I think he hangs up the phone, but then he continues talking. "Oh, alright, let me see if she's awake from her nap. She was getting quite comfortable in here."

The doorknob jiggles as it unlocks, and then he pushes it open. Light spills into the room, and I'm able to get a good look at the man's face. He's tall and muscular. His red hair, as well as his red beard and mustache, contribute to his distinctive appearance. He looks young, around my age. Standing in front of me, he holds out the phone.

"Looks like she's awake. You're on speaker. Go ahead."

"Everly? Sweetie? Are you there?" I can hear the concern in my father's voice, even though he's trying to keep his composure in front of this man.

I swallow the lump in my throat. "Yes daddy, I'm here."

I hear him sigh in relief. "Have they hurt you?"

I look up at the man, who raises his eyebrows at me like he's challenging me. "No, I'm okay."

Before my father can say anything else, the man ends the call.

"Well then, that was fun," he says while coming closer to my chair and kneeling in front of me. "It's nice to meet you, Everly."

So many thoughts are going through my head at this moment, but Declan's voice continues.

Stay calm and don't provoke. It's not worth getting injured unnecessarily.

I give him a fake smile and say, "I wish I could say the same. If you untie me, maybe we could have a cup of coffee and a nice chat."

He grins from ear to ear and says, "Too bad I can't keep you around. I like you Everly."

My heart stops beating again at his words. I was hoping he would just be using me as bait, but by the sounds of it, he doesn't plan on letting me leave here alive.

The man stands up and starts walking toward the door as I say, "Why can't you?"

"What?" He turns around and looks at me.

"Why can't you keep me around?" I ask, trying to hide my shaky voice.

"Your father took someone who is very important to me, so I have to take someone from him who's important," he says, shrugging his shoulders like it's a given.

"Who did he take from you?" I ask.

The man raises his eyebrow before asking, "Do you really not know anything about what your father does?"

I shake my head. "No, he doesn't tell me anything, and I don't care to know."

He looks me over like he's trying to tell if I'm lying, but he continues anyway. "Well Everly, he took a very important business partner away from me. It's someone my business can't live without."

My breath catches. "By took him away... do you mean he killed him?"

The man looks me back and forth in the eye and laughs. "No Everly. You really don't know anything, do you? He took him for himself. You don't kill this type of man. He's too important. Regardless, he has 24 hours to give him back or... well, you know."

I continue to study him before speaking. I need to find a way for him to keep me alive longer than 24 hours. It'll give me time to escape and give everyone else time to save me. I'm not counting on being saved, but every minute counts.

"Wait, so if he doesn't give him to you in 24 hours, then you kill me, right? What happens after that? You mentioned this man is important for your business, correct? So, your goal is to get him back. If you kill me, then there's nothing left to give my father an incentive to give this man back to you. In fact, my father will then be a man with nothing to lose. You know how dangerous that can be," I say calmly, trying to strategize this out as quickly as possible in my head.

I have no idea where I'm going with this, but if I can keep him talking for a minute, I can figure it out and, hopefully, buy more time.

"Interesting perspective. Unfortunately, I already made the threat, and I cannot back down. I'm a man of my word," he says with a smirk on his face.

Of course he would be a man of his word when it comes to threatening to kill someone or do something illegal. These men have their morals twisted.

As he turns toward the door, I continue quickly, "You wouldn't have to go against your word. If I heard you right, didn't you say that you would use me to make him pay? There are better ways to use me to make him pay than to kill me. And this way, you could still get your guy back."

He's silent for a few moments as he looks me over. "You're not wrong. Are you really just saying all this to stay alive?"

Isn't that enough motive? Who wouldn't do anything to stay alive? But I can tell he's curious if it's something more. What more could he think? That maybe I'd want to betray my father and help him? That wouldn't be believable, would it?

I give him a small smile before I speak. "Obviously, I don't want to die, but I really don't want to die because of my father. I'm not interested in what he does for a living and have tried to stay away from it. I'm not sure how much research you've done about my life, but when I turned 18, I left for six years. I only returned because I didn't have a choice." I think for another moment before continuing, "He loves me deeply, as I'm his only child. But I don't approve of his lifestyle. I'd be willing to help right his wrong."

The man puts his hands together under his chin, studying me. "Interesting. I was wondering what you were doing so far away for so long. I got excited when you moved back to New York. You made it a lot easier to capture you. Well, this is all good to know. I'll think about it. Thank you for your help, Everly."

Once again, I stop him right before he opens the door to leave. "Hang on, I didn't catch your name."

He looks over his shoulder at me and says, "Anthony."

I nod and say, "Well then. It's a pleasure to meet you, Anthony. If you decide we could work together with this, of course."

Anthony opens the door, leaves the room, and locks it behind him. The moment he's gone, my breathing is rapid, and I'm panicking. Fuck, fuck, fuck. What the fuck am I doing? Did he actually buy into any of that? If he did, what's my plan now?

After trying to get the ropes off my wrists for who knows how long, I finally decide to give up. I can feel my wrists bleeding, and I see the blood on the floor. I'm just doing more damage than good, and I'm going to need my hands in the future if I'm going to escape this place.

I hear constant voices outside the door, but it's all mumbling, and I can't make out what they are saying. I occasionally hear the name Mr. Morris, which sounds familiar, but I can't place it. Every time I hear footsteps, I stop breathing, thinking that Anthony is going to come back to make good on his word and kill me. I try not to think of the alternative if it's not Anthony that walks in.

The more time that passes, the more I realize no one is coming to save me, and I have to save myself. I wish I knew how long I've been here. Since there's no window, it's impossible to tell if it's day or night. I don't even know how long I was out for when they drugged me. As far as I know, it feels like it's been 24 hours.

My eyes are getting heavy, and I wonder if I should try to take a nap. It would at least pass the time and maybe help me get my strength back up. Just as I start to drift asleep, the doorknob rattles and the door flies open. Anthony is standing in the doorway and turns on the light. I squint my eyes until they adjust to the intrusive light.

Anthony walks around me and examines me. I do my best to hide my wrists, but there's not much I can do with them bound behind my back.

"I see you've been trying to get out of your ties," he says with that stupid smirk on his face.

"I have a terrible itch I was hoping to scratch," I state.

Yeah, that itch is escaping this room and killing everyone out there. One of them killed Declan, and I need them to pay.

Anthony pulls a chair up in front of me and sits down, laughing. "I really do like you, Everly."

It takes all my willpower not to roll my eyes at him and spit in his face. As tempting as it is to do that, I'm smarter than that. Declan trained me to be smarter than that. I can't let him down.

Anthony leans forward. "So, I've been thinking about what you said, and you may be right. I'm curious about how you think I should use you to hurt your father if I don't kill you."

Yeah, that's the problem. I have no idea. Well, I do have an idea, but it's not one I'm going to share. Death may be preferable to that.

"I'm sure there are a few ideas that I could come up with, but I have a feeling you have one. May I ask what you're thinking?" I cringe as I ask, but I need more time to think.

Anthony rubs his chin with his thumb and forefinger like he's thinking. "Well, I could torture you and put you on a live feed. You would still be alive, and maybe that would put a fire under your father having to watch you being tortured. Or I could always let my guys have their way with you..."

He trails off, and I can't hold back my disgust. That's exactly what I was hoping he wouldn't say, but of course he would think of that as an option. Neither of those options sounds good.

So, I think quick, "Explain your relationship with my father."

He laughs again. "There is no relationship with your father."

I force a smile. "I mean, you clearly are enemies, yes? Can you tell me why? Do you want to be enemies with him, or would a truce and working together be something you'd find beneficial?"

He thinks it over for a minute. "We've been enemies for a long time. We both have different specialties, powerful connections. At one point we tried to make a mutual arrangement to combine forces, but he declined."

That's good to know. So, he wanted to work with him once, maybe he will again. As I'm trying to think where I'm going with this, the name I've been trying to figure out clicks instantly. Anthony Morris. Right before my father sent me to the Crawford's house, I overheard him talking to someone in his office about arranging a marriage to me, and it was him! Of course, my father didn't need to think about it before saying no. I was disgusted by the idea.

"So, an alliance would be beneficial?" I ask and hope rises in my chest.

"I suppose it would, yes. But that's not going to happen," he states.

"What if it could?" I ask.

"Spit out what you're thinking," he says.

"An arranged marriage would form an alliance. He would have no choice but to help you out as his son-in-law."

I can tell he's thinking it over, but it doesn't quite hit the spot. "That's not going to work. He'll just kill me."

"Not if we tell him I'm pregnant with your child. He'd never kill the father of my child, no matter how much he hates him." I try to swallow the bile coming up my throat as we talk about this.

"But you're not, and he would want proof," he says.

"But I am. I'm pregnant and he doesn't know yet. It's from a one-night stand. No one would know it's not yours. I can take a pregnancy test right now, and it'd be positive for proof."

"You'd be willing to be part of an arranged marriage with me?" he asks, eying me skeptically.

I mean, no, I'd rather be killed than marry him, but he doesn't need to know that. I just need to keep him talking and keep buying time. It's also beneficial if I say I'll be his because then he won't let his men touch me. I know I shouldn't be counting on anyone coming to save me, but if I could just buy more time. This is all so stupid. None of it makes sense, and I can't believe he is even thinking about going along with it. I thought he was a smart man, but clearly not.

"I mean, how bad could being married to you be? I don't have a boyfriend, and you're handsome. I'm sure we could have a good time together." It takes every effort not to throw up after saying that.

Apparently, that was the right thing to say because he looks up and down my body with the biggest smile on his face. Again, I want to barf, but I keep my cool.

"Alright, Everly, you have a deal. If you take a pregnancy test and are telling the truth, then we can make this happen. If not, well, you know," he says while standing up from his chair and leaving the room.

Well, at least I know the test will come back positive, so I don't have to worry about that. If he makes me take the test, that means he will have to untie me so I can pee on it. I need to think of an escape plan and pay attention to how many men I think are out there because that may be the only time I get to escape. I really hope it doesn't come down to telling my father I'm pregnant because I really want to tell James first. I can't believe I hesitated to tell him for so long. I could die before he even knows.

Chapter Thirty-Three

JAMES

It's been twelve hours since Everly was taken, and I'm going insane. Bash called in reinforcements because I almost killed him to get by him to leave my apartment. Jake and Ben are both here as well, trying to keep me calm and making as many phone calls as they can. We're currently playing the waiting game at four a.m. and I'm not a fan.

Ben places a glass of water in front of me. "You need to drink something, James."

Ben looks as exhausted and worried as I feel. Everyone does. I don't care though as I snap at him. "I'm not drinking anything until Everly is home. She's been fucking kidnapped, and who knows what else is happening to her while I'm sitting here doing fucking nothing."

Jake sits next to me and chimes in. "You've done everything you can. There's nothing more you can do."

I've forgiven Jake and we're in a good place, but right now I just want to fucking punch him.

"I could be out there scouring the streets for her. I need to be looking for her," I yell and stand up.

"We've been over this, James. Where would you look? What would you do? I know it's hard, but you need to take care of yourself so when we get Everly back, you can take care of her," Bash says, sitting on the other side of me.

I lean back on the couch, close my eyes, and sigh. He's right. I know he's right, but I'm finding it hard to see the reason right now. Regardless, I lift the glass of water, show it to them, and take a few gulps. I slam it down while looking through my phone for the thousandth time to see if anything new has popped up.

I haven't heard from Lorenzo since our last phone call. He will call me if there is any new information about where she is. I want nothing more than to text him, but I know there's no update and it will be a waste of his time to respond to me, but I continue to text Asher. He's never been MIA like this before, which is also concerning, but I can't worry about him too.

"I really think you should try to get some sleep, James. We'll take turns doing what we can and fielding your calls. If anything comes up..." Ben starts, but I interrupt him.

"I'm not going to sleep until she's here with me. You all can go to bed. It's late."

"So you can sneak out and start torturing innocent people?" Jake asks, and it isn't a joke even though it came from him.

I shrug my shoulders. As I lean back to look at my phone again, I answer an incoming call from Everly's father on the first ring.

"Talk to me," I answer.

I hear him take a deep breath on the other side of the line and clear his throat. My heart stops knowing he's holding back his emotions, which he rarely has unless it comes to Everly. I feel sick already.

"Tell me you have something more, James. Anything." He keeps his voice even.

"Nothing more from the last call with Lorenzo. What happened Thomas?" I ask, needing to know, but not wanting to.

"Since half my time has run out to get him his man, he sent me a reminder..." his voice trails off.

"What did he do to her?" I ask through gritted teeth.

I'm trying hard to keep my cool, but if he so much as touches her, he's a dead man. Who am I kidding? They're all dead. I may not have killed a man before, but I'm for it right now and would do anything for Everly.

"He sent me a package containing used condoms. You can imagine what the message means," he states.

Bile fills my throat, and I want to throw up. I feel the tears forming in my eyes, which are getting harder to control.

"How many?" I ask calmly.

"Twelve," he whispers.

One for every fucking hour. Hour thirteen is about to come up.

"Where the hell is the guy, Thomas? Give me some information and I'll drag his ass back here myself and turn him over!" I yell.

Thomas raises his voice back. "We've been through this, James! If I had any idea where he could be, he would already be there, and we'd have Everly back. I made the man a promise to let him disappear, and I did, but I would go against my word this once for her if I could!"

I take a deep breath, but it doesn't help. "Call me if anything else happens."

"I'm almost at your place. Be there soon," he states.

As I hang up the phone, I throw it across the room and scream. I turn around and punch the wall, leaving a large hole in it with my fist aching, but I don't give a shit. All three of them come over while Bash holds me back from breaking anything else, and Ben pushes me against the wall to steady me.

I fight against them for a moment because I can't control my rage, but once I look at all of them in the eyes, I lose it. Dropping to the floor, I let the tears stream out. I place my head on my knees and pull on my hair, sobbing and hyperventilating.

I feel them all around me saying something, trying to calm me down, but I can't hear anything they say. I failed her. I fucking failed to protect her again. I promised her I wouldn't fail. I promised Declan I wouldn't fail, and now he's dead and Everly... She's experiencing the unimaginable right now and I'm sitting here doing fucking nothing.

I hear them asking me what happened, and they are all concerned. I need to tell them. They all love her too. We all failed her.

"Thomas called saying they sent him a message..." I pause for a moment to regain control of my emotions before continuing, "They sent him twelve used condoms."

I don't have to explain to them what that means. Their concerned looks for me turn to rage. Each of them has something to say, but I can't understand any of it. Everyone might as well be speaking another language because I can't concentrate on anything right now. I sit here staring at the ceiling doing fucking nothing while the love of my life is missing and being tortured.

Thomas and my father arrived shortly after we hung up the phone. My apartment looks like a police station with laptops, cords, and people everywhere trying to find information. I have no idea how we can find her. They tried tracking the call from Anthony and the package, but of course, both led to dead ends.

Thomas receives a call, and everyone stops what they are doing to watch him.

"Yes?" he answers, and it must be Anthony by the way his body tenses.

There's a brief pause before he replies, "Okay, turning it on now."

He snaps his fingers toward one of his men and points to his laptop. His man sets something up on it and then Thomas looks over at me. I make my way quickly over to find a video call on the screen. My heart stops when I see Everly's hands tied behind her back and Anthony holding her closely. The volume gets turned up and Thomas hangs up the phone.

"How's it going, Thomas?" Anthony asks.

Everly stands in front of him, looking exhausted. Her hair is messed up, and she's wearing a short little dress. It takes everything in me to keep my mouth shut. I clench my teeth together and take a deep breath. She's standing there looking brave, like nothing's wrong.

"We're finding him for you, Anthony," Thomas states professionally.

Anthony tsks. "I don't think you're trying hard enough. I thought I'd give you another incentive to try harder."

"Anthony, please. She has nothing to do with this. I'm doing everything I can, I promise," Thomas states.

Anthony laughs. "Now Thomas, we both know that's not true. You're spending a lot of resources trying to find me and your daughter. You should be using all those to find my guy and give him back to me."

I look over at Thomas as he's saying nothing. There's nothing that can be said because he's right. We're mainly just trying to find Everly.

"Well, maybe this will change things," Anthony says while taking out a knife and placing it against Everly's stomach.

I take a step forward, wanting to lunge right through that computer screen to save her. Fuck, why can't I get to her?

I hear Everly's low voice say, "What are you doing?" Then her voice gets lower as she says, "This wasn't the deal."

Anthony grins as he pulls Everly's chin to look up at him. "Oh sweetie, did you really think I'd fall for your deal? It would have been a good one if it had been years ago, but not now. Now it's too late."

"No! Please!" Everly cries out as he pushes the knife toward her stomach more.

It takes everything in me not to cry out too. My heart is being squeezed, and I can't breathe.

"So, Thomas. Your daughter has a secret she's been keeping, and I think revealing it now may give you a little more incentive to finding my guy. Tell him, sweetheart."

Everly has tears in her eyes as she looks at us through the screen. No, she looks directly at me as her voice breaks, saying, "I'm pregnant."

FUCK! I immediately put my hands up and rub my face as tears form. I can't sit here anymore and say nothing. This may be the last time I get to speak to her. Damn it, I can't think like that.

I kneel in front of the screen and get close to it, gripping the edges so she can see my face. "Baby, we're going to get you back, okay? I love you. We're going to get through this."

Everly's crying now too as she says, "I love you too, James."

It feels like we're both saying these words, as if we know they could be our last words to each other. I can't lose her. I won't.

"Well, well, well, it looks like you're a little liar, sweet Everly," Anthony says while tsking again.

Everyone's quiet, waiting to see what happens next. He whispers something in her ear that we can't hear, and her face is straight, not showing any emotion.

"You know how long you have left, Thomas. I'd work fast before you lose not only your daughter, but your grandchild." Anthony smirks as he ends the video call.

I turn around and place my hands in my hair, pulling on it. I can't believe she's pregnant, and right now I don't know if I'm ever going to see her again. What the hell do I do?

Thomas comes up behind me, putting his arm on my shoulder, asking, "Did you know?"

I shake my head no. I can't speak right now.

"We're getting her back, James. We're getting them both back," he states like he's so sure.

I'm about to say something back to him, but my phone rings and Lorenzo's name pops up.

"Tell me you got her," I plead.

"Not yet, but we found her location. I'm sending it to you so you can be there when we get her out, but I need you to stay back until we do. Do you understand? Her life is at stake here, and my men are trained for this. You are not," he states with authority.

"Understood," I say while getting up and walking toward the front door.

"They are heading in now. We'll get her," he states and hangs up.

I grab my car keys, and everyone follows behind me as I say, "They found her and are heading in now. Let's go."

I call Ryder, and of course, he already has the information. He's meeting us there and reiterates what Lorenzo said about staying back and waiting. As much as I want to barge in there myself, I know I can't. It's going to be torture waiting outside knowing she's in there, pregnant with my child, but I have to trust they'll get her out and they'll get her out alive.

Chapter Thirty-Four

EVERLY

I sit here replaying everything that just happened on the video call with my father and James. Clearly, Anthony didn't fall for my plan about the arranged marriage and used the pregnancy against me. I knew that was a possibility, but I had to try. I hate how James had to find out about it. The look on his face kills me.

Anthony took off my ankle ties for the call so I could stand next to him, and he didn't put them back on. That's one advantage. Now I just need to get these bindings off my wrists. I feel like I'm out of time. I know time passes a lot slower in these situations, but the twenty-four hours have to be almost up, right?

I take a deep breath and try to sit back and relax as much as I can. I need to keep my strength up so I can escape when the opportunity presents itself. Since all I'm doing is hurting myself, I haven't attempted to get out of the ties anymore. However, I still need to find a way to untie myself. I was banking on being untied to take the pregnancy test, but clearly, they aren't going to do that.

I've been doing my best to listen to all the voices outside the room so I can figure out how many of them there are. I've counted three so far, but there could be more in other rooms. My only plan so far is to see if I can get them to let me use the bathroom. I'm hoping I'll be able to see most of them if they let me, but I know there will be some outside of the building as well.

I decide to wait a little to see if someone will come in before I yell out to ask for the bathroom. My exhaustion is hitting me again, and my eyes begin to close. They pop back open the moment I start to doze because Declan keeps popping into my mind. I keep hearing the thump of his body on the ground, along with the gunshots. The look in his eyes still haunts me. He wasn't scared for himself. He was scared for me and determined to save me. Even when his own life was at risk, he was fighting for me.

Tears start streaming down my face again because there's just no way I can control my emotions anymore. I'm trying so hard to stay calm and not be emotional, but thinking about Declan being gone is killing me. I'll never get to see him again. He dedicated his entire life to me, and what did he get? Death.

I'm going crazy because I swear he's speaking to me.

It was my job, Kid. I died protecting you, and I'd do it again if I had the choice.

It was your job to protect me Declan, not die for me! I can forgive you for not being able to protect me, but I'll never forgive you for dying for me!

Not how that works, Kid.

Shut up. It's easier to be mad at you right now.

I can hear him laughing in my head. Ugh, Declan. I'm sorry. I feel like I failed you, too.

The door flies open, and I scold myself for not paying attention to notice someone was about to come in.

Once my eyes adjust to the light now coming in, I realize it's not Anthony. I haven't seen this guy before, but he has a glass of water in his hand and some crackers, I think. My heart rate picks up because this is it. If they are going to feed me, they have to untie me. I need to pay close attention to everything around me.

I scan his body to see a gun attached to his hip, but don't see any other weapons on him. That doesn't mean he doesn't have anything hidden under his clothes.

"I'm supposed to let you drink and eat this. Boss says you need it. I'm going to untie you, but if you try anything stupid, I'll shoot you," he says seriously.

I look him in the eye and nod. His voice sounds like one that was outside the door, so he must be one of the three I've been hearing. Good, because three is better than four.

He puts the food down on the floor beside me and unties my wrists. My wrists burn and I wince as he roughly takes it off. It takes every effort not to headbutt him right now and try to run, but that would be a stupid mistake. I have no doubt in my mind that he would shoot me as I tried to run away.

"Can I please use the bathroom? I really don't want to pee myself," I ask as nicely as I can.

He looks me over for a moment before saying, "Fine."

When I stand up, he holds my wrists behind my back to escort me to the bathroom. As we get near the door, I jump, startled, from hearing gunshots close by.

"What the fuck?" he mutters under his breath as he removes one hand from me.

I don't think as I take the opportunity to remove myself from his grasp and backward headbutt him. He stumbles and grabs his gun from its holster, but I quickly knock it out of his hand, and it flies across the floor. I knee him in the balls, and he stumbles to the floor for a moment as I quickly rush to the gun that's now across the room.

I pick it up, aim it toward him, and he freezes, staring at me.

You picked up the gun, so you have to be willing to use it. Don't hesitate, shoot.

I do as Declan taught me, and I don't think as I pull the trigger. The bullet hits him in the leg, and he screams in pain, but he still comes after me. I shoot him again in the shoulder, and he falls to the floor.

Don't think about it. Go! Are you taking the gun?
Yes.
Then use it and don't hesitate or you're dead.

I run out of the room with the gun at the ready, but no one is around. They must have gone to see what the gunshots were about. I sneak as quietly as I can out one door that leads to another and another. I have no idea where I am, but it seems like a large business building.

I find a staircase and open it. There's still no one around, so I race down the steps as fast as I can. One... Two... Three... Ten... Eleven... Twelve... I'm completely out of breath as I go down flight after flight of stairs. I must have been on the top floor.

I lean against the wall to catch my breath and listen to my surroundings. As I'm running, I hear a few more gunshots, and they sound like they are getting closer. It may be a rescue for me, but there's also the possibility it's another enemy. I need to assume I'm on my own.

As I start down the stairs again, I hear the stairwell door open a floor or two above me. I quickly pick up the pace and run down more stairs. Footsteps pound behind me, and a gunshot cracks through the air with a metallic clang ringing in my ears as the bullet slams into the railing beside me.

I gasp and quickly move away from where it hit. I open the nearest door and duck through it. There's no one on this floor. I run down the hall and duck behind a desk just as the man follows me and takes another shot at me.

I try to steady myself as I'm literally shaking in fear. I've almost been shot, twice. Without any hesitation, I peek around the desk and shoot at the man, who is now just a few feet away from me. It hits him right in the stomach. He drops his gun and wraps his arms around himself as he falls to the floor.

I pick up his gun and run back to the staircase, flinging the door open. I hear more gunshots in the distance as I run down another flight of stairs.

Loud steps vibrate below me, and I stop in my tracks. Crap, someone's coming up the steps. I put my body as close to the railing as possible and hold my gun out. There's no way I can make it to the next door without them seeing me and possibly giving them a good shot at me. I try to steady my shaking hands.

I see a head come around the corner and I shoot, missing him and hitting the wall. He quickly jumps back, looking at me, aiming his gun, but doesn't shoot as he sneaks back around the corner.

"Everly! We're here to help you!" the man yells.

I don't recognize him or his voice. I can't trust him.

"Don't come closer or I'll shoot and won't miss this time!" I yell in a shaky voice.

"We're Lorenzo's men! He sent us to help you!" he yells back again.

Lorenzo's men? What are they doing here, and why would they come to save me? It could be true, but I still can't trust it. They could just be saying that.

I hear the door open underneath me, and they talk in another language. Italian, I think.

A moment later, another man yells out, "Everly, we're here to help. It's me, Matteo. Do you remember me?"

My entire body relaxes, and I can feel the tears forming in my eyes. Matteo... That is Matteo's voice. I remember him perfectly. They really are here to save me.

I hold both guns down at my sides as I say, "I'm coming around the corner with my guns lowered."

I walk down the steps and slowly peek around to find three men standing there. Once they see my guns are lowered, they lower theirs as well. Matteo steps forward and puts his hands on my shoulders, holding me out, and assessing me.

"Are you hurt? Shot?" he asks.

I shake my head no, but I'm not even sure if he could see my response since my whole body is shaking.

"Where's the blood coming from?" he asks while tugging on the dress.

Huh? I look down and see that it's covered in blood. How? It could be my wrists because they have been bleeding pretty badly, but that's a lot of blood.

"I don't know. It might be the two guys I shot," I whisper.

I swear Matteo smiles, but it's gone as quickly as I saw it.

"Let me take these. You're safe now," he says, taking both guns from me.

I forgot I even had a gun, never mind two of them. I don't hesitate to hand them over. I don't want them anymore.

Matteo pulls out his phone and calls someone, definitely speaking in Italian. I can't understand anything that he's saying, but he sounds relieved.

He hangs up and says to me, "Everyone is gone, and we can get you out safely. Follow us."

I look at him and comprehend his words but can't force myself to move to follow. My feet don't want to work anymore, and my brain is finally catching up with me on everything that just happened.

Matteo notices and wraps his arm around my waist to help guide me and hold me up, because I feel like I'm about to fall at any moment. I'm not sure how many more stairs we go down, but it feels like fifty flights.

Before we make it to the last flight of stairs, Matteo says, "You did good. You're strong, Everly. You escaped on your own and didn't even need us."

I laugh, but it's not an actual laugh. "I'm not sure about that, but thanks for coming for me."

Once we make it into the lobby of the building, I see Barry and Ryder, along with a few other familiar security guards. They both run over to me, looking me over while Barry makes a call, I assume to my father.

Ryder takes me from Matteo and leads me out the door. I look around, and it's as if I wasn't just kidnapped and probably killed two people. I expected to see police cars and ambulances, but there's nothing. I suppose they need to keep everything under wraps.

Ryder stops walking for a second and looks at me. "There's a lot of people waiting for you over there. James, your father, and your friends. Do you want me to take you to someone in particular?"

Everyone is waiting for me over there? It's pitch-black outside. It must be the middle of the night. I don't really want to be around anyone right now. I need to process what just happened, but there is one person who always helps me feel safe.

"James," I say, and Ryder nods.

"Where are you hurt?" he asks.

"Just my wrists," I reply.

He looks down at my dress, and before he can question anything, I say, "I shot two guys. It's probably their blood or from my wrists. I'm not sure."

I see pity in his eyes as he looks me over anyway to make sure I wasn't hurt anywhere else. Yeah, like I could just be walking around right now with a gunshot wound and not feel it.

Barry is right behind me, and I look around, not seeing anyone else. We're clearly in New York City, but it seems like an abandoned area.

"Is it safe here for a moment? Can I just have two minutes to myself?" I ask, hoping that Ryder deems it safe.

Ryder and Barry look at each other, nodding.

"Yeah, we can sit over here for just a moment," Ryder says, leading me to the side of the building.

I'm standing against the wall while both of them cover me. Ryder is watching me to the right, while Barry is watching to the left with his back toward me. I turn to face the wall so they can't see me.

The adrenaline is wearing off, but I'm still shaking. I lean my head against the brick wall of the building and try to take a few deep breaths. My mind is racing, and I can't concentrate on anything. I see Declan's body on the ground. I see the two men that I shot and their blood splattering everywhere. I see James' face when he found out I was pregnant, and everything is spinning.

I don't even realize my nausea before my stomach releases the little contents it has in it. I vomit right there on the concrete and sob between each heave. It feels like it never ends as I kneel on the ground.

When it finally subsides, I still don't stand up, keeping my head on the ground. The thing hitting me the most right now is that Declan isn't here. Declan will never be here again. How am I supposed to survive this?

"I'm so sorry Declan. I'm so sorry," I sob and yell out like Declan will hear me.

I feel a hand on my shoulder, and I look up to find Barry looking down at me. I quickly look away because I can't look at him right now. He probably blames me for Declan's death. I blame myself for Declan's death.

"Everly... Declan's in the hospital. He's alive right now and in surgery. His wounds are bad, but he's a fighter," Barry states.

What? Declan's alive?

"What? How? I need to see him," I state, trying to stand up.

Once I get on my feet, I fall forward, and Ryder catches me. I feel a sharp pain in my ankle that I didn't notice before. I think I twisted it while running down the stairs, but it didn't hurt at all in the moment. Ryder guides me with his arm around my waist.

We walk again and round the corner in an alleyway to find a bunch of cars parked and people standing around. Ryder wasn't kidding. There are a lot of people here. I immediately spot James as he runs over to me and pulls me into a tight hug. I let myself finally let go and relax into his embrace.

CHAPTER THIRTY-FIVE

JAMES

I sit in the hospital room with Everly in the chair next to me and Declan in the hospital bed. We've been in this room for three days now with no change to Declan's condition. The moment Everly was back in my arms, I swore I wasn't letting her out of my sight. She immediately wanted to come see Declan and refused to leave his side.

I held her in my arms the entire first day she was rescued. She didn't want to talk about what happened for a while, but eventually she explained a few things that happened to her while she was kidnapped. Thankfully, those used condoms were just a scare tactic, and she said no one touched her in that way. Every person who was involved in her kidnapping is dead. If they weren't, I would've found them and killed them myself.

Everly said the pregnancy is true and I couldn't be more excited. I wish the circumstances of finding out were different, but this is everything I've wanted with her. A family. Once she recovers from the trauma of everything, which she's doing a good job so far, and Declan wakes up, I plan to move up the timeline on proposing to her.

Someone knocks on the door and walks in. It's Everly's father.

He kneels down in front of her and places his hand on her knee. "Hey sweetie, how are you doing?"

She gives him a weak smile and says, "I'm okay."

He returns the same smile. "Good. Come to the cafeteria with me and get something to eat."

She shakes her head no. Refusing to leave the room, she has been eating the bare minimum for the baby. She needs to get out.

I put my hand on her thigh and say, "Hey, I'll call you immediately if anything changes. You should go eat for just a few minutes. Besides, the doctors said that we need to keep talking to Declan, and I have some things I want to say to him alone. Okay?"

Her gaze bounces from me to Declan a couple of times before giving in. Her father helps her up and steadies her as she walks out the door. Everly was checked over, and her cut wrists were treated along with a boot cast for her ankle. Other than that, she is physically okay. As far as they can tell, the baby is okay.

After the door is closed, I do exactly what I said I would do. I don't know if talking to someone in a coma really helps, but in case it does, that's what I'm going to do.

I place my chair right beside Declan as I begin.

"Hey man. Thank you for doing everything you could to protect Everly. Not only were you willing to give your life for her, but your training saved her. You would be so proud of how she handled herself and got herself to safety. Without you, I don't think she'd be here today. So, thank you... Now... I need you to wake up..." I didn't realize how emotional I would be talking to him like this, but my voice cracks.

I clear my throat and continue, "Everly needs you. I need you. You've become a good friend, and I can't imagine you not being here anymore. You're part of our family and... we need you with us, especially now that we are having a baby. I know you will be an awesome uncle, and I know you will also protect him or her. So come on, man, wake up and come back to us."

I place my hand on his arm, hoping that maybe he can feel it. Everly has been holding his hand most of the time that we've been here and constantly talking to him, so I'm doing the same.

Declan has become more than a friend to us, to me. I can't help but think about some of the good moments with him, and I just hope there will be many more. One of my favorite memories with him is when we went after Adam. It was one of the worst days at the time, but looking back, it was also one of the best, all things considered.

"You sure you're up to this?" Declan asked as I slid into the passenger seat of his car.

"Yes, let's go," I replied.

Adam decided not to heed our warnings and continued to bother Everly and harm her friends. It was getting serious, and it needed to be taken care of. I told Everly I wouldn't do anything about it, but obviously that was a lie.

I convinced Ryder to stay back and watch Everly from a distance as I asked Declan for help with this. Ryder didn't know that I was doing this, and obviously neither did Everly nor anyone else. Declan asked for a day off while I told Everly that I needed to do some work with my father. It was risky doing this without anyone else knowing, but it was better having fewer people know.

Personally, I was ready to kill the guy. Declan convinced me we were going to try one more scare tactic, and if that didn't work, then we would end him the correct way. I wasn't entirely sure what the correct way entailed, but it sounded like it was without getting our own hands dirty.

Declan feared since there were so many people Adam had gotten involved, that they would retaliate from his death. We needed to figure out all his contacts that had been involved and who all his friends were to be safe. Plus, he mentioned we aren't murderers. He had a good point.

We were silent most of the car ride to Boston. Halfway there, Declan pulled over because we had a flat tire. I groaned as we both stared at the inconvenience.

It didn't take long before we put on the spare and continued on our way. After we dealt with Adam, we'd bring the car to a friend of his in Boston to change the tire for the drive home.

About an hour from our destination, he cursed and pulled over again. Would you look at that, another flat.

"What is going on?" I asked.

Declan shrugged his shoulders. "I've literally never had a flat before."

Neither have I. What were the odds that both of our luck ran out when it came to not getting flats on the same trip to Boston? Unfortunately, we only had one spare, so we were screwed. Declan spent about ten minutes on the phone with a friend, and we sat and waited for a callback for another forty minutes. We accounted for traffic and unforeseen circumstances, but our timeline was getting close.

Declan walked away, answering his phone. When he came back, he explained his friend was sending someone to pick us up and drive us the rest of the way to Boston, where we could borrow a car. He'd come out, get our car, and have it ready for us in a few hours to be on our way home.

A large white van with no windows, also known as a kidnapper's van, pulled up beside our car. Declan chatted with the woman passenger for a moment, who was friendly enough, and apparently, they were the ones coming to pick us up.

Declan made sure all his weapons were secured inside his car and on his body before we hopped into the back. I'm not going to lie that red flags were raising before the doors even opened.

The driver came around and opened the back for us and we both hesitated. There were four other people in the back, all dressed like... clowns... What the fuck? I looked over at Declan, who just stared for a moment like he was debating if we should get in or not. I mean, this was his friend sending them, right?

The driver laughed. "We're heading to my niece's birthday party, and she loves clowns, so we decided to dress up."

Sure.

Declan shrugged his shoulders and hopped in. If he was okay with riding in the back with complete strangers and clowns, then I was sure it would be safe. Maybe. Those red flags that raised were now flapping around like crazy, but I trusted Declan.

Forty-five minutes into the drive and listening to these clowns talk and joke, I was ready to get out of this van.

"We're going to make a quick stop to drop off our clowns, and I'll drive you where you need to go," the driver said.

"Thanks," Declan responded.

Five minutes later, we stopped at the birthday party, and everyone hopped out, except us. After another five minutes, I noticed he left the van running and considered driving off without them.

"No," Declan said, looking at me.

I laughed. "How did you know what I'm thinking?"

"Because I thought the same, but I'm not screwing a friend of this particular friend," he stated.

I shrugged and leaned back in my seat, continuing to wait. Neither of us mentioned the ridiculousness of this situation. I checked my watch, and it was the time we were expecting to be "running" into Adam. We'd have to change our plan a little when we got there. It wasn't far, thankfully.

The back door of the van opened, and the driver popped his head in. "Hey, so we have a little bit of a hiccup. Since I gave you guys a lift, mind doing a favor back?"

Declan turned to face him more and asked, "What type of favor?"

I had a bad feeling about this...

Thirty minutes later, Declan and I were standing in front of each other in clown suits with a full set of clown makeup on, topped off with a squishy red nose. I glared at Declan, and he didn't say a word about our current attire.

"He said five minutes, in and out," Declan said, but he couldn't look me in the eye.

Yeah, I was having trouble looking him in the eye, too. Not only because he was screwing me over having me wear a fucking clown suit to a child's birthday party, but if I really looked at him right now, I'd never be able to get this image out of my head and look at him seriously again.

We pretended none of this was happening and joined the others outside, getting mauled by five-year-olds. Some because they loved clowns and were so excited to see us, and some because they were scared and wanted to murder us.

Twenty-five minutes later and the cops and fire department were showing up at the house for a fire that started from the birthday girl's candles. How the fuck that happened, I don't know, but we both ditched the scene before we got involved. We didn't have time for this, and Declan was packing his weapons under his clown suit.

After jogging a few blocks away, we stopped to get our bearings. Our clothes were left in one of the bedrooms in the house that was currently going up in flames from a freaking birthday cake candle. We thought for sure the fire would've been put out, but who knew that there would also be an explosion? Everyone was out of the house, thankfully, at least that we knew of. I would continue to pretend they were.

"Now what?" I asked Declan, pretending like we were both not still wearing clown suits.

"We need to find where Adam is. Let me pull up the tracker. Hopefully, he hasn't found it yet," Declan stated, looking at his phone.

I had no idea how Declan got a tracker on Adam, but good for him. I supposed he had more contacts in Boston than New York, since this was where he worked, mostly.

"Huh..." Declan said, zooming in closer on his phone.

"What?"

"It looks like he's walking a block away," Declan said, showing me the phone.

Yeah, we were almost right on top of him. That's awesome. I was about to say let's go get him when I remembered we were sporting clown suits.

"We can't visit him now while wearing these. He'll never take us seriously," I stated.

"It's our best shot. He's right there," Declan said, already heading in his direction.

I followed behind him because what else was I supposed to do? How did we even get into this situation? This was the crap that happened to Ben, not me.

As we turned the corner of a building, a downpour of water splashed over my body. I stopped in my tracks and couldn't move. Are you fucking kidding me? I looked up to see that someone just poured a bucket of water out their window. At least I was praying it was a bucket of water. It was fucking freezing.

Declan turned around and watched me. I shook off whatever water I could and glared at him. He was holding back a laugh and didn't say a word. We both continued walking, and I saw his fucking shoulders shaking. He was laughing his ass off at me right now while I was soaking wet in the freezing cold of winter in the middle of Boston, in a clown suit. I was going to kill him.

Adam must have been on foot because we were catching up to him. Declan was keeping a close eye on the phone to find him, so it wasn't a surprise when I saw him trip because of a dip in the sidewalk. I thought he was going to catch his footing, but the loose clown suit got tangled under his feet as he ended up on the ground, rolling on his side and then forward. To his credit, it was a very controlled roll. Just when I thought he was going to stop and get up, he didn't. He continued rolling into a large trash can that was open on its side and full of trash.

Once his momentum stopped, he rolled himself out of it and stood up, wiping off the pieces of trash sticking to him. His hair was messed up, and he had red stains all over his outfit and on his face. I hoped that was ketchup.

Replaying the entire scene in my head and how nonchalant he was acting, I burst out laughing. He laughed at me for getting water dumped on my head, so I could laugh at a clown rolling into some trash. He smelled awful.

Twenty steps later, Declan pushed me into a disgusting heap of trash on the side of a building. I stopped laughing as I brushed myself off and lunged at him.

"Seriously?!" I yelled at him as we were both fighting, locked in each other's arms, trying to push the other into the pile of trash.

"You thought it was funny, so I let you experience it," Declan said through gritted teeth.

I took a swing at him, and he put me in a headlock. He cut off my air supply, and I tried to get him to let go, but a noise caught our attention. We looked in that direction to find Adam staring at us with wide eyes.

Would you look at that? With all our horrible luck, he was delivered straight to us. Declan let me go, and we both started toward him. Adam ran in the other direction, and we chased him. The clown outfit slowed us down, but it didn't stop us from catching up to him. Declan reached him first, grabbed him, and pinned him against the wall. I came up beside him and glared down at Adam.

The kid was literally crying. I couldn't help the sadistic smile that spread across my face.

"Please, let me go! I'll give you whatever you want! Please, don't kill me!" Adam pleaded for his life and was hyperventilating.

Declan and I both looked at each other. Seriously?

Declan moved his arm up to his throat and pressed down on him harder.

"Jesus, I don't want to die by killer clowns. Come on, my worst nightmare. Take what you want, please," he said, and he looked like he was about to pee his pants.

The kid was afraid of clowns. Maybe this whole situation wasn't as horrible as it seemed.

"You're going to leave Everly and everyone she knows alone. Call off all your friends. If we find out that you haven't, we will kill you," Declan said as he took the knife I didn't even realize he was holding, and sliced a few times under his neck.

Adam wailed and promised he'd never do anything to hurt Everly again. I watched the blood seeping from above his collarbone. It looked like Declan carved an E.

Declan took out a piece of paper and placed it into Adam's shirt pocket. "You will email me tonight the names of every person you know that knows about Everly. In Boston, in New York, in her school, in the fucking world. If I find out you forgot a single one, we'll be back for you," Declan said while pushing him away.

Adam stood there with tears in his eyes and looked at me. I smiled and gave him a punch in the gut for good measure.

Declan and I walked off. That was too easy, but I had a feeling this time it worked.

Breaking me out of my thoughts, I feel Declan's arm move underneath my hand.

Chapter Thirty-Six

EVERLY

I sit across from my father in the hospital cafeteria with a chicken tender plate in front of me. I've only taken a few bites and find it difficult to eat any more. I don't know if it's the nausea from the pregnancy or if it's because of everything that's happening. Either way, forcing myself isn't going to help because I'll just end up throwing it up later.

"What can I do Everly?" my father asks.

"There's nothing you can do," I state the truth.

My father has felt guilty for my kidnapping and wants to do whatever he can to make things right. Unfortunately, there's nothing he can do. This whole thing is an eye-opener, honestly. I have always known the life my father leads is dangerous, but I never really saw firsthand how dangerous it is. He sheltered me as much as he could.

"I'm sorry. I'm sorry this happened. I don't know what I would've done if they had killed you too," he whispers the last part.

My heart sinks. "What do you mean, too?"

My father looks back and forth between my eyes, debating if he should tell me.

He sighs. "I never told you the truth about your mother."

He doesn't need to say more, and honestly, I don't know that I want to know more. I was always told it was an accident, but as I got older, I considered the fact it may not have been. My father has put a crazy amount of protection on me since I was little. I always knew there was a reason he was overprotective.

"Was it like what happened to me?" I ask.

He nods and doesn't elaborate. So, she was kidnapped, and she wasn't saved. I try really hard not to think about what might have happened to her while she was kidnapped and what she must have been feeling. To know that you have a little girl at home that needs you and you can't get to her. I shake my head. I can't think about that right now. I've got too much to work through than to go down that road.

"So, a grandchild, huh?" my father smiles and changes the subject.

I can't help but smile too and place my hand on my stomach. This pregnancy was definitely a surprise, and I was also concerned about telling James, but how could I not want to bring a little James into this world? Just now I'm needing to figure out about bringing it into my world.

"I want my baby to grow up without worrying about all this stuff. Dad, I don't know what to do," I say.

He looks at me like he understands. "I think you need to talk to James about how you're feeling, and I'll support whatever you choose to do, sweetheart. You know that. The world I brought you up in isn't the best, but I'd like to think I've made it better for my grandchild. James' father and I have worked hard to make the company legitimate and move away from all this stuff, so hopefully when we retire, James can keep it that way."

"So, what happened to that guy you took?" I ask.

My father sighs. "That was part of me trying to make things right. We made a deal with him, and he wanted out. My part of the bargain was to give him what he needed to disappear, and I did. I'm trying to do the right thing... I let him go and didn't track him so I wouldn't be tempted to find him. I didn't know this would happen."

Out of everything that happened, my heart is happy that my father was trying to be a good man. I know he's done a lot of shady things in his life, but he's trying. He's trying to make it better for me and his grandchildren. I've grown up not wanting for anything. I don't even need to work if I don't want to. My kids won't need to work if they don't want to. I appreciate everything he has done to provide for me and my future.

My phone buzzes, and I see a text from James.

James

Declan's awake.

I race out of the cafeteria, and my father follows quickly behind me. My mind is completely focused on getting back to Declan's room that I can't say anything to him or think about anything else. I wait for the elevator to come, but it's the slowest damn elevator in the world. I debate sprinting off to the stairs, but this stupid boot on my foot would make the climb up a few floors longer than this dang elevator is taking.

Finally, the doors open, and we get in. I bump into someone on it and mutter a small apology. Once we're off the elevator, I walk as fast as I can to his room. When I open the door, I find doctors and nurses surrounding him. Declan is trying to push them off and sit up. I race to his side and try to gently give him a hug without hurting the three bullet wounds he has. I ignore the doctor's protests.

"Hey, Kid. You did good," he says with a weak smile.

I bury myself in his chest and don't let go as I bawl in his arms.

"Alright, I'm good," Declan complains as I help him onto the couch at home.

A couple of days after Declan woke up, the doctors reluctantly released him to go home. Declan insisted he would be fine. I stayed by his side the entire time, and I'm not leaving him anytime soon. I told work that I wouldn't be back until after the New Year. He's sick of me, and even more sick of James.

"I'll get you a blanket and something to drink. Do you want any food?" I ask while grabbing a blanket from the basket near the couch.

"Everly, I'm fine," Declan says while lying back.

He wants to go to his bedroom, but I refuse to let him. I need him to be in the living room where I can see him 24/7. I know this is all overkill, but it makes me feel better.

James places his hand on my shoulder. "Everly, I need you to go rest, too. You're still recovering and need to rest for the baby."

I want to protest, but James is right. I'm completely worn out and can't tell if it results from everything piling up on me or if it's due to the pregnancy. Funny how every single symptom I have could be a pregnancy symptom. Exhausted? Pregnant. Nauseous? Pregnant. Back hurt? Pregnant. Gaining weight? Pregnant. Finger twitching? I'm positive that one means you're pregnant.

I don't argue as I get comfortable in the chair next to the couch that Declan is lying on. "Fine, but I'm staying here."

I recline the chair and almost immediately want to go to sleep. It's nighttime, so it's dark. James turns off most of the lights and places a blanket on me, kissing my forehead.

"Let me know if you need anything," he says.

I love the fact that he doesn't even argue anymore. I know he wants me in my bed, but he's not going to fight it. He knows that I'm not leaving Declan alone, even though we have a nurse that will come by a few times a day to check on him. Personally, I wanted to have a 24/7 nurse, but that's where Declan drew the line.

James leaves us alone, and Barry heads to his room once we're settled in. Barry has barely slept either. He has taken it upon himself to protect us 24/7. I'm pretty sure he hasn't slept in a week. We had other guards that were watching out for us too, but I think Barry just wanted to be near Declan.

It's late, and we both should be asleep, but I don't think either of us is. We didn't get much time to talk privately at the hospital.

"Declan?" I whisper to see if he's still awake.

"Yeah, Kid?" he responds immediately.

"I'm sorry..." I say, finally getting that apology off my chest.

"There's nothing to apologize for," he says sternly.

"I know you think that, but there is. Declan, you have given up your life to protect me. You make all this money and for what? To never have a day off, not have fun, not have a girlfriend, and not take vacations. What kind of life is that?" I question and start getting emotional.

Declan lets out a pained laugh. "Kid, it's the life I choose. I love this life, even if you don't understand why."

I try to hold in my sobs, which has been an increasingly hard thing to do lately. "Enlighten me."

Declan lets out a breath. "Look, I couldn't protect the people I loved when I was younger, but I can protect you. I was born to protect people. It's what I need to do. You're my family now,

Everly, and I want to protect you. You're having a baby, and I want to protect him or her, too. Don't take that away from me. You're all I have for family."

Well, there goes holding back those tears because now they are free-falling like a waterfall.

"How did you know I was thinking of firing you?" I ask, trying to laugh a little.

"I know you, Everly, but I'm not going anywhere."

We're both quiet for a while, and I'm not sure if Declan is even still awake.

"Declan?" I whisper again.

"Yeah?"

"I love you," I say, meaning it with my whole heart.

"I love you too, Kid."

CHAPTER THIRTY-SEVEN

JAMES

Everly is nine weeks pregnant today. I forced her to go to another doctor's appointment to ensure the baby was doing okay. The doctor said everything looked great, and we were able to hear the baby's heartbeat. I don't know how to explain what hearing that little heartbeat does to me, but... it's everything.

Per Everly's request, I immediately brought her home after the appointment. She's been feeling nauseous and having trouble keeping food down, which the doctor assured me was also normal. I know she used that as an excuse, though, and she just didn't want to be away from Declan that long. He's recovering well, but I can tell he's getting annoyed with Everly.

After getting her settled in the house, I left for the day to run two errands. I wish I didn't have to leave her ever again, but that's obviously not possible. Today, I have two people I'm meeting with, and both make me nervous.

I open the door to the club, and it's quiet inside. It's currently closed since it's the morning, which is the best time to meet. As I enter, there are two people behind the bar with their backs facing me. A man is kissing down the back of the neck of the woman who holds a dish rag. She giggles, and I clear my throat to announce my presence, hoping to make it less awkward.

They both turn around, surprised, but I'm even more surprised by who I see. I do a double take on the woman as I notice that Everly's friend, Paige, is the one behind the bar. Matteo, Lorenzo's brother, is the one all over her.

I'm not one to get involved in relationships, but this one is hard to stay out of.

"James! What are you doing here?" Paige asks, just as surprised to see me as I am with her.

"I have a meeting," I state, nodding toward Matteo.

I don't bother asking her what she's doing here because it's obvious she works here. Everly mentioned that she had quit her old job and got a job waitressing. I helped Everly pay off Paige's student loans without her knowing where it came from, and I also made a few calls to get her old boss fired. Apparently, he was also in a serious accident, so his life is forever ruined. Everly didn't know the details of what happened, but it wasn't hard to guess. I'm sure he deserved it.

Without another word, I follow Matteo into a back office where Lorenzo is sitting at the desk, working on his computer.

When we walk in, Lorenzo stands up with a grin on his face, heading toward me to shake my hand. "It's good to see you again, James. Please, sit."

I sit in the chair across from him, and Matteo pulls his chair around to sit by Lorenzo.

"How's Everly doing?" Lorenzo asks.

"As good as she can be," I reply.

"I'm glad that everything worked out and Everly is safe," Lorenzo says.

I nod. "Yes, thank you for everything you did. You saved her life."

Matteo speaks up. "She held her own. She's a strong one."

I smile, knowing that she is. I'm glad she was able to do what she did to get as far as she did. By the sounds of it, though, she wouldn't have been able to escape if they hadn't gotten there when they did. The gunshots distracted everyone while she took advantage of being untied.

I lean forward seriously now as I say, "Let's cut to the chase. What do I owe you?"

Lorenzo leans back in his chair with his hands folded on his lap, studying me. "Everly was a friend of Lauren's, and I made a promise to Lauren to protect her when I can. With that said, you did call me asking for a favor. So, a favor is usually returned, yes?"

My head is reeling at what he just said. You're kidding, right? Had I just called him and told him about Everly's situation, he would've helped, anyway? Lorenzo is a man of his word, so if he made a promise to protect Everly, he would've done it. I never should have said the word favor, but I wasn't in my right mind. Regardless, I told him he could take my entire empire if he wanted, so he has every right to collect on that. I would do it all over again if I had to.

"Yes," I state through clenched teeth.

I'm not looking forward to seeing what he wants. My father and Everly's father have worked hard to cut ties with people like Lorenzo, and here I am flinging open the gates to Hell, saying come on in.

Lorenzo thinks for a moment before speaking. "James, I think I'm going to keep this favor in my back pocket for a while. I'll let you know when I want to cash it in."

And that's exactly what I didn't want to hear. Owing favors is not something I like. Owing a favor to someone like Lorenzo is as bad as it gets.

Lorenzo leans forward and smirks. "Don't look so scared, James. I'm not going to ask for anything crazy. I think you and I could have a good friendship."

I narrow my eyes at him. "I'm not looking for friendship."

Lorenzo gets serious as he straightens his posture. "You're either a friend or you're an enemy, James. I suggest you pick wisely."

Shit.

I nod and stand up. I don't want this to go on any longer since, clearly, he's not going to tell me what he wants from me right now.

I stick out my hand, and Lorenzo shakes it. "Thank you again for your help with Everly... Friend."

Lorenzo and Matteo both have huge grins on their faces. I'm not going to lie, I'm concerned. I came here to ease my mind about what Lorenzo would want from me, but now I have a feeling I just dragged in some new demons as my father just cast out the old ones.

On my way out of the club, Paige stops me. "James!"

I turn around to see her standing in front of me, and she looks worried.

"Please don't tell Everly. I'll... I'll tell her soon, I promise. I just haven't yet, with everything going on. I was going to talk to her the day she was kidnapped..." Paige starts, but I interrupt.

"I won't tell her, but you need to," I say.

"Thank you..." she whispers.

Before I turn to leave, I continue, "Paige, I'm going to say this only once. I think you need to quit and stay far away from Matteo. This is not a world you want to be involved in."

She looks down at the floor and puts her hands behind her back.

She doesn't make eye contact when saying, "I know."

Ah, shit. She's in as deep as I am. She knows who they are, but she probably loves Matteo.

"If you need anything Paige, any help, come to me, okay?"

This time she looks into my eyes and says, "Thanks, James."

I nod and walk out of that club, hoping that I never hear from or see Lorenzo again.

I sit here in my second meeting to find that I'm more nervous with sweaty palms than I was in the meeting with Lorenzo. Everly's father sits across from me, waiting for me to spit out the reason that I'm here.

I don't waste any time as I nervously say, "I want to ask your daughter to marry me."

Thomas stares at me with his arms folded on his desk. He gives no indication of what he's thinking. An eternity passes and he still hasn't said anything. Did I say something wrong? Should I say more? I probably should, but I don't know what to say, or more like I'm so nervous I don't want to say anything stupid.

After a drop of sweat slides down my temple, Thomas says, "Finally!"

I release the breath I was holding in as Thomas smiles.

"I've been waiting years for this and thought it would never come," Thomas says as he rounds his desk and comes over to me to hug and pat me on the back.

I stand with him and hug him back. Thomas opens some whiskey and pours both of us a glass. I take it to be polite, but don't want to drink much. Ryder and I will be driving back tonight from Boston.

We both take a seat again across from each other when Thomas asks, "Has Everly talked to you about her concerns yet?"

What concerns? What could she have talked to her father about and not mentioned to me?

"No," I state, hoping he will elaborate.

He sighs. "When Declan was in the hospital, she mentioned not knowing what to do about bringing a baby into our world. It seemed like she wanted to leave. I tried to ease her concerns."

Seriously? Leave? Is that with or without me? The fact that she hasn't told me any of this yet is concerning. I thought we were doing really well together. I've been there for her as much as I can, and she's been acting okay. I know she probably has a lot of trauma she's dealing with, but now that Asher's back, she's talking to him about it.

Speaking of Asher, he was MIA until two days ago. After we got Everly back, I put some guys on finding him. It wasn't like him to disappear like that and especially ignore calls when it concerned Everly. My security team was suspicious he could've been involved in her kidnapping, but I had no doubt that was false. Apparently, he went out of the country and was arrested. I can't believe we had no idea, but thankfully it was all figured out and he's back. It's been a crazy few weeks, and it's hard to believe this is our life and not a movie.

I'm brought back to the present when Thomas clears his throat.

"She hasn't said anything yet, but I don't blame her," I say.

Thomas nods. "I just wanted to make you aware. It may be something you need to talk about and think about first. If she refuses to stay, what will you do?"

I don't hesitate before saying, "I'll follow her."

"What about your company?" he asks.

"Ben is more than capable of running it," I say.

Thomas studies me for a moment before asking, "You'd give up your company for her?"

"I'd give everything up for her and now my baby."

"Good."

I'm glad that Thomas and I are on the same page. There are a lot of men out there who believe work should always come first before women. Thankfully, my father and Thomas are not men like that.

I'm hoping that it doesn't come down to leaving my job, but if it does, I won't have any regrets. Everly is worth everything to me, and now she's carrying our child.

I leave shortly after, heading back to New York. The entire drive back, I plan how I'm going to propose to Everly since I'll be doing it much sooner than expected. Next week.

CHAPTER THIRTY-EIGHT

EVERLY

"Everly... I love you... but go away. Now," Declan demands while kicking me off the couch.

Literally. He kicked me off the couch. I'm sitting there all nice, minding my own business, and he pushes me off with his legs.

Okay, so maybe I wasn't just sitting there minding my own business, but he needs someone here to take care of him, especially since after the first couple of days he fired the nurse that came in to help.

"Declan... just let me..." I start, but he interrupts me.

"No. If you don't leave me alone, I'm going back to my room. In fact, I'm sleeping in there tonight. This couch sucks," he states while repositioning himself.

"Stop moving so much!" I yell as I try to hold him down.

I hear someone enter the room, and Declan looks up behind me. "James... can you please tell your girlfriend to leave me alone?"

James comes up from behind and wraps his arms around me, whispering in my ear, "Baby, let Declan rest."

I sigh and finally agree. "Alright, fine. If you need anything, though, tell me."

Declan shakes his head and sits up. "Great, now I'm going to my room."

I want to argue, but I don't. James helps him stand, but Declan walks himself to his room. I can only imagine how much pain he's in right now. Physically and mentally.

James is staring at me, and I glare at him. "What?"

He shakes his head and laughs. "Everly, let him be. He will let us know if he needs anything. He's strong, he'll be fine."

I plop down on the couch, and James joins me. He's right, but it's hard. I feel responsible for what happened to Declan, and I almost lost him. I just want to take care of him.

"Hey, come here," James says while pulling me close.

I lay my head on his lap and relax into him as he strokes my hair. James has been amazing and skipping work to be here. He said he'll go back when I do. Though, two days ago he was gone all day, saying he had some business to take care of that couldn't wait. I may have pushed my luck with Declan that day because I needed a distraction.

"I think we should talk," James whispers.

My heart stops. Oh no, talk? The way he says it indicates it's something serious.

"What about?" I ask, gulping down my nerves.

He sits me up to face him, keeping his arms around me. "How are you feeling? About us? The baby?"

I look at him, confused. What does that mean? I guess we really haven't talked much about the baby and our relationship. We just got back together a couple of months ago. Honestly, it feels like we've been together our whole lives, so it doesn't feel wrong at all. I admit I was afraid at first, but if anything, I feel like this kidnapping and baby have brought us closer. If we could get through that, we can get through anything.

"I feel good about it. I love you, James, and want this baby with you," I say, looking up at him, hoping he feels the same way.

He smiles down at me and nods. "Me too."

He kisses me on the forehead and holds me for a few moments in silence.

He breaks the silence by asking, "Where are you thinking you want to live when you have the baby?"

Is he asking if I want to move in with him? Or something else? Does he know I was thinking of maybe moving out of state?

"Like your place? Or mine?" I ask for him to elaborate.

He shrugs his shoulders. "Or anywhere. Anywhere in the world."

I look up at him, confused. "What about your job?"

He looks at me seriously and says, "I'll go anywhere you are. I don't care about my job."

My heart swells at his words, and I feel the tears burning the back of my eyes. Damn hormones. I cry at everything nowadays.

It means a lot to me that he would be willing to move away if that's what I wanted. He'd give up everything for me and our baby.

When I was talking to my father about leaving, I was just being emotional and not thinking things all the way through. Yes, it might be safer, maybe. I mean, Anthony even mentioned he knew I was in Georgia. He could have gotten me at any time, and it would've been worse. Here, we have all our friends and family. There were so many people looking for me. If that had happened in Georgia, we wouldn't have had all that.

I can't imagine leaving my friends and family again. I've done it once before, and it wasn't worth it. Paige and Ashley both just moved here, too. I want to raise this baby with all our friends and family around. I want us all to raise our kids together, when they have them too, of course.

I lean into James and kiss him, holding his face with my hands. "I love you so much."

He smiles. "I love you too."

"I want to stay here, but we can live at your place. If you want to," I say.

"Are you sure? Wouldn't you prefer living in a house with the baby? An apartment might not be as practical," he says.

To most people, yes, that's true. To me, it's the most practical place to live. James' apartment has security of its own, and then James has his own security. Ben lives right below James with his own security as well. It's the safest place we could live.

It might not have a backyard, but Central Park is right there. We'd make it work, and if we ever changed our minds, we could move.

"Yeah, I would feel safer where you live. It would be nice having Ben right below us, too. One day he's going to get married, and his wife and I could hang out," I reply.

James laughs. "Now that I'll have to see to believe it. I can't picture Ben getting married."

I laugh too, but hit him on the arm playfully. "Hey, Ben is great! He's going to make an amazing husband one day... but... she would have to be at least a little crazy to put up with his brand of crazy."

We love Ben, but he's always getting himself into some weird situations. We still have no idea how he ended up naked in a bush in Central Park.

"So, when do you want to move in?" James asks with a smirk.

We hear Declan yell from his bedroom, "Right now! Take Everly with you right now!"

James and I both die of laughter on the couch, and it feels good. It feels good to laugh again, to have my life back, and to see a future having a family. I still can't believe we're about to have a family.

Paige wraps me in a hug the moment she comes in the front door. This isn't the first time I've seen her since I was kidnapped, but she treats me like it is every time we see each other. Ashley has been the same way when she comes over. I had to convince both of them I'm fine so they wouldn't move into my bedroom. Ashley has been traveling a lot for work, but I know she would've taken time off if I had let her.

We sit at the island with a plate of brownies and cookies that I made. I'm still super nauseous, but chocolate always sounds great at any time. Paige takes a bite of a brownie and avoids eye contact. Then she stiffens when she hears James walk into the room.

"Paige," James nods his head at her.

"James..." Paige says, nodding her head back.

The awkwardness and tension between them are hard to miss. What the heck happened that I don't know about?

James comes over and places a kiss on the top of my head while reaching around for a brownie. "I'll leave you two alone, just wanted to come out for one of these."

He takes a bite, closes his eyes, and moans around the brownie. Dear God, it's been forever since we've had sex, and him doing that makes me want to shove Paige out the door and bring James back to my bedroom.

I know I'm staring too long, and James can read my thoughts. Before he turns away, he winks at me. Damn it. I close my eyes and take a deep breath before turning back to Paige, who has a huge grin on her face.

"You guys are ridiculously cute," Paige says.

I laugh. "Cute? Sure..."

She shakes her head, and we both wait until we hear the door to the office close. Since James has been staying at the house, I turned the library into an office for him to work from home. While he insisted that he didn't need to work, I insisted that he did. I can't have him hovering over me 24/7 because he'll drive me insane. Right at this moment, it clicks. Crap, that's probably what Declan has been feeling. I'll have to apologize to him, but later.

I turn back to Paige, waiting for her to start the conversation. We still haven't talked about why she wanted to meet at the coffee shop the day I was kidnapped. I have a feeling she's ready to share that information.

"So, I need to come out and tell you this, but I don't want you to be mad, and I know what I'm doing, okay?" she says with a concerned look on her face.

Which in turn makes me concerned. She claims she knows what she's doing, but knowing her, it means she doesn't know what she's doing.

I nod and she continues, "I started working at a club after I got fired... It just so happens to be..." Paige pauses, and her voice goes down to a barely audible whisper when she says, "Matteo's."

I cough as I choke on my spit. Did she just say Matteo? No, clearly, I misheard her.

"I'm sorry, did you say Matteo?" I ask for clarification.

She makes a cringy face and shakes her head yes.

My heart races. No, no, she can't be working at his club. Oh my God, what has she gotten into? Has she gotten into trouble? Does she need help?

"Why?" is all I can ask. I told her I wouldn't get mad, so I'll wait for her explanation.

"I didn't know anything about him and his club before taking the job..." she starts, but I immediately interrupt because I remember a previous conversation.

"Matteo is the boss you like?!" I yell, way too loud.

Again, she just nods.

The way she's reacting to my questions shows she knows exactly who Matteo is and what she's gotten herself into. She knows it's wrong. I say nothing, waiting for her to continue.

"Everly... I... I really like him," she states, and I try my best not to panic.

"Paige, do you know what he does for a living?" I ask without judgment.

"Yes," she states confidently.

My mind is racing a mile a minute, but what am I supposed to do? I can't tell her she shouldn't see him anymore because that's her choice. I can't tell her to quit her job, and I know she won't accept James' help or mine to get her a new one. So, I do what any good friend would do when their friend likes someone. I support her.

"Well, if you really like him..." I state, but leave it there because I really don't know how to end that.

Paige's face lights up, and she lets out the breath she was holding in. "I do."

"Alright, then tell me all about him."

Paige smiles the entire time she's talking about Matteo. She starts from the beginning of how she went in after quitting her old job and he gave her a chance as a waitress. She explained how he was so hot and cold at the beginning because he didn't want to drag her into his world, but they both had strong feelings for each other, so they decided to see where it went. That their entire relationship seems to be going fast, and she's scared but wants to give it a try, anyway.

Paige couldn't stay long because she had to work tonight, which makes me reluctant to let her go. I really want to protect her and keep her in a bubble. She's too good for that world, but I don't know what I can do other than be here for her if she needs me.

Except, there is something I can do.

"Hang on. Are you still living with your brother?" I ask as we stop at the front door.

"Yeah, why?" she asks.

"Come stay at my place, here. Please? I'm moving into James' apartment and this house will be empty. I love it, and it's literally going to be sitting here in case in a few years we decide apartment living isn't for us," I say, hoping she will take me up on the offer.

"What? No, I can't just live in your house," she says.

I put my hand on her shoulder. "Paige, please. It would really be doing me a favor. I don't want it sitting here empty, and I'm not getting into the hassle of renting it out. So please, come stay here even if it's just for a little while. It has four bedrooms. Your brother can live here too."

Paige lets out a breath and gives me a giant hug. "Are you sure?"

I have a huge grin on my face as I nod. "Yes!"

"We'll pay rent..." she starts, but I interrupt.

"No, no rent. Seriously, you are taking care of the house for me," I say, hoping she still accepts.

She's quiet for a moment while looking me over and whispers, "Did you know?"

I look at her, confused. "Know what?"

She sighs. "That my brother just lost his job, and we didn't know how we were going to continue affording the apartment."

Oh no, I actually had no idea. I'm so glad I thought of it at the last minute to offer her to stay here while I move in with James. I can't imagine how she's been feeling about that.

"I didn't know, but I'm so glad you can stay here. Seriously, it's yours for however long you want. And if your brother needs a job, you know James will help," I say, not wanting to push my luck for her accepting more help than that.

She nods and gives me another hug. "Thank you. Thank you for being an amazing friend, Everly. I owe you everything. I'll let you know about my brother if he can't find a job."

I'm really surprised Paige is accepting help; she never accepts help. I wonder what has changed, but I'm not going to question it. Now, I'm hoping that since the house is a good distance from the club, maybe she will find another job. Also, at least this way it keeps her from making a mistake and moving in with Matteo, if that would've been an option with them losing their apartment.

CHAPTER THIRTY-NINE

JAMES

With the help of our friends, it took all of five hours to move Everly out of her house and into my apartment. Somehow, Everly convinced Paige and her brother to move into the house, so she left most of the furniture and TVs for them. It's not like we needed any of hers since I have everything we need at my place. I have to say I was shocked that Everly agreed so easily to move in and so quickly.

Declan and Barry will have their own apartment next to ours. On the other side is where Ryder stays. There's also a security office on the same floor, which has multiple security guards coming in and out of for their shifts. There won't be a lack of security on this floor.

Declan and Barry are both on my payroll now, which Thomas was reluctant to do. Not that he didn't want to, he just wanted to continue to pay to help keep his daughter safe. I convinced him, since we'll be getting married soon, that it was now my responsibility to take care of her. Ultimately, he agreed.

Bash huffs and plops himself down on my couch. "Everly, you have way too many books."

"I second that!" Jake yells across the room as he drops a box near the other twenty boxes of books that were brought in.

"Um, there is no such thing as too many books," Everly says while relaxing into the reclining chair.

I smile as I lift her up, sit, and place her back down in my lap. I know I'm sweaty, even though it's freezing outside, but those books really are heavy. I didn't think she had that much to move, but the books alone took half the time.

Jake comes to sit next to Bash as we wait on Ben, who is helping Declan move his things. Declan is definitely a champ because he wanted to help, but we insisted that he doesn't lift a thing, doctor's orders. I'm sure if we'd let him, he would've been carrying all those boxes of Everly's books.

"So, this is it, huh? You guys are moving in, having a baby... is this something you could've imagined being your life almost eight years ago?" Bash asks.

Everly and I look at each other and smile. No, I don't think either of us pictured this happening like this, but I know we both pictured being together and having a family. It was just supposed to be in the right order, but who's to say this is the wrong order? We love each other, always have. That's all that matters.

"I didn't picture it quite like this, but I wouldn't change a thing," Everly says.

My heart swells at her words. Sometimes I look at her and still can't believe that she's mine. That after all these years of thinking I'd never have her again, that she's here right now and mine. Carrying my child.

Ryder comes walking in with a few pizza boxes, and I get up to grab some beers from the fridge for everyone, Sprite for Everly. She said she has been drinking so much ginger ale that it makes her feel nauseous just thinking about drinking it. Sprite seems to help her stomach as well.

"I wonder if Ben needs some help," I say while pulling my phone out.

"He's done helping Declan and will be up soon. He looked a little... preoccupied in the lobby," Ryder says.

Alright, I'm not sure what that means, but I guess we'll find out soon.

Twenty minutes later, we all finished the pizza, leaving a few slices for Ben. He still hasn't shown up, and I wonder at this rate if he went back to his apartment to shower or something.

We're all quiet as we relax on the couch, but when Ben finally walks in, he stirs us all up.

"What the hell happened to your face?" Jake stands while laughing.

I look over to find Ben frowning. It's not the frown that's the issue. It's the red blotchy lipstick all over his mouth, the red blush covering the sides of his face, and the eyeshadow that goes from his eyelids to above his eyebrows. His eyelashes look darker and longer, too, so I'm pretty sure he also has mascara on.

"Don't ask," Ben says as he walks to my kitchen and takes a paper towel, trying to scrub it off.

Everly is dying of laughter as she makes her way over to him and touches his face. "This is waterproof. I'll be right back."

She walks into the other room, leaving us all staring at Ben, who stares back at us.

"Come on, you can't walk in here and not tell us what happened," I say, trying to demand answers.

If he didn't want to talk about it, he should've gone to his apartment first and taken it off before coming up here. Though by the looks of it, he's starving, so he'd rather have us make fun of him than wait much longer to eat because he's currently scarfing down a slice of pizza while he waits for Everly to come back.

"Nope," he states with a mouthful of pizza.

Ryder walks back into the room and stares at Ben, who in turn stares at him. Nothing is said out loud between the two, but there's a whole conversation going on in their minds. Ryder doesn't laugh. He just gives a nod of understanding, pats Ben on the shoulder, and leaves the apartment.

What the fuck?

Ryder definitely knows what happened because he even said he saw him in the lobby. He knew it would take Ben some time.

Before anyone could say anything more, Everly comes back in with a bottle of liquid. She puts it on a cloth and starts scrubbing Ben's face.

After two minutes, his face is back to normal, just a little red from scrubbing off all the makeup. Seriously, how did he go from bringing Declan's boxes up to his apartment to having a full face of makeup that looked like a five-year-old put it on him?

Either way, we all decide to drop it because we know Ben by now. This is not the first, second, or twentieth time he's gotten himself into a weird situation and wouldn't explain it. He's not going to give up the details if he doesn't want to. My brother is smart, but he has weird luck when it comes to strange situations.

Finally... Everly and I are alone after the long day of moving. I let her take a shower first, and then I jumped in after she was finished. I wanted to ask if she'd like to take one together, but I've been trying to be respectful that she's still recovering from being kidnapped and having a rough start to her pregnancy.

I haven't had her since before she was kidnapped, and it's been damn hard. She's so gorgeous all the time, and the fact that she's pregnant with my child... it makes it really hard to keep my hands to myself.

I wrap a towel around my waist after getting out of the shower and open the bathroom door, heading back into the bedroom. I stop breathing the moment I look toward the bed and see Everly lying there, wearing nothing but her lacy purple bra and underwear, smiling at me. She has her head on her hand and elbow leaning on the pillow. Her left leg is lying straight out while her right leg is curved up.

I want nothing more than to go over there and explore every inch of her body. It's what she wants, right? Because why else would she be placing herself on the bed, in the lack of clothing she's wearing, and offering herself up to me like that?

I take slow steps toward her, not breaking eye contact. If she doesn't want this, then she needs to say something before I get to her.

She says nothing, so I put one knee on the bed, lean forward, and kiss her gently. "Baby, you're killing me."

She pulls away and says, "Well, we can't have that."

She slams her mouth back to mine and pulls me onto the bed with her. I climb on top, between her legs, and begin kissing down her neck. When I reach her breasts, I quickly unclasp her bra and take it off, throwing it across the room.

She laughs and pulls me back up. "James, it's been five seconds..."

"And five seconds of all this material between us is too long," I say while heading back down in the direction I was going.

She pants before I even take her underwear off. Once I drag that down her legs and throw it to join her bra on the floor, I grab my towel and toss it as well. That's better, nothing between us like it should be.

I kiss her stomach and around her belly button. I drag my hands around her stomach and feel how her body is already changing from the baby. She has the tiniest bump, and I growl at the thought that I put this baby inside her. I'm so hard I can barely control myself.

"James..." Everly says while I take too long going to where she wants me to.

"Patience baby..." I state, but I know I don't have the patience either.

She digs one of her hands in my hair and pulls, while the other makes its way down to my dick. Jesus, one touch and I'm about to explode.

I groan at the thought I'm not going to last. My hand makes its way down to her wetness, and that nearly undoes me because she's so ready. Fine, this time can be fast. We have all night to do this as much as we want.

I line myself up at her entrance and hover over her. I stop myself before pushing into her, thinking about the baby.

"Is this okay? For the baby?" I ask, not wanting to hurt either of them.

"I think so," she says, which is not convincing.

Fuck, why haven't I looked this up or asked the doctor? I don't want to do anything to hurt either of them.

"James, just fuck me. People fuck while pregnant all the time," she says while lifting her hips, enticing me to enter her.

Damn it. I'd feel better if I wasn't on top. I don't want to squish the baby. Is that possible? These annoying fucking thoughts that have to pop up in my head two seconds before fucking my girlfriend.

"I can be on top if that makes you feel better," she says, reading my mind.

I lay beside her and gently roll her on top of me. I barely lay completely back before she's riding me with my dick deep inside of her. Jesus.

She leans forward, kissing me like she hasn't tasted me in years. With her riding me, our tongues colliding and teeth accidentally clashing, we both find our release together.

I help her lie next to me and kiss her head. "I love you, Everly."

She looks over at me, smiling. "I love you too, James."

We lay there for a few moments, enjoying each other's company, when I notice she's squirming a little like she's uncomfortable.

"Are you okay?" I hope I didn't hurt her or the baby.

She takes a moment before answering. "Yeah, I was just thinking about something..."

"What?"

"I know you have cameras too, but are they here? In the bedroom?" she asks.

"Yeah, why?" I ask, not knowing where she's going with this.

She's always had cameras in her bedroom and all over the house. I know she's used to it, and it doesn't bother her. Everyone we hire is professional about it, and it's more like they just glance occasionally.

She makes a cringing face. "So, like Ryder watches? Oh, God."

She buries her face in her hands, and I have to pry them off her to see what's going on in that mind of hers.

"What Everly? It's no different than it has been."

She shakes her head. "I know... I just... I don't know why I never really thought of it before. Like it's just clicking. James! Ryder was probably sitting there laughing his ass off, watching me lie in your bed before you came out of the shower. I tried out like fifty positions and then stayed like that the entire time you were showering. Ugh..."

I couldn't help but laugh. I'm not going to tell her this, but she's probably right. I can see Ryder grabbing a bucket of popcorn and watching her, laughing his ass off. I don't particularly care for others to see her like this, but it's that or risk something happening. Everyone else will be sure not to watch, and Ryder wouldn't watch either if I told him not to, but I'd hate for something to happen because we were embarrassed to be seen. It's not like they're high-def cameras and they're watching pornos. Okay, maybe I'm now trying to convince myself of all this. Maybe this is weird.

"Baby, he's a professional," I talk louder than I was before so Ryder can hear. "But if it bothers you, we can figure something out."

She shakes her head. "No, it's fine. I mean, at this point, the damage is already done. You're right, Ryder is a good guy and professional like Declan and Barry."

Okay, yeah, I'll be having a talk with Ryder later.

Once she gets up to go to the bathroom, I reach over for my phone that buzzed with a text from Ryder.

Ryder

> I'm a professional James *popcorn emoji*

"Fuck you," I say out loud and stare into the camera.

I can basically hear him laughing on the other side. I laugh too because he really is. He's one of my best friends, and everything he does is to protect me and now my future wife and child. As much crap as we give each other, we've got each other's backs. I trust him with my life and theirs.

CHAPTER FORTY

JAMES

I reluctantly leave Everly this morning so I can set something up for tonight's getaway. I'm taking her to a cute cabin not too far from here, where we will be staying through Christmas morning. I'll be proposing to her tomorrow, on Christmas Eve. We need to return on Christmas Day as she likes to spend Christmas with family, and everyone is gathering in the evening. In time to show off that she's my fiancé, of course.

I'm feeling excited and in a good mood until I'm walking out the door and Everly stops me.

"Hey, Jake is going to stop by in a bit. I just wanted to let you know," she says while wrapping her arms around me.

Well, there goes my excitement. Jake and I have patched things up, and I believe him when he says that he's moved on and not going to try anything with Everly. Not that long ago, we got together for a couple of drinks and really talked through it. He admitted he loved the idea of love versus actually loving

Everly. He was drunk and admitted quite a few things that night.

Regardless, I'll be keeping an eye on the cameras and heading back as quickly as I can. Old habits die hard.

Ryder meets me outside my door, and we head down to the elevator together.

"You're going to leave her alone with Jake?" he asks, trying to start something.

"Do I have a choice?" I ask versus telling him to shut up like my first instinct usually is.

"You could tell her no," he says.

We both stare at each other silently as the elevator descends. Then we burst out in laughter at what he just said.

"Yeah, okay. I'll send you in there to tell her no," I tell Ryder.

"No thanks, I'd rather keep all my body parts intact. She scares me," he says.

I continue to laugh. "Really? Why?"

He cocks an eyebrow at me. "Have you seen her? I've seen her train with Declan. And the way she had no issue shooting those guys that kidnapped her? She's not to be messed with."

He's right. I know he's mostly joking, but I wouldn't want to risk it if I were him. She might take some crap from me because she loves me, but she barely knows Ryder. Also, after last night, I'm not sure that she wants to get to know Ryder.

"How is she doing? Like really doing?" his face turns serious as he asks.

The elevator doors open, and we step out, heading to the car.

"I honestly don't know. She doesn't talk to me much about what happened. She's had a couple of nightmares at night, but nothing too serious. Sometimes I catch her staring off into space, looking upset, and I wonder if she's thinking about it. Today's also the anniversary of her friend's death, so that's another reason I didn't say anything about Jake coming over," I say, wishing that she would talk to me more about it.

"That's right... She's talking to Asher, though, right? Have you asked him?" Ryder asks.

I mean, it's not right to ask someone else about her when she doesn't want to tell me about it. With that said, of course, I asked Asher. He didn't tell me much but assured me she would be okay.

"He didn't say much and basically told me it'll just take time, especially since she had to kill for the first time," I respond.

Ryder gets serious again and nods. He doesn't say anything more, so I figure the topic is done and we move on.

The errands I had to run took a lot longer than I had anticipated. I want to head back to the apartment to be with Everly, but I see that Jake just got there. That should be incentive enough to head back, but I want to show her that I trust her. If I show up now, then she will think I don't.

Ryder and I sit in a restaurant for lunch as I lean my phone up against the wall with the camera on. Okay, I admit I have issues. I just want to know what's going on.

"You trust them, huh?" Ryder cocks his eyebrow.

I scoff. "I just want to see what's going on."

He laughs. "So, you're just nosy, like me. I get it. Sometimes it's hard taking my eyes away from the camera when I'm on duty."

"You watch the cameras even when you're off, Ryder. Don't lie," I state, glaring at him.

He put his hands up in surrender. "Of course I do. For the same reasons you are right now."

Alright, whatever. We've talked enough about these cameras. They're there, we're using them, people see them, we're moving on.

For the first thirty or so minutes that Jake's there, they do nothing but talk. They are at a respectable distance from each other on the couch, just hanging out. I don't have the volume on because we're in the middle of a restaurant. If I'm curious enough later, I can go back and rewatch it.

Ryder and I are almost finished with our meals when I notice Jake get closer to Everly. I place my fork down and grab my phone to get a closer look. He whispers something in her ear, and she laughs, then they look at each other seriously.

She whispers something back, and he whispers again, and it's a damn whisperfest going on. Even if I had the volume on, I wouldn't be able to hear what they were saying. I notice them both glancing over at the camera. Everly nods at whatever Jake said, and then Jake gets up from the couch.

He walks right over to the camera, grabs a chair to reach it, and stares right into it. He has the biggest grin as he moves it to face the ceiling.

"Fuck!" I state while sliding my chair back quickly.

Half the restaurant is staring at me, but I don't care. My heart is now racing, and I need to get back. Why would they move the camera if they weren't up to something? Do they know that I'm watching? Wouldn't they know that I would see the camera was moved? My security team should be all over that.

Ryder stands with me, putting his phone away, shaking his head. He was watching, too. We both head to the car, and I tell him to floor it.

"Come on, James, what are the odds that it's what you think it is?" Ryder asks.

"What else would it be? What's the reason he would move the cameras other than to hide what they are doing?" I ask.

I try really hard not to think about what's happening right now. I take a deep breath and calm myself. Everly wouldn't do that to me. She loves me. This is stupid. There has to be a perfectly logical explanation for why they moved the camera in the living room.

Five minutes into the drive, I get a call from my security team. I answer on the first ring.

"Yeah?"

"Camera 3 has been moved, and the view is obstructed. Would you like me to go check it out?" he asks.

If I say yes and he does, what is he going to find when he walks in there? Or if nothing is going on, Everly is going to know that I sent him in there and, in turn, that I don't trust her.

"No, I'll be home shortly. Let me know if anything else seems weird though or if more cameras go off," I state calmly.

"Yes, sir. So far, everything else is in working order," he states, and I hang up.

I pocket my phone and try to concentrate on not losing my mind before we get home.

Chapter Forty-One

EVERLY

I sit on the couch with Jake, keeping tabs on the time. Jake and I currently have two bets in place. I'm a sucker for bets. I take the bait every time.

Bet number one. James was watching the cameras the entire time Jake has been here. I, of course, told Jake that James trusts us enough to not need to do that. So, I don't think he was watching them. If I lose the bet, then Jake gets to call the baby whatever nickname he wants when he or she is born. I mean, we all know he was going to do that regardless, but I just can't give him any crap for it. If I win, then I get to set Jake up with a dating app.

Bet number two. James will come marching through that door within fifteen minutes of that camera being moved. I'm not entirely sure where James was going, but I'm pretty sure he won't be here within fifteen minutes, no matter where he went. Regardless, he wasn't watching the cameras, so he won't be. My loss means that Jake gets to pick the color of the baby's nursery.

Jake's loss means that he has to go out on a date with whoever I choose for him.

As I look at my watch and see that it's been twelve minutes, I'm not prepared for what happens next. The front door flies open, and James is out of breath as Ryder comes strolling in calmly after him. Damn it.

"Hey," James says nonchalantly while stopping by the island and leaning on it.

I shake my head in disappointment, and Jake has the biggest grin on his face. I can't believe I lost another bet. I suck at them.

"Hi," I state with an accusatory tone.

"How are you guys doing?" he swallows as he tries to catch his breath.

"Seriously? James! Were you watching the cameras?" I stand and yell at him.

"What? Why would I do that?" he asks but looks guilty.

Ugh, damn it, James. I was really rooting for you. Though I think I'm more disappointed that I'm losing two bets to Jake than the fact that James was watching the cameras because he didn't trust us.

"James..." I state, hoping he will just come clean.

He sighs. "Fine, yes, I'm sorry. Why the hell did you move the camera, Jake?"

Jake laughs and puts his arm around me. "So I could win a bet. Actually two. Thanks, man."

James looks over at me with confusion as I say, "You just caused our baby to have the most ridiculous nickname and nursery color."

"What?" he looks even more confused.

I explain the bet to James and what the stakes were. Ryder laughs and walks out the door without saying anything, but we hear his laugh until the door closes behind him.

"I'm really sorry, baby," James says like he means it.

I know he does, but I have to make it seem like it's a bigger deal than it is. Maybe it should be a big deal, but I really don't care that he was watching the camera. I understand, and I have nothing to hide. Maybe it's just because I've been used to being watched 24/7 since I was a kid. Regardless, it doesn't bother me. Losing the bets really doesn't either because I know Jake won't screw with my first child's nursery color and, like I said, he would call him or her whatever he wants to, anyway.

"I think this is my cue to leave," Jake says while giving me a big hug.

He passes James and pats him on the back. "Thanks man."

James looks like he wants to punch Jake. I guess that urge will never go away for him. Once Jake is out the door, I grab James' arm and roughly tug him toward the bedroom like he's in trouble.

"I really am sorry, Everly... It's not that I don't trust you..." James starts, but I put my finger to his lips to stop him.

"I just lost two bets because of you, James. For that, you have to make it up to me," I say, hopefully seductively, like I meant it to sound.

"Oh?" he cocks his eyebrow.

"Mmm. I've been thinking about those skilled fingers and mouth of yours all morning," I say while pulling him down on the bed with me.

"Well, I think I can definitely make it up to you that way," he says just before his mouth crashes to mine.

After three amazing orgasms, which more than made up for losing those bets, James surprises me with a quick trip to get away. We're not too far from home, but far enough that we're in the middle of nowhere in a cute little cabin. It's freezing outside, but it's not snowing. I love when it's a white Christmas, but I'm not sure if it will be this year.

We brought only Ryder along for security because James said we would be safe where we are. I know Declan would've wanted to come, but he still needs rest. We're giving my whole security team some much-deserved time off. They are going to need all the rest they can get once the baby is here. I already know that I'm going to be an overprotective mom.

James and I settle on the couch to relax. I'm exhausted for many reasons. I'm sure the pregnancy plays a part in it, but also today is always a tough day for me. This is the day I found Lauren dead in her bathroom. As the years go by, it gets a little easier to deal with, but the memories will always be there. That's why Jake came over today. He wanted to make sure that I was okay. He has been there for me on this day every year. James hasn't mentioned it, but I know that it's not because he forgot about it. I know he doesn't want to push me to talk about it, and I'm thankful for that. He's doing what he does best, distracting me. If we hadn't come here, then I probably would've gone to her grave and sat there all afternoon depressed. She wouldn't have wanted that.

I jolt awake on the couch, hearing a scream. I look around to find James holding me, shushing me, but the TV isn't on. Did I scream?

"Hey, it's okay, baby. It was just a dream," he says soothingly.

I take a few breaths and realize my heart is pounding and I feel nauseous. I have sweat dripping from my forehead. I must've had another nightmare, but thankfully I don't remember it. Sometimes I just remember the feelings, and other times it's very vivid. Most of the time, it's about when I was kidnapped, and I usually jolt awake the moment I fire off the gun.

"I'll get you some tea, okay?" James asks, and I nod.

As James stands to get the tea, Ryder comes into the room. He looks at James and they nod at each other. Apparently, they can communicate well without words. I expect Ryder to go back to his room, but he surprises me when he sits next to me on the couch.

"The nightmares will eventually fade," he states.

"I hope so..." I whisper.

"Do you want to talk about it?" he asks.

Do I? Not really. I don't talk about it with anyone but Asher. Though Ryder and I rarely have a conversation and he's asking. Maybe I should at least tell him a little.

"I usually wake up when I shoot someone," I say.

He nods. "People think that when you kill for self-defense, it's easier. They're wrong. The reason you had to kill someone doesn't matter. It's hard knowing that you took a life."

Tears start behind my eyes, and I try hard to push them back, but the emotions from the nightmare are still fresh. He understands exactly what I'm thinking and going through. Of course he does. He has probably had to kill people before.

"Have you ever killed anyone?" I ask, even though I know it's a personal question that I probably shouldn't ask.

He looks me in the eye and says, "Yes."

"Does it get easier? Knowing that you took that life. You killed someone's son... possibly husband or father. That they will never see them again..." I trail off because my throat is tight, and the tears are now trailing down my cheeks.

I went to school to become a therapist. You would think that I would know how to deal with my emotions and be able to get over it. Unfortunately, that's not how life works.

"No, it doesn't. But Everly, I talked to Matteo. He said the guys you shot were injured, but they weren't dead. You didn't kill them when you shot them," he says.

I look up at him, but unfortunately, that realization doesn't help as much as I wish it would. "But they are still dead. They killed them."

He doesn't deny it. I know everyone who was involved is dead. That's the way those men in that world do things. They have to in order to survive, and I get it. Regardless, I injured those men to be stuck where they were and then be caught and killed by Lorenzo's men.

"Just remember what you were trying to stay alive for and who. Imagine what would've happened if James lost you, especially after knowing you were carrying his baby. You did what you had to do to protect those you love. Your baby, James, friends, and family. You weren't selfish, you were selfless," Ryder says gently as he places his hand on mine.

He's right. I know that if I had to go back, I'd do the same thing all over again. I don't regret what I did. I just hate that I had to do it, and I hope my children will never have to be put in a position like that.

"Thanks Ryder. I'm glad that James finally let us meet," I say while letting out a chuckle.

Ryder grins wide and says, "Me too. You have no idea how many times I tried to persuade him to let us meet, or I tried to sneak in without him knowing. He always caught me, though."

"Like at the bar?" I laugh.

"Exactly. Did you see his face when I winked at you?" he asks.

"Yes! I was so afraid for you. I thought you were just a random person, but James looked like he was about to go over there and murder you," I say while we continue laughing.

James clears his throat behind us. "Alright, that's enough. There's no need for you to get to know Ryder this much."

I grab the tea from James as he comes to sit down on the other side of me. I'm surprised he didn't insert himself between us.

"Um, no. You kept Ryder a secret from me the whole time. We're going to become best friends, starting tonight." I pause and look over at Ryder. "Would you like to watch a movie with us?"

Ryder's grin grows big as he says, "I'll get the popcorn."

Chapter Forty-Two

JAMES

Last night was an amazing night, even though Ryder crashed our night alone. Thankfully, I wasn't planning on proposing until tonight, on Christmas Eve. I'm so nervous, I barely slept. I don't mind though, because I love watching Everly sleep and knowing she's here in my arms.

I was hoping to take Everly out for a nice breakfast, but her morning sickness was really bad this morning. She woke up vomiting, and every time she tried to get a bite of anything in her system, she immediately threw it up. I called the doctor, and he prescribed some Zofran for her, which I sent Ryder to get.

About an hour after taking it, she's feeling better and was able to keep down some food. She wants to avoid medicine for the baby's sake, but she was so miserable she didn't even fight taking it.

"I'm sorry I ruined our morning," Everly says while sipping some tea on the couch.

I lean in to hug her. "You didn't ruin anything, baby."

She doesn't look convinced, but I really do mean that. Yeah, I had plans, but who cares? As long as we're together, that's all that matters. I hate that she feels so sick sometimes, and she just looks miserable. I wish I could do something more for her, but the doctor said it'll get better in a few weeks.

She gives me a small smile. "I don't know how you can say that when you've been holding my hair all morning while I throw up everything in my stomach. Doesn't sound like much fun for you."

I squeeze her tighter before saying, "Baby, you're the one throwing up and going through all this for our baby. I'll do whatever you need. It's the least I can do. You take care of that baby, and I'll take care of you, okay?"

She sighs and relaxes into my side. "Why are you so perfect, James? I don't deserve you."

My heart skips a beat. I hate hearing her say things like that about how she doesn't deserve me. How does she not see that it's the opposite? I'm not worthy of her, but I'm going to continue trying to be.

"I'm far from perfect, baby, but I'm trying. I love you."

I lean down to kiss her, but she puts her hand to my mouth and pushes me away.

I laugh as she shoots off the couch and says, "James! I just threw up like five times this morning. You can't kiss me! Let me go brush my teeth and get ready."

She already brushed her teeth after every time she got sick, so I'm not worried. I stand and pull her to me, kissing her anyway.

She fights for a moment but gives in quickly. I don't make it last long because I know she's self-conscious about it, and I let her go. Plus, if we get ready quick enough, we should be able to continue with the rest of my plans for the day.

It's getting dark, and my heart is racing. I'm pretty sure it's about to pound out of my chest. I don't understand why I'm so nervous about proposing to her, but I am. I want to make sure it's perfect, and I'm desperately hoping she says yes.

Most people would say I'm crazy to propose after just a few months, but it's not like we just met. We've known each other since we were little kids. We were together for a bit when she was in high school and, yeah, while we took some time apart, I think we both really needed that for ourselves so we could come back together and be better for each other.

Regardless, I wasn't planning on proposing so soon, nor was I planning on doing it this way. I was going to propose to her in about eight months from now when the fair came back around, right on that Ferris wheel, where I made the promise to her.

After convincing Everly to enter this death trap of a ride, we finally made it to the top of the Ferris Wheel. It stopped and Everly's eyes were squeezed shut along with her hand squeezing the life out of mine. It didn't look like she was going to open them until we got off this thing.

"Everly, open your eyes and look," I said.

She did, and I watched her as she looked out in the distance. It's high up, but I hoped that the beauty of it trumped her being scared. There were lights in the distance from the city and it was a perfect night without any clouds in the sky, so you could see the stars along with the almost full moon.

"It's beautiful," she whispered.

I stared at her more than the view. "It is, but not as beautiful as my view."

She's the most gorgeous girl I've ever seen. I've loved her since the moment I met her. The type of love has changed over the years. At first, I loved her like she was mine to protect. She was little, and she had been through a lot. She didn't have any siblings to protect her, so when she was at my house every summer, I took it upon myself to take on that role.

As we grew older, she became more and more beautiful. My feelings for her changed. I began to have a crush on her but pushed that aside. It wasn't right, especially when those feelings started when I was fifteen and she was only thirteen.

Then this summer changed everything. I tried to pretend not to notice her, but she had grown so much this past year. She's beautiful, smart, and funny. I was succeeding, barely, in pretending I wasn't interested in her until Jake decided to go for her. That's why we were where we are today and with what I was about to do. She was mine and always would be. I needed her to know that.

I pulled her into a gentle kiss, with my heart racing. The Ferris wheel moved forward again and stopped a couple times before I let our lips part. I kissed her longer than I was meaning to, but I couldn't deny that I was nervous and stalling.

I pulled the ring out of my pocket, held it in my hand, and kept it covered so she couldn't see it. I took my other hand and placed it on her cheek, holding her face to look directly into her eyes.

"Everly, I want you to know that I've never felt this way for someone before. We've known each other for basically our whole lives, and I can't imagine you not being in my life moving forward. I've fallen completely in love with you, and while we are still young, I know that I want to spend the rest of my life with you. We're not ready to get engaged, but I want to make this promise to you and give you this promise ring to signify it. I promise to love you forever and one day, I'll be proposing for real. Will you accept this promise ring?" I held out my palm to show her the ring.

I knew she couldn't see the ring well in the dark, but I made sure it was perfect for her. It was her birthstone, an emerald, which I knew she loved. I also made sure to get her ring size so it would fit her right away.

She was just staring at me and the ring, taking a moment to answer. I was hoping she was just surprised and not trying to figure out how to say no nicely. My heart continued to race as I waited for her answer.

"Yes, of course," she said as I let out the breath I was holding and slipped the ring on her right-hand ring finger.

She held my face in her hands and kissed me hard. She pulled away and looked me in the eye.

"I love you so much, James. I promise to love you forever, too. No matter what life throws our way, I'll always love you."

We kissed the rest of the way down until it was our turn to get off the Ferris wheel. I stepped out first and held my hand out for her. She took it and stepped off, but we didn't let go of each other's hands for the rest of the night.

That night was perfect, and I'm hoping to make this night perfect too. I've come to terms with things don't go as planned, and sometimes it's for the better. I do my best when I can control them, but I'm slowly understanding that sometimes it's better if things are a little out of my control. Sometimes. Of course, I take back control when I can.

We make it to the little town near our cabin, where there are Christmas lights strung everywhere. It's Christmas Eve, so a lot of the shops are already closed, but we didn't come for the shops.

"James, it's freaking freezing. Are you going to tell me what we're doing yet?" she asks with her arms hugging her body.

I know it's cold, but soon she won't be thinking about it. I look at my watch as we sit on a little bench in front of a Christmas tree in the square. The guy should be here any minute now. I wrap my arms around Everly to keep her warm and rub my hand up and down her arm. She's completely bundled up with probably ten layers underneath, but she's always cold, anyway.

I see the horse-drawn carriage in the distance and pull her to face me so she will be surprised when it stops in front of us. I smile as I look into her beautiful eyes and see that bright red nose from the cold air. I lean forward and kiss her. Her lips feel like I'm kissing a popsicle, and her nose is colder than ice.

"We'll be warm shortly," I say as the carriage finally pulls to a stop in front of us and I stand up.

She stands and follows me toward the front, where I shake the driver's hand and hop in the back of the carriage, helping her inside. I've already talked to him about where we're going and where to stop. I also made sure he had warm blankets for us. I help Everly up and sit her next to me, putting two of the blankets on us, hoping it'll help warm her up fast. She doesn't say anything, but she doesn't have to when she has that smile on her face and leans in to kiss me.

CHAPTER FORTY-THREE

EVERLY

I'm not a super sappy person or romantic. Don't get me wrong, I love romance, but I'd be happy just cuddling on the couch with the man I love for the rest of my life. But when James does things like this, it makes my heart melt, and I realize what I'm missing out on.

We're currently sitting in a horse-drawn carriage with two very large white horses pulling it. They are beautiful, and I'm thankful they have such thick coats because it's freezing outside. They don't seem to be bothered by it.

I lean my head on James as the carriage pulls us around the square. There are Christmas lights strung all around the trees and buildings. It's beautiful. We were sitting on a bench in front of a large Christmas tree. I thought for a moment I saw a few snowflakes while we were kissing on the bench, but I think I was imagining them because I haven't seen anymore.

We rode around for about twenty minutes before pulling to a stop in what feels like the middle of nowhere. James gets out of the carriage and helps me out. He leads me over to a beautiful gazebo with lights strung all around. There's a cute little Christmas tree inside of it, and there's some seating with a fire pit behind it.

"I'm surprised you're allowing me near fire," I tease.

James' face becomes serious as he says, "We're not going to get too close, and I'm having someone take care of it for us, so we don't need to touch it."

I gasp and feign being hurt. "You don't trust me with it?"

"No," he states without a hint of joking around.

Well dang, okay. Let's move on.

"So, what are we doing out here?" I ask.

He looks nervous, like he's not sure what to do next or what to say. I love nervous James. He always seems so in control and sure of himself, but there have been a few times lately that he's not. It's nice, but I'm not sure what he could be nervous about tonight. It's Christmas Eve, and he just planned the most perfect and beautiful evening.

He leads me over to the gazebo, and we stand in the middle of it. The fire pit is a decent distance away, but I can still feel the warmth from the fire. It feels nice, especially with how cold it is.

James is staring at me while we stand here, and my heart races. Why is he just staring at me, and why is he so nervous? He's making me nervous, which in turn is making me nauseous, and that's not something I need right now.

I look away from him for a moment out into the distance, and my heart skips a beat in excitement at what I see.

"James! It's snowing!" I say a little too excitedly.

He looks out and smiles. "It is."

He leads me out from under the gazebo toward the back, closer to the fire pit, but not too close. I look up to the sky and stick my tongue out, letting a few pieces land on it. I don't know why that's always my first reaction to snow falling, but it's something I've always done since I was a child. I don't remember much about my mother, but the snow always reminds me of her. I wonder if we used to go outside in it and catch snow on our tongues together.

I look back toward James, who's watching me and smiling. I feel silly, so I stop. James pulls me in closer and kisses me. By the time we part, the snow is falling much harder and coating our clothing. He's looking nervous again as he pulls away from me and puts his hand in his pocket. He pulls out a little box and immediately falls to one knee as the snow falls around him.

Oh my God! My heart is racing as I realize what he's about to do. He's about to propose, right? Oh my God, he's about to propose!

James clears his throat, opens the ring box to face me, and says, "Everly... We've known each other basically our whole lives, and I can't imagine another day of my life without you in it. Things may not have gone the way we were hoping, but I wouldn't change anything because it led us to this moment. I love you so much, and I'm going to love you for as long as I live. Baby, will you do me the honor and marry me?"

I'm completely stunned and just stare at him. I'm pretty sure my mouth has hit the ground, but my face is so cold and frozen I'm not sure. Either way, I probably should give him an answer because he's looking more and more nervous the longer I take to respond.

"Yes..." I whisper, because that's all I can do.

James has the biggest smile on his face as he stands up and grabs my left hand. He slides the ring on my ring finger and then pulls it up to his mouth to kiss it.

When he lets go, I look at the beautiful ring. It's perfect. It's not too flashy, but it has a large diamond in the middle and two small diamonds beside it. There are more diamonds inside the band going down the sides. It's exactly the type of ring that I've always pictured myself wearing, and I'm wondering when James bought it. I have a feeling he's had this ring picked out for a long time because it's exactly what I described to him back in high school.

My heart is still racing from the excitement as I pull him in for a kiss. I wrap my arms around his neck and kiss him more passionately than I ever have before. I can't believe this man is mine and mine forever. I don't deserve him, but I'm going to do everything I can to be the perfect wife for him. Wife. Husband. I smile at those words. Soon we'll be husband and wife.

He pulls away from the kiss. "Do you want to ride back on the carriage, or do you want Ryder to drive us back to the cabin?"

I laugh. "James, we need to get back to the cabin as quickly as we can because I'm about to jump you, and it's way too cold for that out here."

He laughs too as he pulls his phone out and sends a quick text. I assume to Ryder. When he finishes, I pull him in for another kiss, but it ends too quickly because Ryder is already pulling up with the car.

James opens the door for me, and I get in as he grabs the buckle and buckles me. He rounds the car and slides into his seat.

After we're both settled, Ryder looks back at us and asks, "So?"

I want to mess with him, but I don't have it in me. I'm just too excited.

I lift my left hand to show him the ring and say, "So we're getting married!"

Ryder grins wide and says, "Congrats, you two."

The drive back really isn't that long, but it feels like it when you want nothing more than to jump your fiancé. Fiancé. I can't believe I'm engaged to James. I know I've been engaged before, but it never felt like this. James and I were meant to be.

When we pull up at the cabin, Ryder keeps the car running. I have to use all my willpower not to jump out of the car while waiting for James to come around to open my door.

"I'll give you two some privacy," Ryder says to me as James is rounding the car to my door.

"Thanks Ryder," I say while grabbing James' hand to help me out.

James doesn't even get the front door to the cabin closed before I literally jump on him, kissing him. I wrap my legs around him, and he closes the door fully with his foot. We don't part while he carries me to the bedroom, laying me gently on the bed.

"I need you to fuck me right now, James," I say desperately.

He laughs as he strips some of his layers off. "I won't be fucking you tonight."

My heart literally stops. "What?"

He leans forward, his face inches from mine, and says, "I'm going to make love to my fiancé."

I can't handle it anymore as I pull him in for another passionate kiss. Even though I have about ten layers of clothes on, he removes them in under a minute. I crawl up onto the bed, and he lies on top of me, with nothing between us.

He slowly, torturously kisses every inch of my body. When he makes it back up to my lips, I push him onto his back and do the same to him. As much as I want nothing more than him to be inside me right now, I want to savor this moment. I want to explore every inch of him as he just did me.

When I make it down to his erection, I plant a few kisses on it before sucking him into my mouth.

He pulls on my hair, moans, and says, "Everly... Jesus, baby. I'm going to come already."

I don't stop as I slide him in and out of my mouth and sucking him, teasing him with my tongue. James groans as he pulls me off and lifts me up to his face.

"I'm not coming in your mouth tonight," he says while kissing me and pushing me on my back.

He leans over me, aligning himself with my entrance. "James, I thought…"

"I talked to the doctor. It's fine right now as long as I don't put pressure on your stomach," he says.

When did he talk to the doctor? And oh my God, that's so embarrassing. I don't even want to know how that conversation went.

James eases into me slowly. He rocks back and forth torturously slow, but it feels so good. It's so much more than just sex. It has always been with James, but even more so tonight. He's taking it easy, probably mostly for the baby, but also, I know he wants to savor this time. The first-time making love to his fiancé.

His breathing picks up, and his thrusts become erratic. "Everly…"

My rapid breathing matches his as I say, "James…"

After a few more moments, we both are riding our high and crashing together. He slows and pulls out of me as he kisses my forehead and rolls over, pulling me into his chest.

"Jesus, Everly. That was… amazing," he says, still out of breath.

Yeah, I know what he means. It felt different from what it has been in the past. I've always loved being with him, but tonight was... I don't know how to explain it. It was different. Amazing.

"I love you, James," I say, tipping my head up to kiss him.

"I love you too, Everly," he says against my lips.

After the post-sex bliss wears off, I get excited again about the fact we're about to get married.

"So, did you have a date in mind for the wedding?" I ask James because I know he likes to have things planned and be in control when he can.

"No, I was going to leave that up to you," he says.

I'm surprised. I think about it for a moment and try to picture our wedding. A spring wedding would be beautiful, but I'm pregnant. By that point, I might be a giant whale, and I don't want that. We could wait until after the baby is born, but I don't want to have a wedding after he or she is born.

"February," I say.

James gasps. I guess he wasn't expecting me to say for it to be so soon.

"This February?" he asks.

"Yes, is that a problem?" I ask, hoping that it's not.

He smiles. "Baby, I would get married to you tomorrow if you wanted to."

I laugh, "Well, we already have plans tomorrow, so I think February will have to do."

CHAPTER FORTY-FOUR

JAMES

Ryder pulls up to my parents' house and parks the car in the driveway. We came straight from the cabin because we didn't want to leave any sooner than we had to. I kept Everly up all night because I couldn't get enough of her. She didn't complain, though. I let her sleep in this morning because she needs it. I couldn't help but watch her while she slept. She's perfect.

The Hales and Crawfords have always spent Christmas together, and occasionally Everly and her father would join us. It has been a long time since we all did this, but tonight everyone is here. It's the perfect night to announce our engagement, showing off she's mine. My fiancé. Shit, fiancé. I love the sound of that. I'm going to love the sound of wife even more. It's hard to believe I'm about to walk in to have Christmas with my family, with my beautiful pregnant fiancé on my arm.

I open the car door and hold my hand out for her to take, which she does as always. Once we enter the foyer, I take her white fur coat and hang it on the coat rack by the front door. She looks stunning tonight.

She's wearing a long, fitted red dress with a slight V-neck that shows just a little cleavage. Her hair is curly as it lies across the front of her shoulders. She put on extra makeup, but she doesn't need it. She looks beautiful without it.

"What?" Everly asks.

I smile. "Nothing, I'm just admiring you. You look beautiful, Everly."

I lean forward and kiss her forehead. I wrap my arm around her waist and lead her inside the house toward the sitting room, where we hear everyone has gathered.

"James! Everly!" My mom comes over and gives us each a hug.

"You're late!" she yells at me as she pulls back from the hug.

"Sorry mom, we were a little busy," I say while smiling at Everly.

She's blushing, and damn if that doesn't make me happy. I love seeing her blush. Everyone else says their hellos, but we're interrupted when my mom lets out a loud scream. She rushes back toward Everly and holds up her hand with the engagement ring on it.

"Is this what I think it is?!" she looks at me with such hope in her eyes.

I don't have to say anything because Everly excitedly answers, "Yes!"

My mom gives us both big hugs again and then goes back to studying the ring. She pulls Everly off to the side and they hug like ten more times before sitting down. My father and Everly's dad come over to congratulate me, and I couldn't be happier. The proud look in her father's eyes means everything.

I wanted to make an announcement, but that ship sailed the moment my mom noticed the ring. Maybe we should've taken it off when we got here. I should've known that my mom would notice it. That's okay. This works too.

Once the bodies part and I can see Everly again, I notice a shy girl sitting next to her. I'm assuming that's Amelia.

"Is that your girlfriend?" I ask Bash, nodding toward her.

"It is, that's Amelia," he states proudly, and he looks so in love with her.

"You love her," I state and don't question.

He nods. "I never understood how you could be so sure about you and Everly, but I get it now. She's it for me. We've only known each other for half a year, but I know she's it."

I pat him on the shoulder. "I'm glad you worked it out with her. Now come introduce us."

After dinner, we all sit around the Christmas tree. We decided years ago to do a white elephant Christmas exchange versus having to buy gifts for everyone. There are no rules other than you have to bring one gift. There's no price limit or anything. It can be funny, or it can be something practical. I have no idea what Everly brought, but I always bring something practical. Usually, some prototype from work.

We go through a couple of rounds, and all the gifts are normal so far. There's perfume, home decor, and puzzle books. It's my turn, and nothing that's already in play is something that I particularly want. I have no idea which one is Jake's, but I always try to figure it out so I can avoid it. He's gotten good over the years at making sure his is wrapped nicely, and he somehow always keeps it hidden when he comes in the door.

I pick a gift that looks like it's in a box the size of printer paper. I begin to open it, and Everly has a huge grin on her face. I shake my head, knowing that this must be hers and, by the looks of it, it's something silly.

When I open it, a couple of items fall to the floor. I pick them up. One is a large pack of fancy colored pencils, and the other is bookmarks of some half-naked guy on them. I look back at the rest of the gift to find a coloring book of the same guy and a Little Golden Book of Dwayne Johnson. I cock my eyebrow up at Everly as she's hysterically laughing.

"What did you get, James?" my mom asks, trying to peek over.

I hold up the coloring book and the book, shaking my head. I hear my mom say, "Oh my," and can't help but laugh as well. Yeah, yeah, we all know the ladies love The Rock.

I lean over and tickle Everly until she stops laughing. "Thanks babe."

"I didn't know you'd get that. I was hoping it would be your dad or something," she says, laughing again.

I laugh too at the image of my dad getting this gift.

It's Amelia's turn, and she gets up, heading toward me with her hand out. "Hand over my man. He's mine!"

I laugh and gladly hand the items over to her.

When she gets back to her seat, I see Bash looking at her like he's jealous. "Your man?" he asks.

She shrugs her shoulders. "I mean yeah, it's Dwayne Johnson. Enough said."

"I knew we'd be best friends," Everly calls over to Amelia.

Well, since she took mine, I guess I have to pick another. I decide to go with a smaller box this time.

I nearly have a heart attack when I unwrap it and open the lid. Everything goes fuzzy as I suck in my breath to hold it and close my eyes. What the fuck just happened?

"Glitter bomb!" Amelia shouts and laughs.

Everyone else is laughing, including Everly. She at least gives me the common courtesy of wiping away whatever is in front of my eyes and all over my face.

When I open my eyes, I see glitter everywhere. I mean everywhere. It covers the couch, the floor, my lap, my arms, and I'm positive it's all over my face.

"Who the hell gave this gift?" I ask, looking around.

Everyone has their hands up in a surrender motion, shaking their head, except Jake. Fucking Jake.

"Real mature Jake," I say as I shake my head and glitter flies everywhere. Everly is completely covered too, but she's a girl and clearly doesn't mind.

I finish opening the gift and pull out like ten bracelets. Really? I read a couple of them, and they say things like "lover," "swiftie," and "fearless."

"What are these?" I look over at Jake and ask.

He mocks surprise and says, "How do you not know?! They are Taylor Swift bracelets James!"

Everly starts grabbing the bracelets and putting them on. I just shake my head and join in on the laughter because what else can I do? While the glitter was highly annoying and clearly, I won't be wearing these bracelets, I'm having one of the best nights of my life. I have all my family, friends, and fiancé here, who is carrying my baby.

"So, you want to get married on Valentine's Day?" I ask Everly as we lay in bed.

We decided to stay the night at my parents' house because it was getting late, plus my mom insisted. She wants more time with Everly to talk about the baby and now to plan the wedding.

"I hope that's okay with you. I kind of just said it to give them a date and thought it would be romantic," she says.

I kiss her and say, "Baby, I told you last night, I'll marry you whenever you want. You pick the date, and I'll be there."

"You better be!" she hits my arm and laughs.

She rolls on top of me, and I think she's going to kiss me, but she picks at my hair.

"What are you doing?" I ask, confused.

She smiles. "I'm picking out some glitter you missed."

I swipe my hand a few times through my hair like that's going to help, but I know it won't. After we came upstairs, I took a shower and washed my hair and body about ten times. Each time I kept finding more and more glitter. It's like it multiplied every time I tried to wash it off. Everly joined me in the shower to help, but she got more glitter on her too. I'm pretty sure we were in there for over an hour. Though, washing the glitter off each other wasn't the only thing we were doing in there.

I roll her to the side and kiss her again. I play with her hair as I just stare at her. She's so beautiful, and I still can't believe she's mine.

"What?" she asks.

I bring our bodies closer together so we're pressing against each other before I kiss her. "I love you, Everly. I can't wait until we get married and have this baby, starting our family. I know I told you this before, but I need to again. I'm all in, Everly. I'm all in, and I hope you are, too."

Tears form in her eyes as she looks back at me. She's been so emotional, but I can tell this is the good kind of emotional.

She kisses me and says, "I'm all in, James. I'll forever be all in."

ALSO BY

Want to find out the gender and name of James and Everly's baby?! Join my newsletter and get the free bonus chapter here! https://dl.bookfunnel.com/nyr6kbdmrl

Check out the first two books in the series, if you haven't already! fALLINg into Summer and fALLINg into Senior Year. Read these two stories for Everly's POV to see where it all started!

Want to see more of Bash and Amelia? Read fALLINg for the CEO for their story!

Amelia

It was supposed to be a one-time thing while on vacation, to forget and feel something good for once. I didn't expect to see him again, so imagine my shock when I start my new job and walk in to find him as my boss... the CEO of the company. Now I'm working side-by-side with the man who turned my world upside down. He's confident, charming, and sees right through every wall I've built. I've been burned before and recently ended an abusive relationship. Falling for Bash might be the most dangerous thing I've ever done.

Bash

I've been over the one-night stands for years, but I couldn't help myself when I met her on vacation. I wasn't supposed to want her. She was a mystery, a spark I couldn't stop thinking about. Then she shows up as a new employee... a beautiful, walking disaster with a past that haunts her. I should keep my distance, but I can't. There's something about Amelia that draws me in. She's been hurt, and whoever did it left scars I'm determined to heal. She doesn't know that I need her as much as she needs me.

If you'd like the inside scoop of upcoming books and releases, join my Facebook group:
www.facebook.com/groups/snchristensenreaders/

Follow me on TikTok
@authorsnchristensen

ACKNOWLEDGMENTS

There are so many people I want to thank for making it possible to write and share my stories with the world. With every book, I've been blessed to find people who stepped into my life at just the right moment, encouraging me in ways that shaped each story. I could easily fill twenty pages naming names, but please know this: whether you've supported me from the very beginning or encouraged me during this book in particular, I am deeply grateful for you. Each and every one of you has left a mark on my journey, and your encouragement means more than words can ever capture.

First, and foremost, to my Lord and Savior Jesus Christ who died for my sins so I may have eternal life. I give Him all the glory for blessing me with the gift of storytelling and the opportunity to share it with others.

To my biggest supporter since I was little, Aunt Karen. You have always believed in me, not just in my writing but in every dream I have ever chased. You spent countless hours editing my books, listening to my endless story ideas, and cheering me on. These books would hardly be readable without your time, patience, and love. With every new story, your excitement for my characters grows, and you remind me to keep going even when doubt creeps in. I could not ask for a greater champion.

To my husband, who read my stories as I wrote them, listened to every crazy idea that I had, and bounced back ideas. For taking care of the kids and allowing me to dedicate time to writing. For being understanding and taking on whatever role was needed when I was exhausted and stressed.

To Kim, for being my first official beta reader and going through each book with a fine-tooth comb to make sure the timeline is just right. For loving my characters and continuing to encourage me to write more even when I want to give up.

To Lexi, who has been part of my life for so many years but became an even bigger part of it just when I needed you most. You helped shape this book into what it is today with your encouragement and support. You took the time to read through every chapter, to talk through every detail, and to cheer me on at every step. Your friendship means more to me than I could ever put into words.

To Kelli, who was my first reader of these books and for being invested in the story and my characters. For understanding me and my anxiety by being there for me and texting as many times as I needed to support me.

To all my friends including Adrianna, Ashley, Wes, Sydney, Wendi, Jordin, and Kelly for believing in me and being excited for me to write these books. For continuing to support me through my writing journey and allowing me to share my excitement with you.

To my children, who have been patient with me and never once making me feel bad for spending time writing instead of time with you. To Amara, who constantly asked me how my book was coming along and being proud of me for being a writer. To Aiden, who graciously allowed me to go write and made me smile every time I finished for the day by being excited to see me again.

To my mother and father, who both believed in me from day one when I said I wanted to write a book. For always encouraging me to write the moment I said I wanted to be an author when I was little. For being excited and proud of me for my accomplishments.

To my ARC readers, for taking the time to read, review, and be honest about my books before it was released. For all the kind words and excitement for upcoming books and loving my characters the way I do.

And finally, to all my readers. I wrote these books because it was something that I'm passionate about. When I put them out there, I never expected anyone to actually read them. So, thank you for taking the time to read my stories and for getting invested in my characters. I can't wait to continue the stories of the characters and see where they take us.

S. N. Christensen

ABOUT THE AUTHOR

S. N. Christensen lives in a town outside of Atlanta, Georgia. She holds a BA in English and MA in Secondary Education. From a young age, she has dreamed of being a writer. She loves writing in the fantasy, thriller, and romance genres.

When she is not writing or reading, she can be found teaching at her church preschool and serving at her church. When she is at home, she loves to spend time with her husband and two children playing games and crafting.